MELODY

A FIRST CONTACT NOVEL

David Hoffer

PROLOGUE

Twenty-five years ago

Clear water streamed down a wall of frosted glass that glowed with a deep blue light. The water bubbled and flowed over the etched shapes of a dolphin, an octopus, and a school of smiling fish. I remembered being like one of those creatures, living deep within a faraway ocean with others who were just like me.

But today, I stood with my brother inside the hospital lobby waiting for my dad who was talking to a man at the counter. I looked up at my brother, Eric, who was holding my hand. "I'm not afraid."

"You never are," he said, but didn't look me in the eye.

Dad returned from the counter and tousled my hair. "Come along Stephen. We don't want to be late for your appointment."

"Why are you doing this?" Eric asked.

"Because nothing else has worked," Dad replied. "We're lucky the doctor is allowing Stephen to have this treatment." Taking my hand from Eric's, Dad led me along the hallway where we turned opposite the direction we usually took. "Don't you worry about a thing, buddy, you'll soon be good as new."

I don't think he believed that, but I smiled anyway, wanting to please him.

"There's nothing wrong with him," Eric insisted.

Dad slowed his pace and lowered his voice. "You heard what the psychiatrist said: your brother needs help before his delusions get worse."

Within Eric's mind a whirling finger of crimson sprouted from the center of a growing storm. Or so I imagined. The doctor had told me that what I saw inside of people wasn't real, nor was the music I heard playing in my head. They were symptoms of an illness, she said, like having a cold. I wasn't sure about that, but my father believed her, and that scared me. What if I wasn't who I thought I was?

Crimson deepened to purple, a sure sign that Eric was about to lose it. Delusion or not, I'd seen this before. Quickly looking around to make sure nobody could overhear me, I said, "Dad's right. I need to get better."

Eric's shoulders slumped, and the finger of purple faded back into the swirl of color that moved within his head. Dad tugged at my hand, and I hurried to keep up as we walked to the end of the hall. Pushing open a heavy door, Dad gestured for me to enter. I did as I was told, but looked over my shoulder to make sure Eric followed. He did, dragging his feet.

Inside the room was a silver table surrounded by computer screens, cords, and machines. The lights were way too bright and it smelled like pee and bleach. I didn't like it.

Two ladies turned toward us as we entered. The one holding a clipboard gave me a friendly smile which I tried to return. The other woman was my doctor. She was old, dressed in green, and had a gray streak running through her hair. She patted my head then extended her hand to my dad.

"Mister Fisher, it's a pleasure to see you again," she said.

My dad didn't let go of her. "I appreciate your including my son in this trial. I've tried everything, medication, therapy, but the symptoms only get worse. I don't know what else to do. You should have heard what he told—"

"Yes, yes, I understand," the doctor said, untangling her hand from his. "While the early onset of schizophrenia is extremely rare, rest assured that your boy's not the first I've treated. Though the procedure is experimental, it's precisely targeted and perfectly safe. I'm confident this will change his life, and yours."

My dad said nothing, only took a deep breath. Leaning over me, the doctor reminded me that her name was Samantha. I stared at my shoelaces, ashamed to be the cause of so much trouble. If I could turn invisible, now would be the time.

"Feeling brave today?" Doctor Samantha asked.

Wanting to assure her that I was, I raised my eyes, but the words caught in my throat. A man was wheeling a cart toward the table. Scary things were on top of it, flashing and beeping. Some were sharp. I pointed. "What's that for?"

"Tools for us to help you get better," the doctor said.

"Oh," was all I could think to say.

Doctor Samantha introduced the woman beside her as a nurse. After greeting me, the nurse held up a flimsy gown. "You have to change into this. Would you mind if I helped you?"

I did mind but nodded anyway just to get this over with. After lifting the shirt from my arms, the nurse took off my shoes and pulled my pants around my ankles. Embarrassed, I stepped into the waiting gown as quickly as I could.

"Everything's going to be fine," Dad said, and squeezed my arm. "Try to relax and do what the doctor tells you. I'll see you once you're finished. Okay buddy?" Struggling to hold back tears, I bobbed my head.

"Call out if you need anything," Eric said, shooting a distrustful glance at the doctor. "We'll be waiting right outside."

"Thank you," I said, meaning it, then waved goodbye as Dad herded Eric toward the door.

"Would you like help getting onto the table?" the nurse asked.

Wanting my dad to see me being brave, I shook my head and climbed up all by myself. But when I turned around, all I saw was the metal door swing shut. The nurse gently pushed on my chest until I was lying face up on the table. The thin fabric covering my back didn't stop the cold metal from giving me a shiver. She fit leather straps around my wrists, telling me it was for my safety. Something sharp pierced the inside of my arm. But I didn't cry out, even when a tube was put into me. Doctor Samantha then placed moist things on each temple. They were cold. When I tried to touch one, my hand tugged at a strap connected to the table.

"They're called electrodes," Doctor Samantha explained.

"What are they for?" I asked.

"They create a tiny electrical current, which will make those delusions go away."

"Will it hurt?"

"A tingle, if that. And one of my associates is giving you a sedative to make you more comfortable. You shouldn't feel a thing."

That didn't sound so bad. "Okay," I said, feeling sleepy.

After telling me to open wide the nurse placed a piece of rubber between my teeth and instructed me to clamp down. She then pulled a strap over my forehead and secured each of my ankles. Nobody had warned me about this. I felt afraid. It occurred to me that maybe I shouldn't have shared anything with this doctor. That was such a good idea I wondered why I hadn't thought of it before. Good thing I didn't tell her what I had come here to do. Who knows what she would have thought about that?

"This will be over before you know it," the nurse said.

A man's face hovered over me, the same person who pushed the cart. "How are you feeling?"

I felt lightheaded and too tired to answer. Darkness crept from the edges of my vision until the light from the overhead lamp became a circle, growing ever smaller. Though I tried to fight it, the outside world became a speck. Then darkness fell.

◆ ◆ ◆

I woke up with my head on fire. Gasping, I tried to pull off a mask that somebody had placed over my face. But I couldn't move my arms, nor could I talk. My body slammed against the table and I felt the doctor fumble with the electrodes on my head.

Another symptom of my sickness was being able to reach inside of people. This I did, demanding the doctor to make the pain stop. But instead she flew against the table where she slumped to the ground, along with the man. The nurse reached for the strap to release my arm. But the moment her hand brushed mine crazy whirls of yellow and white invaded her mind, mirroring the agony that burned inside of me. She staggered backward while opening and closing her mouth like a fish. Blood dripped from her ears.

I was now alone with what seemed to be an ice pick stabbing into my head. Music, my constant companion, faded into nothingness. Who was I, where was I, and what was I supposed to do? As I searched for the answer I lost track of the question. Then, as if I looked through a waterfall, the distorted image of my brother took shape. Grasping a tattered thread that reached into a place I could no longer recall, I called out to him – help me, please.

PART I – THE FATHER

CHAPTER ONE
Present day

"What do you like best about school, Clay?" I asked. "Do you have a favorite subject?"

My thirteen-year-old patient slumped deeper into the lounge chair and stared at the ceiling with his arms crossed and mouth sealed into a line. Throughout the session he'd been responding with a defiant stare, discomfiting silence, or if I was fortunate, a monosyllable. Not once had he looked me in the eye.

"I hear you like to draw," I said. "Is that true? I'd like to see some of your pictures."

With an impatient sigh, Clay made a show of looking toward the door, reminding me that we were well past our scheduled time. But I sensed a profound problem bothered this boy, well beyond the former psychologist's diagnosis of depression.

"What do you do in your spare time?" I persisted. "Do you like music, have a favorite band?"

A dismissive shake of his head was the reply, none of my business the message. I sympathized, having myself endured a parade of psychiatrists that probed and prodded my adolescent mind.

"Ever find yourself wishing that you didn't exist?" I asked.

"Yeah, like right now," Clay sneered.

Progress. He spoke. "That's a good one. Do you sometimes think people talk about you behind your back?"

"You're wasting your time, Doctor Fisher."

"I don't mind."

"Maybe I do."

Just watching the boy, I felt sure that something tormented him.

Seconds turned into a minute as I puzzled over what lay beneath that hard shell. Clay bore my scrutiny stoically, being an expert at keeping to himself.

"What's troubling you, Clay? I have a feeling you don't know how to ask for help."

"My mom forced me to come here," he said, though his eyes bounced off the empty chair behind my desk. It was nothing more than a flicker, lasting less than a millisecond. But it was enough. I can often tell what people aren't saying, and the more suppressed the emotion the easier it is for me to detect. Everybody has it: the ability to read an expression, a tone of voice, or visual inconsistency so fleeting that most people would hardly notice. But I had paid attention and knew what troubled Clay with a surety of seeing my own reflection in the mirror.

"You hear a voice, don't you?" I said, and it wasn't a question.

Clay's body went rigid. "Did you see that in a movie? Thought your kind went to college."

"Many suffer from the same affliction, Clay. Rest assured, you're not alone."

Clay half rose from the seat, torn between stalking out or admitting the voice existed.

"You can go," I said. "But ignorance only makes the voice stronger. I can teach you where it comes from, and more importantly, how to manage it. But to do that, you need to sit down."

"Nobody can help me," he said, frozen in place.

I said nothing. After a tense few moments, Clay dropped back into the chair. He pulled his legs up and wrapped his arms around his knees. "How did you know?"

"Let's just say it was an educated guess."

"What's wrong with me?"

"There's nothing wrong, just like there's nothing wrong if you catch a cold or break a leg. What you're experiencing is a hallucination caused by a misfiring of circuits in your brain. That's all there is to it." Clay exhaled, which I hoped meant he found comfort in that knowledge. "Where does the voice come from?" I asked.

"A shadow," he murmured.

"It's typical for the manifestation to come from the outside," I reassured him. Unlike the voice that spoke to me. "Is the shadow with us now?"

"Sitting in the chair behind your desk," he said, and fractionally lifted his chin. "It says it doesn't like you."

Unable to help myself, I looked toward the chair…nothing. "What else does the shadow say?"

Clay clenched and unclenched his hands. "To hurt myself."

I chose my next words with care. "Voices can often be critical; it's the nature of the affliction. Don't do what it suggests or believe what it says. How long has this been going on?"

"Since always."

I found myself clenching and unclenching my hands. My own voice was born after having suffered pain on a metal table, and it treated my mind as a screen to flash terrible images as tangible as the young man sitting before me

"Is it possible," Clay started, then glanced at the empty chair.

"That what you hear isn't your imagination?"

He nodded.

"It's only as real as your subconscious thoughts. Understanding that these hallucinations are due to the dysfunctional wiring in your brain can help correct what you see, and possibly, quiet that voice."

For the first time, Clay's eyes met my own. "Can I ever get rid of it?"

That was the same question I often asked myself. Never could I shut down the voice, only muffle it through the generous use of medication reinforced by a disciplined repression of thought. "It's more likely you'll have to come to terms with it. Though we need to spend more time together, I'm confident that as treatment progresses you'll be able to see this as I do…an illness to be managed."

Clay expelled a long drawn out breath. He nodded.

"Do you…" I began to ask, then thought better of it.

"Do I what?"

"You don't happen to hear music, do you?"

Clay blinked. "Should I?"

"No, no," I said, flushing. Truth was, I heard music, even now, playing softly in the background, as if it came from behind a closed door. "You've made great progress today, Clay. Next step is to come up with a treatment plan that'll work best for you, if you'll allow me to help."

"Thank you, Doctor Fisher."

"Call me Stephen. Now, if you don't mind, I'm late for a birthday party."

◆ ◆ ◆

Hidden amongst a sea of balloons, my wife Fran, was at the patio table cutting slices from a white-frosted birthday cake. Eric stood beside me in a darkened corner of the backyard, both of us looking upon my five-year-old daughter. We all wore pointy party hats.

Danika lifted a new computer tablet up and over her head. Swaying unsteadily on her feet, she pointed the camera somewhere between the waning crescent of an aging moon and the bright speck of Jupiter. "Help me!" she implored.

I dropped to a knee and looked up at the screen. The tablet was a gift for her birthday, as was the app she was using that identified celestial objects wherever the camera was pointed. But all I saw was a black canvas dotted with unremarkable stars. There were no galaxies, planets, satellites, or anything most people would find interesting. Danika was not most people. "Honey, what is it you want to do?"

"Take a picture," she said. "But I can't move the lines."

Steadying her elbow with one hand I used the other to drag the cross-hairs on the computer screen over a random white speck. "There you go, you found a star. Good job."

"That's not it!" Scrunching her lips together she bounced her head to the right. "That way, down a little, up a little" –I followed along with my finger– "Not that one. Oh, let me show you." While trying to point at the screen she lost her grip on the tablet sending it flopping to the ground. "Oh no, is it broke?"

I picked up the computer from the lawn and wiped away the stray blades of grass. "It'll be fine. How 'bout we take a look at the moon? There are craters—"

"No."

"We can look at the sea of tranquility."

"The moon's made of rocks," she said, knitting her brows together.

"She's got you there," Eric said, suppressing a smile. "Mind if I give it a go?"

"Not at all," I said, handing him the tablet. Eric then did what I should have done in the first place…he hung onto the screen while Danika moved the cross-hairs over her quarry. It took seconds.

"Okay," Eric said. "Say the words."

"Take the picture, please," she said. The app obediently made a clicking sound, freezing her piece of cosmos onto the display. Placing both hands over her mouth she exclaimed through splayed fingers, "That's it!"

"The perfect picture for the perfect birthday girl," Eric said. "Of a beautiful star, just like you."

Danika smiled, like the angel my astrophysicist brother imagined her to be. "There's three of them," she said.

Eric tapped an icon on the screen. "Well, look at that, a trinary star system. Aren't you clever. What you see in the sky is what's called an orange dwarf, not as big as the sun but just as bright. The second is too dim to see. But it's the third that's the most interesting. It's what we scientists call a neutron star." She gave him a blank look. "A star that died," he explained.

Danika bobbed her head. "That's right."

"The system even has a name, which is special because most aren't so lucky. It's called HR 7448."

Danika repeated the name with such fascination that it gave me a chill. There was a world of difference between the playful engagement of a creative mind and an involuntary descent into disorder. I'd seen it often enough with my own patients. What was my brother fueling?

"There's planets," Danika said.

"There's bound to be, sure," Eric agreed. "Most systems have at least one."

"There are five, and one has an ocean, like here."

"Maybe so," Eric said, passing the tablet to Danika. "You're the smartest little girl I know."

Danika beamed while embracing the tablet to her chest. "Thank you!"

"Honey," I said, "why don't you go show Mommy your new present."

"Okay!" Danika wrapped her arms around my brother's neck, squeezed, then raced to the patio table where Fran waited. Climbing into her mother's lap she began talking a mile a minute.

"You're Danika's hero," I said to Eric.

"That was always my plan," he said. "Funny she picked out that system. It's the only interesting thing in an unremarkable area. Astronomers avoid the neighborhood."

I chuckled, more at him than the joke. Astrophysicist humor, I supposed. Detecting movement in the corner of my eye, I peered into the shadows. Birds lined the fence, still as the night and silent as their silhouettes set against the silvery light of the moon. I felt sure they were staring.

"Stephen?"

"Sorry?" I said, "what did you say?"

"I said Danika has quite the imagination."

"I hope that's all it is." I looked back at the fence. The birds were gone. Then again, were they ever there? After years of therapy I still had trouble trusting my own senses. With a sigh, I confessed to Eric my greatest fear, "I'm concerned Danika may be like me."

Eric regarded me for a long moment. "As far as I can tell she's perfectly normal, Stephen. Relax, let her grow up. You'll be glad you didn't do anything to fix something that was never a problem."

"But I can't shake the feeling—"

"You need to hear it," Danika interrupted, having sprung up at our feet.

"Um, hear what, honey?" I asked.

Danika pointed to the spot in the night sky where she had taken the picture. "It will help you remember—"

"Stars don't talk," I said.

"This one plays a song," she insisted, and her expression was as serious as the statement was nonsensical.

A shiver crept up my spine. Dropping to my knees, I lifted her chin with a finger. "Honey, we've talked about this. You know as well as I do that—"

She thrust my hand away, knowing what I would say, that her imaginary world wasn't the same as the real one. "Why don't you believe me?"

When I didn't respond, her chin fell, and she kicked at a clump of grass. Moisture glistened in her eyes.

"Danika—" I began.

"Stephen," Fran cut in, the warning clear in her tone. "You know that it's her birthday, right?"

"Maybe I can help," Eric said, and bent to be at eye level with Danika. "The pulsar won't sound like much, mostly static and, well, I guess, pulses. But I think you'll find it interesting. Tell you what, I'll point a special telescope at it, then we can take a listen together. Consider that another gift for your birthday."

I shot him a hard glance. Of all people, my brother should be the first to understand my fear. What the hell was he doing?

Scurrying over to Eric, Danika wrapped her arms around his legs. "Thank you!"

CHAPTER TWO

Heads turned as Doctor Dolores McCann accompanied her high-ranking guest into a repurposed conference room within the campus of NASA's Jet Propulsion Laboratory in Pasadena. This room served as mission control for a project near and dear to Dolores' heart. Nodding greetings to the assembled engineers and technicians, she noted that none recognized the new boss, except for Tara, the manager of the AMIGO project, whose eyes lingered on the man.

"Everybody," Dolores said, and paused a beat to assure she had their attention. "I'm privileged to welcome the new NASA administrator, Victor Mercer, who's dropped in to witness our first engineering run."

Victor casually held up a hand while correcting Dolores under his breath, "Acting administrator, actually," a reminder that he had yet to be confirmed by the Senate. Dolores hoped he wouldn't be, for as far as she was concerned the man's only qualification for office was having once been a pilot in a squadron commanded by the new President.

While directing the administrator toward the back of the room, Dolores explained the basics. "AMIGO is the largest space-based laser interferometer ever built. The device can search out ripples in space-time with a sensitivity a thousand-times greater than anything in existence."

"What is AMIGO, exactly?" Victor asked.

"Oh, sorry, it stands for 'A Massive Interferometer Gravitational Observatory,' a name I coined twenty-two years ago when the project first—"

"I meant what purpose does it serve?"

Dolores blinked, not only at having been interrupted twice, but also that the new boss wasn't familiar with one of NASA's largest projects. Still, the fact he asked was a good sign. Better to cure ignorance than wallow in it.

"It detects gravitational waves, ripples in the fabric of space-time produced by massive celestial events, like the collision of neutron stars, black holes, or an exploding supernova. Measuring the disruptions help us understand how these objects form, which gives us an insight into the nature of gravity, particularly near the horizons..." As Dolores spoke, she noticed Victor's eyes glaze over. "Anyway, think of AMIGO as a new sense to hear what the universe has to say."

"Ah," was the disappointing response. "Would you mind if I say a few words to your team, Doctor McCann?"

"Not at all. I should have suggested that you do." Dolores lifted a hand, intending to get her team's attention, but the new administrator was already striding toward the front of the room. Busy chatter quieted to a low murmur as Victor Mercer reached the small podium. With a practiced and emotionless smile, he turned up his palms.

"We have a new vision for NASA: to develop the technologies, knowledge, and infrastructure to explore space and protect the homeland. Though similar words have been used in the past, my intent is to repurpose them to meet the challenges of the present, reduced budgets and greater competition in a world of threats. I expect everybody to bring their A-game to work each and every day, to be flexible, and embrace change rather than cling to old ways. I look forward to leading this organization and working with you to bring this vision to life."

A heavy silence blanketed the room, made more awkward by a half-hearted clap from a newly hired and doe-eyed engineer. Homeland? Shouldn't the vision encompass the entire planet? Regardless, Dolores took up the applause while nodding energetically for others to do the same. Wouldn't do to have JPL perceived as not supporting the new boss. The Administrator then extended his hand and made small talk with members of her team. Dolores found that encouraging, as this project needed his support, especially given the upcoming budget reauthorization. Moments later, Victor returned to Dolores' side.

"It's fortuitous you were able to join us today," Dolores said, but otherwise was at a loss for words, small talk never being her forte.

Victor absently nodded while seeming to appraise every square inch of the repurposed conference room, critically, she thought.

As the team busied themselves with preparations for the test, Dolores felt obliged to explain what was about to happen. "For the first time we'll be receiving telemetry from the spacecraft. Our task is to assure the component systems work end to end, instrumentation, communication, software, and the like." She pointed to the main screen up front, where an empty two-dimensional chart was displayed. "If AMIGO is working as designed, meaning actively listening for a cosmic event, a horizontal line will render on the chart."

"I didn't come to see your test, Doctor McCann," Victor said.

Before she could ask why he had come, a voice cut through the room. Tara, the project manager, announced, "Move the antenna."

"Instructions are being sent now," a technician said.

"Received," another replied. "Confirmed complete."

"Re-configure the laser lock," Tara instructed.

"Locked. Moving to establish ground communication."

"Okay, here we go," Tara said, and bit on a nail. Dolores gripped her hands together, feeling tense. For this was the primary objective of today's exercise…to establish communication with ground control. Once complete they would test components already proven operational by the prototype, AMIGA, little sister to the larger AMIGO.

After a beat, the technician said, "Receiving telemetry, processing now."

A small cheer broke out as every member of the project team lifted their eyes to the center screen. A smooth flowing wave form appeared on the chart – not the horizontal line that was expected. Stifled gasps erupted. Two of the more junior engineers high-fived. But Dolores knew better than to celebrate. Celestial events happened in sub-second bursts, recorded much as a seismograph records an earthquake. It was inconceivable that they stumbled upon an event the moment they activated the equipment. She looked at Tara, whose grim countenance communicated all there was to say – failure.

"You'll pardon me a moment," Dolores said to Victor. Not waiting for a reply, she walked toward Tara.

"I can use thrusters to try countering the wobble," Tara said as she approached.

"Do that," Dolores agreed, "but not until I get our guest out of the room."

"He seems like a handful."

"I can handle him." Dolores looked again to the screen where the sinuous waves still flowed. "Crap."

"I don't get it. Each spacecraft is, or was, operating perfectly."

"A micrometeorite, perhaps," Dolores said. If true, she prayed it hadn't hit a vital component. "Let me know what you come up with, and soon. I have a feeling I'm going to be asked."

"Will do," Tara said.

Dolores returned to Victor's side. "Shall we adjourn to my office."

"Yes, let's do that," Victor agreed. After striding to the exit, he held open the door for Dolores. "There are a few things we need to discuss."

Once they entered Dolores' office, the new administrator wasted no time second guessing the project team. "Looks like you have a problem with a spacecraft. If I'm not mistaken, and my gut is usually right about these things, that'll be an expensive fix."

"That was just the first of many operational tests," Dolores retorted. "I'm confident the root cause will be identified, and an appropriate course of action taken."

"I'm not. This mission has been full of unpleasant surprises, Doctor McCann. Tell me, how much has been spent on this project, since inception, I mean? Twenty-two years ago, isn't that what you told me? That's quite a long time. Only took eight to land a man on the moon."

"The project began five years ago," Dolores replied, her pulse racing. "Up to that point, it was a series of false starts, with funding allocated, pulled, then allocated again. Not to mention the lengthy effort involved in putting the original proposal together."

"Twenty-two years' worth?"

"Pushing the frontier of science requires a long lead time."

"All right then, let's go with five years. How much was spent in that time?"

Dolores purposefully went high to avoid being accused of going low. "South of six billion."

"Five billion, eight hundred sixty-four million, which includes a five-hundred million dollar overrun. I'd say the project has been mismanaged."

"The overrun was wholly due to the failure of the first launch vehicle," Dolores said, trying to keep her temper in check. She failed. "Do you often ask questions to which you already know the answer?"

"That's my background as a lawyer. I also find it a handy technique to judge the competence of subordinates."

"I've been perfectly transparent about this project. Which goes for every project I've been involved with."

"That's only to be expected, not boasted about," Victor said. "As is coming in on budget and on schedule, despite the risks, which you failed to manage. Which brings me to the subject at hand. The new administration believes what used to pass for transparency is no longer sufficient. To that end, I've ordered all in-flight projects to be reassessed. We're going to do what in my judgement has never been done at NASA: clearly establish the benefits of a mission before a penny is spent."

"You don't consider scientific advancement a benefit?"

"Hard benefits, Doctor. Something more substantial than" – Victor used air quotes – "a new sense to hear what the universe has to say."

"I think you misunderstand the purpose of this organization."

"I expected you might feel that way, which is the reason I wanted to tell you this in person. NASA is in urgent need of fresh thinking. To do that I need new leadership. You've come a long way, Doctor, rising through the ranks to become the director of JPL and VP at Caltech. Most would consider that the pinnacle of a career. Ever consider enjoying the fruits of your labor, maybe take a cruise, tend a garden, bounce grandchildren on your knee?"

The blood drained from Dolores' face. JPL was her home, and AMIGO her baby, which she intended to defend as if it were her flesh and blood. "I don't have grandchildren, nor do I have a garden."

"A shame. Regardless, I've spoken to the president of Caltech and we've come to an arrangement. Expect to receive a retirement package. I'm told it's quite generous. I strongly advise you to consider it."

"And when I decide retirement isn't for me?"

Victor's chin jutted forward. "At NASA's next steering committee meeting, I expect a full report on the status of this mission. To be quite candid, I'm not optimistic about chances for continued funding. I'll grant you that time to think about your personal situation. We have a new mission, Doctor, and I need new leadership to carry it out. Am I clear?"

"Perfectly," she said through clenched teeth.

CHAPTER THREE

Driving slowly along a tree-lined street I scanned both sides looking for the daycare center. A car passed us by with an irritated blare of the horn. From the booster in the back seat, Danika asked, "You don't remember where it is, do you?"

"Just because Mommy usually takes you doesn't mean I don't remember," I said. In truth, I knew about where the daycare was located and was beginning to suspect we were travelling in the wrong direction. Looking over my shoulder I executed a perfectly safe but highly illegal U-turn.

"I mean you don't know who I am," she said.

I looked ahead for a familiar landmark, finding nothing. "Your name's Danika, you're five years old, and you were born in Santa Barbara. You love music and don't have a favorite color because you like all the colors."

"That's not what I mean!" she said, kicking the back of the seat. "I don't understand what's wrong with you."

"I'm lost," I admitted. Not only lost but late taking her to daycare.

"You're also going the wrong way," Danika said. "It's at the top of the hill, before you get to the rose garden."

"Oh." I said, knowing she was right. I pumped the brake earning a honk from a car following closely behind us.

"Do you know where you're from?" Danika asked.

I pulled over to let the traffic pass then did another illegal U-turn. "Same place as you, honey."

"That's right!" she piped, prompting me to smile. For a moment I thought this was going to be one of those conversations where she'd try getting me entangled in her imaginary world. From the rear-view mirror Danika waved at me, then two fingers slid into her mouth, as she was nervous about going to daycare.

"Mommy will pick you up in a couple of hours," I said, trying to reassure her. With a smile, Danika nodded. Then she began to hum.

I returned my attention to the road, where traffic had grown dense. Apparently, I wasn't the only parent who was late dropping off their child. Her humming grew louder, echoing in my head. Gripping the steering wheel, I tried to stay focused. But it was no use. Waves rippled over the skin covering my hands. I tried blinking past the hallucination only to watch flesh melt away into nothing. A mass of tendrils appeared from beneath, weaving and swaying in a grotesque parody of what should be hands.

Danika screamed.

I looked up too late to see that I had run a red light and that a semi-truck was about to plow into the passenger side of my car.

CHAPTER FOUR

During her seventy-two years of life, Dolores had collected a doctorate and three advanced degrees, none of which offered a solution to the failure analysis report that sat on her desk like roadkill. AMIGO had malfunctioned. That much was obvious but the why remained a mystery. All Tara and the project engineers had produced was a list of probable causes, most of which required total replacement of the three spacecraft making up the gravitational wave detector. If true, that would spell disaster for the project and the inglorious end to a dream spanning decades.

As a child, her father had taken her out of the city and into the mountains to view a cosmos unspoiled by city lights. Once darkness had fallen, the night sky came alive and that was when she first looked into a telescope. She beheld the rings of Saturn. At first, she thought it was a trick, and insisted her father show her the aperture to make sure he had not taped a picture to the end of the telescope. He hadn't, of course, and that evening Dolores discovered a universe far larger than the walls of her bedroom. Since that day, she had striven to understand her place in the cosmos, eventually landing the job at JPL. Now the legacy she hoped to leave behind was about to go up in ashes.

The project team needed more time to confirm the root cause of the problem and come up with a workable solution. But time was up. She checked her watch; only five minutes until the meeting with the executive budget committee, where pencil-wielding accountants would lay the blame at her feet. The perfect stage for the new administrator to use the failure of AMIGO as an excuse to push Dolores into retirement. Not one of her colleagues, not even those she considered friends, would dare object, out of fear of becoming targets themselves.

Word had gotten around about the bullseye on her back, but no amount of criticism could match the burden she placed on herself for this disaster.

Tara barged into the office. Her usually coiffed hair was ruffled and she had dark circles under her eyes. After putting her laptop on Dolores' desk, Tara pulled out a chair and plopped into it. "I've got an update," she said.

"No 'Good morning, Dolores' or 'How was your weekend, Dolores?' because I'd tell you it wasn't good. Sorry, Tara, but it's much too late for an update. We're done."

"You're going to want to hear this."

"Not unless you tell me we have a new administrator."

"I can't help you with that, but I do have other and better news. I spent my weekend looking over the raw telemetry from the prototype AMIGA and compared it to the signal data collected from AMIGO."

"Given you were going to waste a weekend, I would have preferred if you focused on the root cause of the problem."

"There is no problem, Dolores, that's what I'm trying to tell you. The waveform AMIGO detected may be an aberration but it's not a malfunction. The gravitational wave observatory is working as designed." She flipped the laptop around. "I have proof."

Dolores passed a cursory glance at the numbers streaming down the screen, the digital representation of input collected from the prototype. "These are spurious signals, Tara. Actuation fluctuations, thermal variations, magnetic gradient effects, and noise from a dozen other sources. I appreciate the effort, but desperation is making you see patterns where there are none."

"The noise is why we couldn't detect it," Tara said. "The prototype isn't nearly as sensitive as AMIGO, but it did pick up the larger wavelengths. Look here" – she stabbed a finger at the screen – "the higher amplitudes repeat within the data stream at regular intervals. When I compared the telemetry between the two instruments, I found a one hundred percent correlation." She walked through the numbers in a hurricane rush, but it wasn't until Tara overlaid a graph of the data collected from AMIGA with the data from AMIGO did Dolores see the pattern.

"Both instruments are picking up the same signal," Tara said. "It's real."

"All you've proven is that the malfunction exists in the prototype. If you would've caught that earlier, we could have avoided the problem we have today."

"I thought you'd say that," Tara said. "So, I used both detectors to triangulate the signal back to the source, a trinary star system within the Draco constellation. There's a pulsar in that system, Dolores, a neutron star theoretically capable of producing gravitational waves. Explain that."

"I don't have to because it doesn't make a lick of sense. A continuous disruption in the fabric of space isn't possible. It would be like…somebody banging two black holes together."

"Regardless, we have confirmation of the signal from an independent source."

"Back up," Dolores said. "The instruments may be separate, yes, but they share similar components and have the same operating system. They share the same problem —"

"You need to hear it," Tara interrupted.

"What?"

"The gravitational waveform magnified into the human auditory range."

"What possessed you to do that?"

"Desperation. Two weeks ago, Eric Fisher, a professor at Caltech, sought my approval to reserve time at the radio observatory in Owens Valley. Said something about wanting to record a song for his niece. Over the weekend something nagged me about that request and I checked it out. Turns out Eric pointed the dish at the same star system where the gravitational waves originate. He didn't find anything, just the usual background noise, but the coincidence got me wondering. So, I decided to see if I could find a song. I mean, what did I have to lose? Took me only a few minutes—"

Dolores tapped her watch, for the meeting had started. "Tara, as fascinating as I'm sure this is, I need to attend my execution."

"Right, anyway, that was the reason I spent the weekend comparing data." Tara flipped the laptop around. "Brace yourself," she said, and tapped a key.

A slow haunting rhythm filled the room, the pitch rising and falling in a transcendent melody that took her breath away. Parting her lips, Dolores leaned into the chair and let the music flow through her. What she was hearing wasn't possible, she knew, but every moment that passed proved her wrong. By the time she thought to look at her watch, it was fifteen minutes past the start of the meeting.

"This isn't natural," Dolores said.

Tara stopped the recording then looked at Dolores in silence for a long moment before the corners of her eyes creased into a smile. "We've uncovered a new phenomenon."

"I want you to double, no, triple check every one of those data points," Dolores directed. "Bring in a separate team to do an independent analysis. Also, I want you to power up little AMIGA to collect additional telemetry. Confirm everything. Whatever money or resources you need I'll find – somehow."

"Yes ma'am," Tara said, and her eyes sparkled with an enthusiasm that keenly reminded Dolores of the young intern she had taken under her wing. She knew exactly what Tara was thinking.

"Let's not get ahead of ourselves," Dolores warned.

Tara said it anyway. "First contact."

CHAPTER FIVE

S itting on the couch in the bleak gloom of a barren dawn I reached for the bottle, the last survivor standing among its fallen comrades. After twisting the cap off, I watched foam slowly rise over the rim and dribble onto my bare chest. A narrow line of liquid streamed down the lines of my abdomen to soak into the elastic band of my boxer shorts. Hoping to dull the deadness inside, I tipped the container to my mouth and let the bitter liquid flow. But to no effect, other than to increase the pounding inside my head.

The ceremony was four days past. The air had been warm, the breeze still, and the church full. A four-foot casket wreathed with pink roses and white lilies had lain silent in the central nave. I couldn't bear to look at it and only stared at my hands as the priest spoke consoling words from the pulpit. Outside a train passed with a warning blare, the sound stretching on and on until it faded into the distance. My wife attempted to grasp my hand, but I pulled away. I didn't deserve her sympathy. After the service, friends offered condolences and spoke well-meaning platitudes, which I found excruciating. My brother stayed by my side the entire time, offering only blessed silence. I appreciated his doing that because in that moment I wanted nothing more than to escape back to the refuge of my home where I now slumped, alone.

There was a knock at the door.

My chest tightened, and gut fluttered. Days ago, my wife had fled to her mother's house to receive the solace I was incapable of providing. I looked to the door, hoping and dreading that she had returned. But the silhouette framed within the glazed window was tall and thickset. I imagined it as the reaper, come to collect another soul.

That would be both fitting and welcome. I finished off the drink with one long swallow.

A face leaned close to the glass and a muffled voice called out my name. I ignored the specter just as I ignored the insistent hammering on the door. Placing the empty container on the table my hand searched for another, sending bottles clattering to the floor. Whoever was on the porch raised their voice, telling me they knew I was home. Annoyed, I rose, stretched my limbs, and hobbled to the foyer where I flung open the front door.

An apparition wreathed in shadows towered over me. I flipped on the porch light. It was a man. He wore a trench coat and his closely shaved scalp accentuated ears that were too small for his head. Beside him stood a crop-haired female dressed as his twin. A hand whipped toward my face. But instead of a scythe, it was an open wallet showing a badge along with a picture that matched the face of the man who held it before me.

"Stephen Fisher?" the man asked.

I gripped the door frame and squinted at his identification but failed to read the words as they seemed to be moving.

"My name's Connor"—he motioned to the side— "and this is Agent Hudson." The woman's nose crinkled as her attentive eyes swept me up and down. Realizing I wore only boxer shorts, I shuffled behind the door.

"Are you Mister Fisher?" he asked again.

"Maybe. What is it you want?"

"There's an urgent situation that requires your presence."

Situation? I ran a hand through my hair, having no idea what he was talking about. "You better double check that address. Pretty sure I'm not the person you're looking for."

"We know who you are," Hudson said, an edge to her voice. "You never answered our calls." I was about to reply that nobody had called, when I realized I wouldn't know, for I'd muted the phone.

"Sir," Connor said, "I'd appreciate if you'd come with us. It won't take long…a few minutes is all. Standard procedure."

Stepping back a pace I forced my addled brain to consider what was happening. Clay leapt to mind, and I wondered if he had acted on that voice in his head. It wouldn't be the first time one of my patients got into trouble, and he was one of many. But in my judgment, most of my patients were a danger only to themselves. Even if Clay had surrendered to the voice, I was bound to confidentiality for all.

"Sorry, I can't help you," I said, and shut the door.

Hudson forced it back open. "We'll be the judge of that."

Connor laid a hand on her shoulder. "Mister Fisher, you're not being accused of anything. All we wish to do is have a friendly conversation."

"I won't discuss patients," I told them both.

Connor bounced a glance off Hudson, who gave a slight shake of her head. "Sir, I don't want to do this, but I can have a judge issue a subpoena. Then you'll see us again, probably later this morning." He shrugged, as if it were all the same to him. "I assure you that conversation will be less pleasant."

What more could he do that I hadn't already done to myself? Too tired to stand and not concerned enough to care, I turned my back and retreated toward the couch. "You do that," I said.

"You might be interested to know this involves your brother," Connor added.

I stopped mid-stride. "What did you say?"

"I'm referring to an Eric Fisher who works at Caltech. I believe he's your brother."

My breath stilled, and I turned to face him. "Is he hurt?"

"No sir, he's perfectly fine. We spoke with him last night. That's why we're here."

Whatever relief I might have felt was lost in exhaustion from days without sleep. "Who are you again?"

"Agents from the Special Security Force. We serve a branch of the military."

His answer left me more bewildered than before. "Never heard of it. What's this about, exactly?"

"It's a sensitive matter," Connor said. "And not something I'm authorized to discuss here."

"You said you wanted to talk, so talk."

"My compatriots prefer to meet with you in person, Mister Fisher. Like I said, this will only take a few minutes."

I couldn't fathom what possible trouble Eric might have gotten himself into. He was the good son, with excellent grades and a blessed life. My father had once called him the "steady one," which I took to mean that I was the opposite. Also, Eric would have called if there were trouble. I turned, and my eyes fell to the mobile phone sitting on the coffee table by the couch. I walked over and picked it up. There were several missed calls, and a text from my brother – "You're going to be asked questions by people you don't know. Don't worry, it's a misunderstanding. Call me."

"If you'd come with us, sir," Connor said. He beckoned toward the street where a glowing halo of fog from a streetlamp cast its dim light on a sport utility vehicle parked at the curb. Hudson stretched her head past my door and peered inside my home. Looking for what, I had no idea.

"Fine," I felt compelled to say.

After I clothed myself we were on our way. Hudson drove while Connor took shotgun. I was placed in the back seat. Once we left the city limits of Santa Barbara and entered the empty expanse north of Goleta, I grew concerned. "Where are we going?"

"Vandenberg Air Force Base, sir," Connor said.

That was an hour away. "You said this would take minutes."

"Yes, sir, for the interview."

"That wasn't the deal. I've changed my mind, take me home now."

"Like I said, sir, this is urgent."

"I don't care."

"I'm afraid my superiors will, Mister Fisher."

I again insisted he turn around only to hear him respond with a refusal. When I accused him of kidnapping, Hudson reached over and slammed shut a plexiglass partition that separated the front and back seats. Connor cracked it open. "Relax, we'll be there soon," he said, and closed it tight.

I pulled at the door handles, which didn't yield. I looked for a lock, which I couldn't find. I then hammered on the partition until the adrenalin powering my defiance began to fray. The agents ignored me. That should have concerned me more than it did, but I felt wrung out like an old washrag. Unable to do anything about the situation, I sank into the cushions and stared at the horizon.

Morning light feebly tried to break through a thickening marine layer, much like the cares of this world tried to penetrate my indifference. Streams of gray mist sauntered past and droplets of water formed on the windows, coalescing into lines of moisture which snaked down the surface like tears. Shadows of structures and trees floated by as if they were ghosts in the fog. Feeling numb, it seemed as if I watched myself watch the world go by.

Before I realized it, the vehicle slowed and passed through the gates of the base. After traveling for some minutes we approached a hulking five-story building. With straight lines and squared corners, it seemed to be made from a jumble of blocks. Even the fountain adorning the entrance flowed over a series of symmetrical shapes. Etched over the marbled entryway were the words, USSF Space Operations Command. Above that was the insignia of an eagle with two rockets gripped in its talons. What had Eric done to get these people's attention?

Hudson drove around the building and halted the vehicle in a red zone at a side entrance. She then popped out and opened the rear door. Gripping my forearm, she tried pulling me from the seat, resulting in my head smacking against the frame.

"No touching," I said, pulling her fingers off me.

After getting to my feet I rubbed my eyes, trying to sooth the hammering inside my head. My mouth felt like sandpaper. Hudson crossed her arms and I could tell she was about to say something rude when a finger tapped on her shoulder. "I've got this, dear."

An older woman stepped around Hudson and placed herself before me. A silver ponytail hung over one shoulder and eager eyes locked on mine. "You must be Stephen Fisher. Thank you for joining us. I apologize for the ungodly hour." With a smile she extended her hand. "My name is Dolores McCann."

CHAPTER SIX

Dolores regarded Stephen through the drizzle of a thickening fog that stubbornly hovered in the air, as if it were reluctant to touch the ground. With the disheveled hair, thin frame, and worried lines etched on his face, he looked to be the embodiment of sorrow. The whiff of drink and body odor only reinforced that impression. Now that she met him face to face, she was convinced more than ever before that this interview would be a waste of time. Worse, it was cruel to have dragged him from his home. It was obvious this man knew nothing of gravitational waves and less about an extraterrestrial transmission. His role in the detection was, as his brother had claimed, completely coincidental.

Stephen glared at the hand that hovered between them. "Why bring me out here?"

An obvious question and one for which she didn't have a satisfactory answer. She dropped her hand to her side. "My team has come across an anomaly, Mister Fisher. Though I don't expect you know anything about it the military insists on due diligence—"

"Doctor," Connor interrupted, "this interview needs to be conducted inside."

"It shall be," she assured him, "but not until our guest is put at ease."

"Who are you?" Stephen asked.

"You know my name, so I presume you're asking why I'm involved. I'm employed by Caltech, Mister Fisher, working with a team at the Jet Propulsion Laboratory."

"The college where my brother works."

"Yes, he's a professor there."

"What did you do to him?"

"Nothing, other than having spoken to him about this very subject. Right now, I expect he's getting ready for a class."

Stephen jerked his chin toward Connor. "Does he belong to you?"

Dolores did her best to keep the bitterness out of her voice. She never wanted the military involved with the investigation; it had been forced down her throat. "He belongs, as you say, to a branch of the military called the U.S. Space Force."

◆◆◆

It had started at a meeting with the NASA executive budget committee. Tara had presented evidence that the telemetry received by AMIGO wasn't due to a malfunction but was an accurate recording of anomalous gravitational waves. Victor had accused them both of manufacturing the data to save their jobs. But other members of the committee prevailed, and a stay of execution was granted.

Dolores was given one week to make the case. In that time the project team collected corroborating evidence that put the conclusion beyond dispute, not only proving the existence of the gravitational waves but that they were artificial in nature. After a series of seemingly endless meetings, the brass at NASA became persuaded that AMIGO had detected a transmission generated from an alien intelligence.

Dolores recommended the discovery be made public and that further investigation be done in collaboration with international partners. Surprisingly, at least for Dolores, Victor had agreed. But during this time news of the transmission had bubbled up to the executive branch. It was the President himself who made the decision to put the military in charge of the committee formed to investigate, specifically the head of Space Operations Command for the U.S. Space Force, General Beckman. And he treated the transmission as if it were enemy correspondence.

Victor had been ordered by the General to publicly declare AMIGO a failure and announce that funding had been suspended indefinitely. Privately, Dolores was directed to continue operations but lock down the project. The General declared that from here on out all information was on a need to know basis. Dolores was furious. The only silver lining to this foolishness was that she retained leadership of the science and engineering team, one part of a council otherwise made up of military and intelligence types.

◆◆◆

"Say something nice to Mister Fisher, won't you Connor?" Dolores asked.

Connor obliged, albeit stiffly, "Your cooperation is appreciated."

Stephen scowled and ran his gaze along the road, as if considering walking off the base. She didn't blame him. Quite frankly, she would have joined him if she could take the investigation with her.

"Whatever anomaly you found has nothing to do with me," Stephen said, and rubbed his hands over his arms.

"Though I expect that's likely," Dolores said, "I'm afraid my colleagues will insist on asking you a few questions. My advice, if I might be so bold, is to get this over with. Will coffee help? The cafeteria makes a fine latte, or an espresso if you'd prefer."

A glimmer of life appeared between Stephen's puffy eyelids. Shouldering her purse, Dolores gently tucked an arm into his and escorted him along a cement path darkened by moisture. Connor followed behind. The other agent—Dolores never caught her name—returned to the vehicle and drove off.

With a coffee firmly in his hand, Dolores escorted Stephen into the conference room set aside for the interview. It was nothing special, just four chairs and a table set within windowless walls, but it was a vast improvement over the space Connor had first recommended…the one used to interrogate suspects. A member of the investigatory council waited within, Obadiah Wallner, in charge of data acquisition for the National Security Administration. Neither greeting them nor rising from his seat, Obadiah just pocketed a smart phone and folded his hands. Dolores felt obligated to make an introduction.

"May I call you Stephen?" she asked. He barely lifted his shoulders, which she took as permission. "This is Obadiah, part of the team investigating the anomaly. Sit anywhere you like."

With a groan Stephen collapsed into the chair closest to the door.

Connor took the seat opposite while Dolores settled into the chair beside Stephen. From inside her purse, Dolores fished out a bottle of aspirin and placed two pills in front of him. Stephen didn't hesitate, he swallowed them in one gulp and rubbed his eyes.

"Mister Fisher," Connor began, "what you're about to hear is classified and must be held in the strictest confidence. You are not under any circumstances allowed to discuss this conversation with your friends, your colleagues, not even your wife. Do you understand me?"

"I have no interest in your secrets," Stephen said.

Connor slid a sheet of paper and pen across the table. "Regardless, your signature is required."

Stephen barely glanced at it. "I didn't ask to come here."

"I insist."

Dolores interceded. "It's a formality, Stephen. Whether it's necessary or not, I signed it, as did your brother."

Stephen took the pen and scribbled on the dotted line. Connor pulled the sheet toward him, then heaved a breath. He turned it toward Dolores. Stephen had signed her name on the paper. Which would have made her laugh had the situation been less tense.

"Doesn't matter, get on with it," Obadiah directed.

With a curt nod Connor reached into a satchel and withdrew a thin sheaf of typed sheets. "Mister Fisher, an encrypted transmission was intercepted by equipment operated by NASA's Jet Propulsion Laboratory. Since the transmission didn't originate from a domestic source, we suspect it emanated from a foreign satellite."—Dolores nodded along, pretending to agree with the absurd cover story— "I was hoping you might shed some light on this matter."

Focused on the coffee, Stephen sipped at it with his eyes half closed.

"Mister Fisher," Connor prompted.

"What?" Stephen yawned.

Connor repeated himself.

"How would I know anything about that?"

Connor traced his finger down the sheet. "On Saturday, September fifteenth, you were alleged to have identified the exact location where the transmission originated. Do you recall the events of that day? I believe it was somebody's birthday."

Stephen froze. He placed the mug of coffee on the table.

"Your brother told us that he brought your daughter a gift that day," Connor continued. "A computer tablet, I believe."

Stephen's gaze fell to his lap. "She took a picture."

"Which you helped her to take, is that correct?"

"She couldn't hold it still."

"Why did you choose that spot in the sky, Mister Fisher? Was it purposeful, was there a reason?"

Stephen examined his hands until the silence became thick, and increasingly uncomfortable. "It was my fault, you know."

Dolores winced at the pain she heard in that quiet voice. Shame filled her for being a part of this farce. Who cares if they took a picture? A coincidence in no way implied causality. "I'm sorry for your loss, truly."

Stephen didn't reply.

"Did someone, or something, tell you to take that picture?" Connor asked, remorseless. "This is important, Mister Fisher. It's the only reason you're here with us this morning. I have to say, it seems very odd you happened to pick out that one spot in the sky where the transmission originated. Stranger still was that you asked your brother to investigate. You know he works at a college with access to sophisticated equipment. What was it you hoped to hear? Who asked you to do it, and why?"

Despite her feelings on the matter, Dolores found herself leaning forward, wanting to hear the answer.

Long seconds ticked off the clock. Finally, Stephen raised his eyes only to study a picture on the wall of a launch vehicle with a white plume set against the backdrop of the Pacific Ocean. He stared at this for some time before, inexplicably, tapping on the microphone sitting in the middle of the table. His gaze wandered to Obadiah. "I never did hear what you do."

Obadiah steepled his fingers on the table. "I work in cryptology, Mister Fisher. Why do you ask?"

"Cryptology," Stephen repeated to himself, quietly. His eyes then drifted to the ceiling which he contemplated for a long moment. "You call it an anomaly."

"Indeed," Dolores confirmed, finding herself holding her breath.

Stephen swallowed. "Does it, by chance, sound like…I don't know, music?"

Connor clenched his jaw. Obadiah subtly straightened in the chair. Dolores kept her expression carefully neutral. "That's a strange question," she said. "Why would you think that it sounded like anything, Stephen?"

Stephen slumped into the chair like so much putty. "Never mind."

Dolores eyed Obadiah, who acquiesced to the unspoken suggestion with a nearly imperceptible nod. She then looked to Connor.

"Do it," Connor said.

Pulling the small laptop computer from her purse, Dolores powered it up and plugged it into a console on the table. She then found and tapped on the acoustic recording Tara had created from the transmission.

A slow haunting rhythm took over the room. It was lovely, mesmerizing even, and Dolores marveled that it originated from more than a thousand light years away. To hear it was to know it was otherworldly.

Stephen shrunk away from the computer. Obadiah and Dolores exchanged a knowing look, for they both saw it, the recognition so obvious on his face – Stephen had heard this music before.

Slowly lifting his hand, Stephen stared at it with widened eyes. His body began to shake violently, and his eyes glazed over.

Dolores rose to her feet. "He's having a seizure."

CHAPTER SEVEN

I arrived home from work and had just dropped my briefcase to the floor when I heard a shriek. With a patter of bare feet my daughter burst from the bedroom and ran down the hall into the foyer. She was dressed as Cinderella. After a quick pirouette, her face bloomed into a toothy smile.

"Very pretty," I said.

With a flourish, she handed me a piece of paper. "I made this."

Sketched in crayon was a stick-figure drawing of our family holding hands. The sun smiled from the corner and grass grew at our feet. There was also a dog we didn't own. Just in case I didn't notice Danika stood on her toes and pointed. "I would name her Princess Freckles."

"You realize somebody would have to take care of her."

"I would feed Freckles, play with her, and make sure she had water."

"Every day?"

"Yes. Now I want you to come here." Grabbing my hand, she began pulling me into the kitchen.

Steam rose from a pot on the stove and the air smelled of garlic and onions. At the counter Fran was grading papers from her fourth-grade class. She paused to greet me. I kissed her then handed her the picture. Fran studied it carefully, complimented Danika profusely, then tucked the drawing into her purse.

Pleased, Danika hopped into a chair at the dining room table. An electronic keyboard was on top. This was another gift for her birthday, as consolation for not getting a dog.

"You like your present?" I asked.

"I love it," Danika replied. "Are you ready to hear my song? I think you'll like it."

"She's been practicing all week," Fran said.

I took a seat. "Okay, let's hear it."

"Record me," Danika said. "I want to hear what I sound like."

"Sure thing." I pulled out my cell phone. "Break a leg."

"Daddy!"

"That means good luck, you know, in the entertainment business."

"Oh. Thank you."

I started recording. "Anytime you're ready."

Danika placed both hands on the keys, took a deep breath, and closed her eyes. Seconds passed. Fran and I looked at one another. Not often had we seen our daughter this composed. Raising a finger of her left hand, Danika began....

It started slowly, as a single tone in the voice of strings. A second note joined the first, then a third, producing a discordant chord. The fingers of her opposite hand introduced a higher octave, the effect being of wind chimes clanking in an erratic breeze. I had heard this before. I looked to Fran. "Did you teach her this?"

"No, she said that you did," Fran whispered. "It's beautiful, don't you think?"

I didn't think so at all. I found the sound disquieting, disturbing even, and my pulse began to race. My daughter then began to hum. Retreating into myself, I tried placing where I had heard this, but all I came up with was a memory of a memory...not of the sound, but of the hole it once occupied.

As the pace of the music quickened, an amber shimmer manifested around my daughter. I shook my head, trying to clear the hallucination, but the shimmer only intensified until I could no longer make out the sweet face of my child, only a maelstrom of color that spun in the air like a wheel.

Unwilling to do so, but feeling compelled nonetheless, I raised a hand before my face. The skin bulged and bubbled as if something percolated from beneath. Anxiety wrapped a steel band around my chest and fear tightened it. Unable to avert my gaze I watched as my skin peeled away to reveal silvery tendrils burrowing within the flesh. One paused and raised a pointy end, trying to look me in the eye.

"Get out of me!"

There is no me, there is only you, and there is nowhere to go.

White sparks flickered at the edges of my vision turning to searing tongues of fire that stabbed into my brain. My hands shook, and I dropped the phone to the floor. From a distance I heard Fran ask if I were okay. I wasn't. I wanted to run, away from the voice, away from the music, and especially, away from the pain.

The ground rushed toward me.

◆◆◆

"Can you hear me, Mister Fisher?"

I opened my eyes to find a mustached face hovering over me. There was a blood pressure cuff strapped to my arm and a monitor attached to my chest. I was in an ambulance. It was moving. My eyes flicked to the badge on the man's shirt, identifying him as a paramedic. I replayed events in my head, the last one being of music that sounded exactly like what my daughter had played for me on a keyboard. How was that possible?

"What happened?" I asked.

"You passed out, Mister Fisher," the paramedic explained. "The authorities at Vandenburg thought it best that you get checked out. We'll be arriving at the hospital in a few minutes. How are you feeling?"

So, I had another seizure. These had grown more frequent of late. "Just tired. We still on the base?"

"They don't have the facilities at Vandenberg. We're heading to a medical center nearby, in Lompoc."

Over the paramedic's objection I lifted myself into a sitting position. I then began peeling the sensors off my body. He tried stopping me, but I batted his hand away. "There's nothing to worry about," I said. "I have these fits now and again. It's my fault for neglecting my anticonvulsant medication. I just need to get home and get some rest."

"I strongly recommend you let the doctors check you out, just to be sure there's not a problem. You never know, and it's best to be safe."

"I'm fine."

The ambulance slowed to a halt. As I climbed out of the back a triage nurse stopped me at intake. We engaged in much the same conversation that I already had with the paramedic, but she wasn't appeased until I signed a form absolving the hospital of liability. All the while I noted Dolores McCann standing at a distance, watching and listening to what was transpiring. Once I thanked the nurse and paramedic for their concern, I began walking toward the street. I also pulled out my cell phone and executed a quick search on the internet.

Dolores joined my side. "Might I offer you a ride home?"

"No offense, but I think I'll pass." Exhausted, I took a seat at a bus stop and hailed a car using an app on the phone.

"May I ask you a question?" she asked.

I sighed, wanting nothing more than to get home. But I had a question of my own, concerning a growing suspicion. "All right, but I get to ask mine first."

"Fine. What is it?"

"I googled you, Dolores. You don't just work at JPL, you run it. Which begs the question, why would the director of such a prestigious organization come all this way to talk to little ol' me? I'm a nobody. Unless, and feel free to correct me if I'm wrong about this, your transmission didn't come from a satellite. My guess is it's coming from"—I waved a hand in the air— "somewhere faraway. Does that sound about right?"

Dolores regarded me a long moment before taking a seat on the bench beside me. "The military has their own way of doing things, Stephen. Regardless of what I think, secrecy is considered a means to an end. I expect that will eventually change, but for the moment, it is what it is."

"That's bullshit."

"Maybe so, but I caution you that Connor meant what he said about talking too freely. For that same reason, I'm afraid there's not much more I can tell you."

"Did my brother buy your story?"

"People tend to believe what they're told, especially when it's consistent with their preconceptions."

"Like not believing in little green men?"

She shrugged. "Your brother's a scientist, as am I. Facts guide my beliefs, as well as what I can see with my own eyes. My turn. Have you heard that music before?"

I expected the question and had already considered my answer. Given Connor had dragged me from my couch on a suspicion, who knows what he would do if I confessed to having heard that music before? Plus, how could I explain something I didn't understand myself?

"No," I lied.

"I see," Dolores said.

She doesn't believe you.

I flinched, not expecting to hear the voice. It had been some time since it last spoke to me. Stress must have brought it on. Also, how long had it been since I'd taken the antipsychotics? Two weeks, at least. Ever since the funeral. As disturbing as the return of the voice was, it was easy enough to remedy – I ignored it.

Seeing the car approach, I stood and waved it over. Dolores kept her eyes fixed on me. As I opened the back door, I paused, my curiosity getting the better of me. "That transmission of yours, it comes from the star system where my daughter took the picture. Is that what you're trying to hide?"

"I would hope you can work that out for yourself," Dolores said.

"I see," I said, mimicking her. "Goodbye, Dolores."

"Be well, Stephen."

I got into the car and didn't look back.

Wipers flung themselves back and forth in a futile effort to keep the windshield clear of the rain which had grown intense since leaving the hospital. Finding it mesmerizing I leaned against the headrest and tried to relax. But my mind churned.

How had my daughter known about that music? Over miles of road I kept coming to the same conclusion – she must have heard it before, whether it was on television, radio, or she had found it somewhere on the internet. Word of the transmission must have leaked, despite Dolores' claim of secrecy. Certainly, that would be big news. It might also explain how Danika picked that star system from out of the sky, though, that seemed a stretch.

"Which exit, sir?" the driver asked.

"State Street," I replied. Taking the designated off-ramp, the driver wound his way through downtown.

A ray of sunlight peeked through dark clouds billowing overhead and the rain lightened to a thin drizzle. Abruptly, the driver swerved to avoid a woman stepping off the curb. She held a child in one arm with her eyes glued to an electronic screen. I wanted to shout out the window for her to wake up. Didn't she know that her life balanced on a thin fulcrum of probability, and any wrong turn could rob her of everything she loved? I certainly did.

"Make a right at the next street," I said.

The moment the driver turned my day got much worse. For at the end of the cul-de-sac were strangers wearing blue jackets. One handed a heavily laden container to another crouched in the back of a white van parked in the driveway of my home. At the curb was a sport utility vehicle of the same make and model as the one which took me to Vandenberg. And leaning against the hood was the familiar figure of Agent Hudson. She sipped at a mug while looking at a man on top of a ladder leaning against my house. He was trying to pry the satellite dish from off the edge of my roof. Blood rushed to my head. Who the hell did these people think they were? And what was it they hoped to find?

"What's going on there?" the driver said.

"Drop me off here," I snapped.

The car came to a sudden stop. I tossed some bills onto the front seat then exited the car without a word. The driver took off. And there I stood, on the sidewalk frozen into immobility, unsure how to proceed in a world that had been turned upside down.

People I'd known for years peered over fences and through window curtains at the spectacle unfolding in front of my home. Greg, my next-door neighbor, stood on his driveway pretending to irrigate rose bushes that grew in the sliver of soil between our two properties. Despite the cold he wore his usual outfit...a faded t-shirt, ancient short shorts, and flip-flops. Water overflowed from the already saturated flower garden to stream past his flip-flops and into the gutter. Catching my eye, he angled his head toward the SUV parked at the curb.

A lone mug now sat unattended on the hood. The woman, Hudson, had her gaze locked on me while she spoke into a handheld radio. Another agent, this one restraining a German Shepherd with a leash, joined her at her side. They both began walking toward me. For an insane moment, I considered running. But I'd done nothing. If anybody had something to hide it was them.

Hudson held out a badge. "Mister Fisher, I have a subpoena granting me the authority to search your premises as well as your person." Reaching into her jacket, she produced an official looking document. I took it. It was a search warrant signed by the Honorable T. Rawlee Atkinson, Jr. There were several typed questions, one of which concerned what was concealed on my person or property. The hand-written answer referred to an Attachment A, which was nowhere attached.

I handed back the paper. "This is ridiculous."

"Hold out your arms," Hudson ordered.

The second agent slackened the dog's leash, which snuffed inches from my hand. The dog was big, and its eyes glittered, as if it sensed my defiance. I did as commanded. Starting with my armpits, Hudson patted me down in a practiced manner, noting the rectangular form of the cell phone straining against my slacks. In that moment it dawned on me what was on it, a recording of Danika playing the keyboard...evidence that I had heard the music before.

"Please empty the contents from your right-side pocket," Hudson said.

I had no choice. Taking the phone from my pocket, what once might have been freely given was confiscated from me. Hudson passed the phone off to her partner, who placed it in a plastic bag and retreated toward the waiting van, the dog in tow. I moved to step past Hudson, who blocked me with an upraised hand. "You may observe, but under no circumstances are you to interfere. Do you understand me, Mister Fisher?"

"What I *understand* is that you have no right to invade my home."

"You've been warned."

Giving Hudson a wide berth I headed straight for Greg, who I knew would tell me everything that had occurred while I was gone. With his legs planted wide and eyes bulging out of their sockets he looked about as pissed as I'd ever seen him.

Greg lived in a stygian world of shadows, where elections were rigged, politicians hopelessly corrupt, and the activities of citizens were surveilled by a government concerned solely with holding onto power. He also believed in Bigfoot, the Loch Ness Monster, and jackalopes. Up until today I thought he was paranoid. Sidling next to him we both watched as an agent struggled to fit what remained of my satellite dish into the van parked in my driveway.

"Bastards," he growled. "At first, I thought they were coming for me."

"How long have they been here?"

"Forty or so minutes. They've spent the time emptying your home of your electronics, files, and papers. I tried to intervene, but they warned me off. Knew my name too." He shrugged, as any soldier might, though Greg's sword was a keyboard, and his battle horse a faux leather captain's chair. "I'm recording them from a camera I hid in the front window," he said, nodding to himself. "Any idea why they're searching your house?"

I was tempted to tell Greg what had happened, but good sense intervened. Wouldn't do to have him implicated in my problem. "I think one of my patients got himself or herself into trouble," I lied, then told him what I believed to be true, "Pretty sure that these people have no idea what they're looking for."

"A fishing expedition."

"Yep."

"Bastards," he repeated, earning a hard look from the agent stuffing my belongings into the van. Giving me a sidelong glance, Greg added, "Fran's inside. She arrived about fifteen minutes before you got here."

My wife. She had returned home only to find me gone and her house overrun by strangers. I thanked Greg before hurrying across the driveway and walking toward the open door of my home.

Fran stood in the foyer. Brunette hair fell onto alabaster shoulders and her eyes were turned down in what I imagined was permanently etched grief. With arms tightly wrapped around a three-ring binder her mouth was stretched into a grim line. Behind her I saw opened cabinet drawers, cushions that had been flung off the couch, and empty book shelves with their contents spilled over the floor. "Bastards" was right.

Fran's eyes widened when she saw me. "Tell him he can't take the binder."

I stepped through the door to find another agent facing off with my wife. The man's eyes fixed on me, registered recognition, then returned to Fran. "Ma'am, you need to hand me those notes."

"It's okay," I said, and gently took the binder from Fran's arms. Flipping through the leaves I found memories of Danika inside: pictures, letters, and artwork carefully preserved inside plastic sheet protectors. So, this was the reason Fran had come home, to collect what remained of our daughter. Turning the binder around, I held up one of the pages to the agent. "I can't imagine your people have a need for drawings from a dead child. Why not let my wife mourn in peace?"

Hudson chose that moment to step through the door. Taking in the situation with a glance, she immediately used the radio to call for reinforcements. In the space of a few seconds two agents showed up at the door, including the one with the dog. "Either hand that binder over or I take you into custody," Hudson said. "Your choice."

A molten anger welled within me. Under false pretenses these people had taken me from my home then invaded it. I clamped the folder to my chest. "Get out!"

Hudson ran the tip of her tongue over her teeth. She gestured to the other agents when Fran intervened. "You can have it," Fran said.

"Smart lady," Hudson said, and yanked the binder out of my grasp. "Next time I won't be so nice." With an irate wave, Hudson dismissed the agents, then followed them out of the house. I slammed the door and flipped the bolt.

"What in the world is happening?" Fran asked. Her lips trembled as she swept a pitying gaze up and down my disheveled form. "You look terrible."

My rage receded only to be replaced by guilt amplified a hundredfold by shame. I leaned against the wall and slumped to the floor, like a sack emptied of contents. "I'm sorry," was all I could think to say.

Fran walked to the window and peered through the shutters. I heard doors slam and vehicles pull away. "Why would they take our things?" she asked.

"They came this morning," I said. In a stream of uninterrupted words, I told Fran everything that had happened. Most of it, anyway, for I was beyond tired, and recollection of who said what had grown confused. I told her about the agents, about Dolores, the transmission, and where I thought it came from. I didn't mention my seizure, or the voice. It was odd to hear myself tell the tale aloud, as if I were explaining something that happened to somebody else. Odder still was that Fran listened in silence, all the while staring at the floor, not even reacting when I told her about the music, the same Danika had played for us a lifetime ago.

Once I finished, Fran knelt beside me. "When's the last time you took your meds, Stephen?"

"I'm not making this up."

"When?"

"A while ago," I admitted.

Fran pointedly looked toward the table, where beer bottles lay on their sides. Others were strewn across the floor. "You had a few drinks, I see."

"That's not, I mean, I did have a couple…" I rubbed my eyes, fighting to remain coherent. "Sorry, what did you say?"

"You look like hell, Stephen, like you haven't slept in days. You also don't smell so good. Why don't you go wash up and get some sleep?"

All that had happened to me became immaterial at that moment. "Does that mean you're going to stay?"

Fran appraised me for a long moment before her lips formed a forlorn smile. "We'll see, Stephen, we'll see."

Encouraged that she didn't say no, I did exactly what she suggested, though I didn't make it to the shower. Once I got into the master bedroom I fell face first onto the mattress.

CHAPTER EIGHT

In the failing light of an early evening Dolores watched streams of gray mist saunter past the window from inside the conference room situated on the topmost floor of Space Operations Command. Seen on the screen covering the adjacent wall Victor Mercer sat behind a desk three-thousand miles away at NASA headquarters working at a computer. Obadiah was speaking with someone on a cell phone. Clicking her fingernails on the table Dolores glanced at her watch. It was an hour past the time the General had called for the impromptu meeting. Anxious to get on the road, yet dreading the commute home, Dolores began to collect her things. She was tired and there remained a mountain of work awaiting her back at JPL. She would just have to dial in from the car, despite the General's insistence they attend the meeting in person. As she was about to take her leave, General Beckman strode into the room, followed closely behind by Connor.

Obadiah pocketed the phone. Victor closed his laptop. With a resigned sigh, Dolores settled back into her seat. The General took his accustomed place at the head of the table while Connor slid into the chair opposite Obadiah. Wearing combat fatigues and a grim countenance, the General folded calloused hands and looked Dolores directly in the eye.

"Before we get to the business at hand," the General said, "I'd first like to understand how that man knew about the transmission."

"You're talking about Stephen Fisher?" Dolores asked.

"Who else?"

"An excellent question," Dolores said, and one she'd been asking herself. "I take it you heard about the interview?"

"I didn't have to hear about it, I listened in to the conversation from my office." Wiping a stray strand of hair over his balding head the General's gaze shifted to the screen. "It seems clear that Eric Fisher knew about the transmission and told his brother. If true, and I think it is, that means word leaked out of NASA. Victor, I expect you to track down the source and remove that person of responsibility before the leak becomes a sieve. Connor here will lead the investigation. I expect your security people to be made available to him."

Victor sat upright in his chair. "Yes, of course. NASA will cooperate fully," he said, then his eyes pierced Dolores. "I suggest the questioning start with the personnel at JPL. They are the only ones who know of the transmission."

Dolores shook her head, earning a disparaging stare from Victor. There was a big problem with the premise, and Obadiah said it before she had to.

"The events of the day in question occurred weeks before the transmission was picked up by AMIGO," Obadiah said.

"There was nothing to leak," Dolores confirmed.

"Then the signal must have been detected earlier than you know," Victor said. "Could have come from the ground-based interferometer. Or maybe AMIGO was activated before you were told about it."

"Eric Fisher denied foreknowledge," Connor reminded them.

"He might've lied," said Victor.

The General turned his attention to Dolores. "Is that possible?"

"That Eric lied? I suppose, but why would he?"

"No, Doctor. I'm asking if the transmission could have been detected earlier."

Dolores crafted her words to minimize embarrassing Victor. After all, he was her boss. "The ground-based laser interferometer detects the same phenomena, yes, but it's nowhere near sensitive enough to have detected the gravitational waves of this transmission. It's just not possible. As far as AMIGO goes, the three spacecraft weren't in a position to be operable. They weren't even powered up."

"Double-check anyway," Victor said.

"Yes, Sir," Dolores replied, knowing full well there was nothing to check.

Beckman persisted. "Assuming there was no leak, Doctor, then how the hell did Fisher know where the signal originated?"

"A coincidence," she said, earning a raised brow from Connor and a tilt of the head from Obadiah. "Both the brothers said it was the daughter who pointed the camera at the sky. Must have been random chance is all." It had to be, she thought.

"Connor also thinks that Fisher," the General continued, "and I'm talking Stephen Fisher here, recognized the transmission the moment he heard it. Explain that to me."

"I've been thinking about that. Could be he heard a similar tune on the radio, the internet, or an old vinyl record. Who knows? And what does it matter anyway? We should make the transmission public. People would willingly come forward with information and might raise questions we would never think to ask. We should also tap into the international community, pick the brains of top experts in every field. Progress would be quicker and results superior to anything we're going to come up with on our own."

"We've been through this," the General said, an edge to his voice.

"Doesn't mean you're not making a mistake."

The carotid artery pulsed in the General's neck, so distinctive that she could count each heartbeat. "You've been quite clear on your position, Doctor McCann. There's no need to repeat yourself. Until I understand what we're dealing with, news of the transmission will be kept under wraps. There may come a time to share what we know, but now is not that time. I think you will appreciate my position once Connor shares what he's learned."

Dolores looked to Connor, whose face was stone. "Oh, and what's that?"

"We obtained a warrant to search the premises of Stephen Fisher—" Connor began.

"You did what?" Dolores interrupted, appalled. "That man came here voluntarily, and now you search his home. How is that remotely okay? Doesn't even sound legal."

"Let him finish," Victor said. "I want to hear this."

Dolores shook her head. "The signal emanates a thousand light years away. Am I the only one who thinks employing the tactics of a police state doesn't help with the investigation?"

"You have to admit," Obadiah said. "The man's behavior was odd."

"Continue," the General ordered, his voice curt.

Connor tapped on a console splitting the overhead screen into two halves. On one side was Victor, his lips pinched in lingering disapproval. On the other was the frozen image of a young girl sitting at a dining room table in front of a keyboard. Dolores knew without having to ask who that girl was. She looked like the father.

"This is Danika Fisher," Connor said. "The video you're about to see was found on a mobile phone in possession of Stephen Fisher." Obadiah leaned forward, as did Dolores, noting that General Beckman kept his eyes pinned on her. Connor touched a key.

The child began to play. It started simply, with a long a drawn out pull of a bow over a stringed instrument. She added a second note, then a third, creating a chord that exactly mimicked the sound of the transmission. Dolores gasped, and as she listened, her objections melted into irrelevance, as did her considerable annoyance. Then the child began to hum in time with the music. "How is this possible?" she murmured.

"Maybe now you won't object to my tactics," the General said.

Dolores' mind churned, not only at the impossibility of what she was hearing but at what it could mean. The girl knew. How, she had no idea, but what was more significant was the song, which rang in perfect harmony with the music. She looked to Obadiah, Associate Director in charge of data acquisition for the National Security Agency. Having risen through the ranks of the Cryptologic Services division, Obadiah was the only one on this council who could understand. Already staring her full in the face, Obadiah lifted an eyebrow. Dolores nodded her agreement.

General Beckman stopped the recording. "What is it?"

"The first step to understanding any signal is knowing where it begins," Obadiah said. "The transmission is a continuous waveform that could have been transmitting for years, decades, or eons. We have no idea where it begins or if it will ever end."

"That doesn't help," the General said.

"The child's voice might offer a clue for us to decrypt the signal," Dolores explained. But how the child knew the music was beyond her. Did Stephen teach her this? If so, how did he learn of it? And from whom? Questions only led to more questions.

"Get on it then," the General said. "We need to find out what more the man knows. He's obviously hiding something."

"We don't know that," Dolores said, though her insistence sounded weak to her own ears.

"After having heard the transmission he chose not to disclose the recording. Don't be thick, Doctor." The General turned to Connor. "I want a close eye kept on Fisher. I want to know what he does, what he says, and want him tracked everywhere he goes."

"Yes, Sir," Connor replied. "Though, I don't have agents to cover—"

"That problem's been solved," the General interrupted. "I've spoken to the Vice President who has arranged that domestic intelligence resources be made available to your organization. Liaison officers have been appointed. I'll send you the names."

"Thank you, Sir."

"What more did you learn about the child?"

"The daughter had little contact with outsiders," Connor said. "The family kept her very close. Any clue to how she knew that music was lost the moment she died."

"And the body?" Beckman asked.

"She wasn't cremated, which is good. As we speak my people are tracking down the cemetery. Forensics assures me the soft tissues would remain intact…."

It took a while for Connor's words to sink in. And the moment they did Dolores found herself on her feet. "Tell me you're not planning on exhuming that child's grave!"

Beckman glared. "You're charged with science, Doctor. I suggest you leave security to the experts."

Dolores couldn't help herself. "You're spending time chasing ghosts when we should be studying the transmission. For what possible reason would you dig that girl up?"

"You have to ask?"

"Oh my god, you want confirmation that she's human?"

"We investigate every possibility, no matter how remote."

"The procedure is surgical," Connor said, using an infuriatingly reasonable tone. "The drill is guided through the earth by sonar. Only a small sample will be taken, otherwise, the body will remain undisturbed. The family will never know."

As he spoke, Dolores imagined the drill biting through the dirt, the paneling of the casket giving way, and the body being violated. Her voice rose an octave, "I refuse to be a part of this."

The room went still, until Victor smoothly broke the silence. "You're welcome to make that choice."

Beckman slapped a hand on the table. Dolores jumped. "Unimaginably powerful. That's how you described beings able to manipulate gravitational waves. I'd imagine our technology would seem quaint to them, like, what did you say, tinker toys?"

"Sticks and stones," Dolores said, albeit, reluctantly. She knew where he was going with this.

Beckman's expression morphed from red-faced anger into an impatient stare. "Given that power have you ever considered these entities might already be here? What if they're not friendly, Doctor? With power comes danger. I've got the scars to prove it. And for as long as I'm in charge of this council my first priority will be keeping this nation safe. You decide, stay, or go, but you make that decision now."

Connor averted his gaze. Obadiah subtly shook his head, his normally impassive eyes holding the barest of pleas. Doubts assailed her. What point was she trying to make anyhow? To prove that she was queasy about disturbing the dead. She was. But violating the body of an innocent child was only a symptom of the real problem - the utter paranoia that infected this investigation. It was disgraceful. Worse, it was unproductive. She should walk out. But the only thing keeping her from doing exactly that was what she knew would happen after: a person just as qualified would be slotted into her place, leaving her to miss what could be a turning point in human history. Passing a hand over her blouse, Dolores tried wiping the stain from her conscience. She sat down, her illusion of influence gone, the choice made. "I'm not going anywhere."

The General pursed his lips in that condescending manner Dolores had seen before, having dealt with Beckman types her entire career. She didn't know her place, it seemed. "This council will do whatever is necessary to learn the purpose of the transmission and assess the threat. It's past time you understood that, Doctor."

CHAPTER NINE

There was a scream. I looked up too late to see that I had run a red light and that a semi-truck was about to plow into the passenger side of my car.

Throwing out my arms I sat up. I was at home, in bed, and entangled in sheets drenched in sweat. My breathing was shallow. But it was only a dream, and a new morning. It took a moment's reflection to recall how I'd gotten into bed, and another to recall the events that preceded it. There was a council, a transmission, music, a hospital, then agents desecrating my home. I had seen Fran. Sweeping aside the covers, I looked out the window. Shadows of wind-blown clouds drifted over a lawn sparkling with dew. Scanning the room, I noted that the mess from before was gone. And a plate of food and glass of water waited for me on the nightstand. A welcome sight as I was famished. Better yet, it meant Fran might still be here.

The bottle of water I drank in a series of gulps, satiating a desperate thirst. The pastry and banana I consumed in a few bites, leaving two blue pills placed prominently in the center of the plate. This was a message from my wife.

I mused on the behaviors which Fran could have construed as a recurrence of my psychosis: withdrawal from friends and family, check; depression, check; paranoid delusion of being persecuted by a military committee investigating a mysterious extraterrestrial signal, check. A trifecta of mental illness. Or so she thought. Then again, maybe she was right.

I stepped into the bathroom to judge what had greeted my wife at the door. Reflected in the mirror were whiskers too short to be called a beard, a mass of unruly hair, and a t-shirt yellowed with stains under my armpits. Add poor hygiene to the list of symptoms. No wonder Fran hadn't believed a word I said. Dumping what I wore into a pile, I showered and groomed, striving to match the image of the man my wife thought she had married. Rummaging through the closet, I found what could pass for clean clothes. Once I was dressed, I ran a comb through my hair and re-checked my appearance. Not great, but presentable. The pills I dropped into my pocket.

I headed down the hall and into the living room. There I paused. The books were back on the shelves, the floor was clear of clutter, and the pillows on the couch were perfectly arranged, almost like the search had never happened.

"Franny," I called. There was no response.

Having spent a lifetime second guessing reality, I marched out of the house and looked up to the edge of the roof. Sure enough, the mount of the satellite dish dangled from screws torn from the fascia board. Not that I really doubted the search had happened, but I needed to be sure.

A cool breeze brushed my cheek as I breathed in the fresh air, enjoying an unusual contentment. The scent of the ocean reminded me of happier days. Birds whirled through the air, their chirping louder than usual. The grass shone a neon green under a sapphire sky. And the bed of roses glowed with luminescent reds, pinks, and whites. Whether it be due to a good night's sleep or because I had seen my wife, everything seemed more alive than usual. I took the pills from my pocket and regarded them. Forgetting to take the medication surely was a reason for this lucidity. I liked it. Loath to return to mind-numbing darkness, I flicked the pills into the shrubs, telling myself I could take them at any time, especially if the voice returned, which I didn't expect. For now, I would revel in the light.

My stomach growled. After reentering the house, I bee lined to the kitchen where I began pawing through the refrigerator. The milk was sour, the greens wilted, and an unknown fruit was covered with mold. It resembled a chia pet. The yogurt looked okay, though it was well past the expiration date. As I gave it an investigatory sniff, I heard the front door open. Fran entered the kitchen. I hustled over to take the grocery bags from her arms. In silence, she began putting the food away while I cleaned out the refrigerator, both of us going through the practiced motions of a past life.

"You slept twenty-two hours," Fran finally said. "How are you feeling?"

Meaning, was I still the lunatic she had met at the door yesterday? Believing it more important to reconcile with my wife than try convincing her that what happened to me was real, I replied, "Much better."

Fran rewarded me with a wisp of a smile. "Good," she said, then proceeded to prepare an omelet for both of us.

As we ate our meal, Fran occasionally wiped a hand over her cheek, hiding the tears. I pretended not to notice, thinking it best to keep my mouth full and unoccupied with dangerous talking. She would approach whatever there was to say in her own time, I knew. Surveying the kitchen, I noticed the things that were missing: knick-knacks from the shelves, pictures of our family, some books but not others, and for whatever reason, the dish rags. But it was the absence of our daughter I missed most of all, whose voice and antics once enlivened our home. That was a hollow space that could never be filled.

Fran picked at her food then dropped her fork onto the plate. Placing both hands over her face, she said, "Stephen, I can't take this."

"How 'bout we go for a walk?" I suggested, hoping it wasn't me she couldn't take.

To my great relief, Fran nodded.

After collecting the keys, I slipped into my shoes and joined Fran, who was waiting out front. Ignoring the quizzical glances from our neighbors, we strode down the sidewalk, both of us knowing the destination without having to speak. Walking in comfortable silence, we soon arrived at the memorial garden, an island of beauty hidden amidst the busy streets of the city. Down a meandering path we came to a wooden gazebo overlooking a pond. Grasses edged the still water and lilies floated serenely on the surface. A raft of ducks hurriedly swam towards us, knowing we were good for a meal. Pulling two quarters out of my pocket, I bought a handful of feeding pellets from a coin operated dispenser and poured the pellets into Fran's waiting palm. She absently flung them into the water one by one, making sure the shyest fowl got their fair share.

After a time, she said, "I called a lawyer."

"Oh," I said, surprised.

"To look into what happened yesterday. Greg gave me the reference, claiming she was the best in town. Anyway, this lawyer checked in with the police who informed her that no charges had been filed against us. They couldn't even confirm we were the subject of a search warrant. The lawyer asked me if we might be involved in another investigation. I wanted to tell her that wasn't possible, then I thought of your practice." Fran dumped the remaining pellets into the water and turned to face me. "Some of your patients aren't good people, Stephen. I know you have a hard time believing that, but it's the truth. I want you to talk to this lawyer, to be sure that we're protected."

Ah. So, that was it then. Fran had devised an explanation to neatly explain away what had happened to our home. Understandable, given my first instinct was to blame a patient. The story also buttressed her suspicion that my claims from yesterday were nothing but figments of my imagination.

"Sure, I'll call the lawyer," I said. "Good idea." But it wasn't for the reason Fran supposed, but because I wanted to consult the lawyer about an altogether different matter, a concern that had arisen since our little walk to the park.

"Thank you," Fran said, and let loose a relieved breath as the tension so tightly wound within her began to relax. As we strolled out of the park, Fran's hand found mine. Warmth filled my soul.

I chose not to spoil the moment by mentioning the woman who pretended to read a book on the bench near the gazebo. Or the man sitting at a bus stop across the street whose eyes followed our every movement. Or the sedan that crept two blocks behind us as we walked back to our home.

CHAPTER TEN

Dolores felt the tug of gravity as the elevator propelled her small team toward what she feared was to be her peremptory dismissal. Since she'd objected to the search of Stephen Fisher's home, not to mention invading the grave of his child, Dolores hadn't heard from anybody on the council, not even from her supposed boss, Victor. They did, however, hear from an analyst working in Obadiah's organization, Michael, who requested access to the archived telemetry and real-time data pouring out of AMIGO. At this point, it seemed the function of her team had devolved into being nothing more than operators of the gravitational wave observatory.

She sipped at her coffee for comfort, like a child hugging a teddy bear. Why the silent treatment? Had she been too vociferous with her objections? She'd thought prostrating herself before the General would have papered over that conflict. Maybe she'd been too insistent with subsequent demands for people and equipment to study the transmission. If so, that would be ironic given she'd been provided nothing. Or maybe somebody had divulged the existence of the transmission. Her stomach lurched at the thought. That would explain everything…the silence, the sudden meeting, and last-minute demand that she bring along her team. It was the perfect excuse for the General to take full control of the investigation. Now that she thought more about it, she felt sure that's what was happening.

"Good god, Dolores, lighten up."

Dolores dropped her eyes to look upon her diminutive friend, Megan, knowing she would make one hell of a scene if they were about to be fired. That lifted her spirits a little.

She first met Megan thirty years ago as part of a team designing a sensor to detect life on other worlds. Since then, they had become fast friends. A biochemist by training, Megan had grown to become one of the world's foremost astrobiologists. Dolores had just this month recruited Megan to handle the biologic aspects of the investigation, putting her one step closer to forming a multi-disciplined science and technology team. Optimistic thinking, she realized now.

The elevator shuddered to a sudden stop, sending coffee splashing onto her blouse. While wiping it off with a napkin Dolores couldn't shake the feeling this was an omen for what was to come. She placed a hand over the elevator bumper to allow Tara and Megan to step onto the floor before following with leaden steps.

"You realize the General will want a briefing on what we've learned," she said.

Megan swung around and planted her four foot eight-and-a-half-inch frame directly in front of Dolores. "Tara figured out the transmission repeats itself, what, every twenty-six days?"

"Twenty-five days, six hours, and twelve minutes," Tara corrected her.

"That's a big deal," Megan said. "I'd call that a breakthrough. Tell your General that."

"Michael figured that out before we did," Tara said. "Claimed he couldn't tell us because the information was considered confidential. Sorry to break it to you, Megan, but we've never been a part of this team and never will be." Lowering her voice, she hissed, "Next thing you know we'll find our homes being searched."

"Best keep that to yourself," Dolores warned.

"Then tell him your theory, Dolores," Megan said, and smiled, as if trying to instill some of her own overwhelming confidence into them both. "I happen to believe you might be right, or at least, you're onto something."

Dolores dismissed the suggestion with an impatient wave of her hand. "Nothing more than conjecture, Megan, totally unsubstantiated. What little credibility I have with this council, or had, will disappear if I start waving my hands around without evidence to back me up. We need proof."

"Nonsense," Megan said. "This is uncharted territory. Defend yourself by speaking up. From what you've told me, the people on this council are idiots."

Tara sniffed her agreement.

"Don't either of you make the mistake of thinking they're stupid," Dolores said. "Least of all, that fellow Obadiah. They're just focused on the wrong priorities."

"Same difference," Megan insisted, then swiveled on her heel and strode down the corridor leaving Dolores and Tara to look at one another. With a sinking feeling, Dolores quickened her steps to catch up to Megan and passed through the open doors at the end of the hall.

Dolores scanned the room. At the table was Obadiah and next to him sat an intent young man hunched over a laptop. At least he was young as far as Dolores was concerned, thirtyish or so. Dolores assumed this to be Michael. General Beckman had his back to the door speaking with Connor.

Megan marched up to the General. "I've heard a lot about you," she interrupted, and pumped his limp hand. "I look forward to being part of this team." Beckman looked to Dolores, the incredulity on his face clearly asking, "Who the hell is this?"

"General, everybody," Dolores said. "This is the newest member of my team, Megan McCullough, an expert in chemistry and astrobiology." She gestured to the side. "And you all know Tara."

"An astrobiologist," the General said. It wasn't a question, but rather, a judgement on the usefulness of that profession, and by extension, of Dolores herself.

Before Dolores could explain, or rather defend, her judgement, Obadiah interrupted. "This is Michael," he said, gesturing to the man tapping at his computer. "One of the best cryptologists at the National Security Agency."

"Um, hello," Michael said. His gaze lingered on Tara's mid-section a tad too long, before his attention returned to the keyboard. Single, Dolores guessed. And judging by the rumpled clothes and oily sheen of his hair he'd been that way for a while. While everybody took their seats, Dolores heard Connor chuckle while telling the General something about linebackers. An eye-roll from Tara confirmed it. They were talking about football. Oh god.

"First order of business," the General said, clasping his hands before him. "I've already consulted with your boss, Victor, and we've agreed the operation of AMIGO will be transferred from the Jet Propulsion Lab to personnel in the National Security Agency. I'd like a detailed plan by the end of the week and operational transfer completed in less than thirty days." He paused a heartbeat, his eyes pinned to Dolores. "Do you see a problem with that?"

Though Dolores had expected the worst, it still felt like a punch in the gut. Tara bowed her head, her long hair screening her face. Megan's cheeks flushed pink. Obadiah stared straight ahead, avoiding her gaze.

"You wanted this from the beginning," Dolores accused.

"Don't take it personally," the General said. "The NSA has resources which dwarf your own, in people, facilities, computers, you name it. This move will position this council to make much faster progress—"

"Progress?" She couldn't keep the frustration out of her voice. "You insist that anybody on the team have a top-secret security clearance. That's not only unnecessary, it's wasting time. Of the twenty-six names I gave to Connor" — all experts who'd spent considerable time thinking through issues involved with first contact— "none have been approved. Almost like you're purposefully obstructing our role in the investigation." What the hell, if she were to be fired, she would go down fighting.

"Security is the primary reason I want operations transitioned," Beckman snapped. "It's no secret that I want a tighter lid kept on this project. I fear civilians can be, shall we say, undisciplined."

With unblinking eyes, he stared at Dolores, the message clear - she wasn't to be trusted. But it made no difference. The General wanted control, simple as that, no matter how well behaved she was. Still, why drag them to Vandenberg, to rub her nose in it?

"You could have told me this in an email," Dolores said. "Why bring us here?"

The General jerked his chin toward Obadiah. "Director Wallner has something to share with your team."

This caught Dolores by surprise. After a moment of deliberation, her curiosity focused around a singular suspicion. "The recording of the child, you found something."

"What you're about to hear can't leave this room," Connor warned.

Dolores' heart fluttered. She turned to Obadiah. "You deciphered the signal using the child's song?"

Obadiah shook his head. "Not exactly, no. But you're right about the recording. Turns out it allowed us to identify a pattern in the signal." He tapped on Michael's shoulder. Michael's head snapped up from the laptop and his eyes fluttered, shocked to find himself the center of attention. "Explain what you found," Obadiah directed.

"Oh, right, yeah sure," Michael said. After tapping a key, he flipped the laptop around. The screen showed a series of three-dimensional multi-colored bars flowing left to right. Having stared at a similar graph for hours, Dolores knew this was a depiction of the gravitational wave. Numbers scrolled vertically below the graph at the same pace as the horizontal bars. Michael dragged his finger over the screen. "The child sang twelve measures, delimited by a series of distinct pauses. Using those measures, we were able to identify a time-boxed series of frequency modulated patterns repeated within the transmission."

Dolores sat back, stunned. "How did she know?" she asked, more to herself, than anybody in the room.

"That can't be a coincidence," Obadiah said.

"Twelve measures," Megan said, thoughtfully.

"Yes," Michael confirmed.

"Did you find patterns within the individual frequency modulations?" Tara asked.

"Fifty-four," Michael answered, "interspersed at irregular intervals. I was about to get to that."

"Why is that significant?" Obadiah asked.

"In a moment," Tara said. "Did you find anything else?"

"No, I'm afraid that's all we came up with," Michael said.

"You have no frame of reference," Megan interjected. "No context."

"How could anybody?" Michael said, defensive.

"Which is why I brought this to your team," Obadiah said.

Tara leaned into the display, brushing her hair behind her ear. "The amplitude doesn't show any type of pattern, does it?"

"None," Michael confirmed.

Tara broke into a faint smile, which Megan amplified into a Cheshire grin. They both looked to Dolores, who shook her head. The General, who up until this point seemed indifferent to the conversation, straightened in the chair. "What is it?"

"The twelve patterns might provide context," Tara said. In answer to the General's blank look, she added, "Meaning, if there's a message, it could be based on a duodecimal numeric system. From a mathematical point of view, it's simpler and easier to conceptualize than using decimal. Makes sense."

"Might also mean our alien friends have twelve fingers, tentacles, or whatever it is they use to count," Megan said.

"Absurd," the General said.

"No more absurd than this"—Megan wiggled ten stubby digits in the air— "Why do you think we count in chunks of ten?"

"Which tells you what?" Obadiah asked.

Megan opened her mouth to reply when Dolores cut her off. "Let's not get ahead of ourselves."

"Dolores has a theory," Megan said, ignoring her. "And I'd wager she can make sense of the transmission."

"Is this true?" Obadiah asked.

Dolores shrugged, but it fit, all of it…the numbers, the patterns, the random amplitudes. A ray of light slipped through the clouds of resentment and her heart pounded.

"Spit it out, Dolores," the General insisted.

Not daring to hope her guess was correct, Dolores proposed a bargain. "Tell you what, give me Michael's data and give my team two weeks. If I'm wrong, you lose nothing. But if we figure this out, JPL stays in charge of AMIGO."

The General frowned and looked to Obadiah, who returned, what for him was a vigorous nod. "I still expect a transition plan," the General said.

"Of course," Dolores agreed, having no intention whatsoever of following that order.

CHAPTER ELEVEN

Fran and I passed the days in a routine filled with household chores, preparing meals, watching television, and long walks. Each of us took comfort from the other in the small talk of everyday life. She never again brought up the attorney, nor discussed the search of our home. I suspect she feared cracking the eggshell of my sanity, which was fine, as it was more important to heal the rift between us.

When we weren't together, I spent my time researching how Danika might have known the music I heard at Vandenberg. I fast forwarded through her television shows, listened to her favorite songs, and played her computer games, but found nothing that sounded remotely similar. Believing she must have heard it somewhere, I scoured the internet looking for news of the transmission. Again, I found nothing. I even called JPL and asked to speak with Dolores McCann. But every person I spoke with claimed to have no idea how she could be reached. Some told me she was on special assignment, others that she had retired, and more than one implied she had left under a cloud. The responses left me back at square one, more puzzled than before.

As I lay in bed staring at the ceiling, the rhythmic breathing of my wife brought me comfort but no peace. How had Danika known? Flipping over, I buried my face into the pillow, forcing myself to relax. But that only increased my aggravation. Conceding sleep was out of reach, I slipped out of bed, being careful not to wake Fran.

Making my way to the kitchen I pulled a yogurt from the refrigerator and began spooning in mouthfuls. On edge and off balance, I felt like an actor on a stage who'd forgotten his lines. I had no answers and no idea where to look for them.

My eyes wandered to the backyard. Trees glimmered silver from the reflected light of the moon and elongated shadows lay on a frost-covered lawn. The blades of grass looked brittle, as if they would shatter when stepped upon. A hawk moth flickered past and settled onto the desiccated remains of a tomato plant. Deciding that pastures were greener elsewhere, the moth fluttered into the air and disappeared over the fence. Stillness returned to the night, but not to my thoughts. How did she know?

At the edge of awareness, a shadow flickered, and a whisper beckoned, as if somebody murmured from behind. Startled, I dropped the yogurt onto the floor. I looked over my shoulder. There was nobody there. Going to the entryway, I peered into the living room. It was empty.

You should follow, my inner voice said.

I ignored it. Returning to the counter I ripped a paper towel from the dispenser and began wiping up yogurt.

Ever wonder if the answers to your questions wait inside the place you most fear?

"I'm not listening."

You know where that is.

The voice referred to the shrouded place I had escaped from as a child. I could literally see it now, a shimmering curtain of iridescence that separated me from madness. This was the place where the Stranger lived, the name I had given the voice. Memories of my time there were few, but enough to recall the price I paid to break free: being strapped to a steel table while suffering a pain so great that even the reminder sent a dagger through my head.

You also know who it was that whispered.

"That was nothing but a delusion, like you."

There is no me, there's only you, and the delusion is believing that what you hear isn't real.

"Go back to where you belong."

The whisper came from your daughter.

I dropped to the floor and rubbed my eyes, wanting to believe it. "You're trying to fool me."

You can only fool yourself.

A lump formed in my throat. In truth, I did recognize that whisper.

I had heard it before, in the quiet of my mind. Only wishful thinking, I had supposed. But knowing the voice wasn't real didn't stop me from hoping a piece of my daughter still lived.

You're afraid.

"I'll get lost if I go there."

You're already lost.

"You can't be trusted."

Then you don't trust yourself. Be bold, be brave, follow the shadow.

Contemplating entering that shrouded place caused me to break out in a cold sweat. But the chance of reconnecting with my child, however slight, proved irresistible. Throwing away years of discipline, and all caution, hope compelled me to tear the curtain aside.

Foreign thoughts slid through and around me, each a temptation to lose myself in wondrous delusion. Turning aside the distractions, I closed corporeal eyes to concentrate on the flicker of a shadow. Like the wings of a moth, it tried to slip away, but I held it firmly in my mind, turning it round and round until the darkness took form. It was a perfect sphere. A wavering finger of light appeared within, sputtering like a candle flame in a breeze. I forced myself to follow.

The floor dropped out from under me and fear metastasized into terror as I plunged into a well so deep that if time were wind, it would have been whistling past my ears. I had no idea how much time passed as I fell into this lightless well; it could have been an hour or a day. Then the sense of motion ceased as abruptly as it had begun.

I found myself floating within a cavern of emptiness. Moving my limbs, or what I imagined to be limbs, I encountered only empty space. Then, a faint luminescence brightened the interior, birthed from hundreds of golden orbs that covered the ceiling above, like unblinking eyes that awakened to pass judgment on me. Issuing from each came a fog that filled the emptiness. The fog thickened and grew spindly arms, which shimmered and began to spin in a complex and multi-hued dance. My breath quickened, and my chest heaved. I had seen this maelstrom before.

It was my daughter.

Falling to metaphorical knees, I tried begging her forgiveness, but the words wouldn't come. In a voice as distant as the fog was amorphous, I heard her say, "You belong with me."

To my distress, the disembodied form dissolved into the mist from whence it came. Golden orbs retreated into shadow and the fog dissipated into the darkness. I called for Danika, only to find myself mute.

Reality intruded, and my eyes flew open. My heart dropped. My child was gone, as was the certainty that what I beheld was real. In a moment of panic, I raised a hand before my eyes. But there were no tendrils, only fingers and skin. I sighed, thankful that I had returned whole. Just as I suspected, the vision was nothing but a trick of the Stranger.

If you can't trust yourself, then trust this…

An image percolated to the forefront of my mind. I knew where it lived. Getting to my feet I strode to the end of the hall where I paused. Since the day my daughter had died, I hadn't the strength to step inside her bedroom. Turning the knob, I entered and closed the door. I flipped on the light. My eyes immediately went to the bed, half expecting to find her asleep. But there were only sheets, tossed aside exactly as they had been when Danika had awoken that morning. Toys lay scattered across the bedroom floor and three books lay face down in front of a bookshelf emptied of contents by the agents that invaded our home. My gaze shifted to the nightstand. Three sand dollars were set in front of a clock with an owl for a face and arms made of wings. Two were broken in half and the third was whole but scarred due to a spot of black tar common along the shore. These were Danika's special treasures, the shell with the spot being the first she had found as we strolled along the beach. I picked it up and ran my finger round the edge, imagining that day. But none of these things were the reason I was here. I set aside the sand dollar and lifted my eyes to a sheet of paper stuck to the wall.

This was the drawing I had given Fran the day Danika played her song. Fran had taken it from her purse and hung it in Danika's room as a memorial to our lost child. Carefully, I peeled the scotch tape from the wall and held the paper up to the light.

Sketched in crayon were stick-figure drawings of our family holding hands, plus the hoped-for dog. Each of us had bubbles for heads and circles for hands. I pulled the paper close. Inside the head-bubbles were intricately drawn spirals emanating from a common center.

Moving my eyes down the sheet, I looked within the circle-for-hands to find finely drawn lines, each of them with a distinctive beginning and end. I stared at the images, imagining what I saw in the throes of my own madness: colors swirling in people's heads and tendrils wriggling within their flesh. I stuck the drawing back on the wall, convinced that what I suspected was true – my daughter had seen others as I did.

What might have been diagnosed as a shared psychosis couldn't be reconciled with the simple fact that I never told my daughter anything about my hallucinations. Nor did I ever tell my wife. Though I couldn't explain how Danika saw the same things that I did, I knew what I must do. One way or another I would learn how she had known about the music. It was the only part of her that still lived.

Though I doubted my daughter in life, I would not fail her in death.

CHAPTER TWELVE

It didn't take two weeks to prove Dolores' theory correct; it took seventy-two hours. When she called General Beckman to inform him of the news, he ordered her to appear at Space Operations Command for a meeting the very next morning. Once again, she and her small team sat around the same conference room table as General Beckman and the council. But this time Dolores felt no anxiety or self-doubt, for her team had uncovered something astounding.

"My team has uncovered something truly remarkable..." the General began.

Adorned with stars on his shoulders and multi-colored bars on his chest, the General addressed the overhead display where the Vice President of the United States, Janise Martinez, presided inside the White House Situation Room along with several other serious-minded people. The only person Dolores recognized was Victor, though the faces of the others were familiar from her having seen them on the news. As the General continued to read from the script Dolores had provided, Obadiah leaned into her ear. "To the left of the Vice President are the Secretaries of Homeland Security and Defense. On the right is the Director of National Intelligence, my boss."

"Should I be nervous?"

"I think so, yes."

Wondering if Obadiah was joking (and if so, that would be a first), Dolores looked at him. But the enigmatic mask was already in place as he held himself still and silent, like a sphinx sculpted from obsidian. She returned her attention to the General.

"Doctor McCann, who leads our science and engineering team, will expound on what was discovered," the General concluded. With a polite tip of his hand, acting as if she were always a valued member of the committee, he beckoned her to take center stage.

Eyes made larger by the magnification of the screen followed Dolores as she stepped up to the podium. After politely greeting her remote audience, she got right to the point. "The recording of the child is what I'd liken to a Rosetta stone. But rather than hieroglyphics inscribed on a rock, the key to deciphering the language hidden within the transmission turned out to be a song."

Feeling much like the professor she had once been, Dolores scribbled two equations on the adjoining whiteboard: $0 + 0 = 0$ and $0 + 1 = 1$.

"The NSA identified twelve frequency patterns that were scattered throughout the transmission. Up front, my team assumed those patterns to be numeric in nature. Further, we speculated the primer would take the form of an equation. Turned out, both these assumptions were correct." Using the dry-erase pen, she tapped on the whiteboard. "These were the first two equations extrapolated from the transmission. The numbers we knew, the operator we didn't. But that was only a matter of simple deduction. In this case, zero plus zero equals zero but only zero plus one equals one. Thus, the first operator must be addition. Simple as that."

"Math," the Vice President said.

"Yes, the universal language," Dolores confirmed.

"Like teaching a child to read," Megan interjected.

"Exactly," Dolores agreed. "Those two equations were only the start. Once we, and by we, I mean" – she swept her hand to encompass Obadiah, Tara, Megan, and to be a good sport, even included the General – "figured out the basics, we applied the same logic to identify a total of fifty-four operations. Not only arithmetic, but logical operators, Boolean values, and conditional statements – 'if this, then that' type of logic. Essentially what we uncovered was the primer, a key to teaching us what's written in the transmission."

"Which was what?" the Vice President asked.

Dolores beckoned for Tara to join her at the podium. "I'd like to introduce our expert in signal processing, Madame Vice President. This is Tara. It was her insight that allowed us to answer that very question." With that, Dolores stepped aside.

Blushing profusely, Tara stepped up to the podium. She spoke in a rush, "The logical operators almost certainly mean the transmission is a virtual machine, a self-contained message based on logic gate matrices designed to lay on top of a binary system. If true, and that remains to be proven, the amplitude variation in the data stream is surely the input."

Dolores looked over the audience, only to find blank faces, including and especially, on Janise Martinez herself. She then repeated what Tara already said, "It's a computer program, Madame Vice President."

The universal equivalent of "Oh" formed on the Vice President's lips. After a couple of seconds, she asked, "What does this program do?"

"We don't know...yet," Dolores said. "It will take considerable resources to get to that answer, in computing power, people, time. Most of all, insight—"

Beckman quickly approached the podium, a little too close to Dolores for comfort. "We're pulling together a plan, Madam Vice President," he interrupted, "which will be submitted shortly for your approval."

The Vice President nodded. "I'll speak to the President, but I'm confident that whatever it is you need you'll get."

Murmurs rolled from one end of the Situation Room to the other, growing more animated with each voice. Ideas were floated concerning the function of the program, that it was a message, a warning, a gift of technology, or Pandora's box. Victor suggested it could be all the above, even a taxonomy of the alien world. The Secretary of Homeland Security suggested the program might be an Artificial Intelligence, which sparked a flurry of discussion that rose in volume as the perceived threat increased. Dolores found the idea interesting – minus the threat. A civilization powerful enough to generate a gravitational wave had no need to threaten anybody. The Secretary of Defense cautioned the program might be a virus designed to infiltrate our security systems. The General heartily agreed, sparking Connor to expound on techniques to guard against cyber-warfare. It took effort, but Dolores avoided rolling her eyes. While conversation amongst the notables ebbed and flowed, Tara and Dolores found themselves increasingly sidelined. They made their way back to their seats.

"Excellent job," Obadiah said.

"Thank you," she said in a quiet breath, then asked the question that loomed ever larger in her mind. "What was the result of the DNA analysis?

"From the child?"

She nodded.

"One hundred percent human," Obadiah replied, as if expecting the question.

"And the father? My guess is that samples were collected during the search of his home."

"The same, as with the mother. We also confirmed the child as their progeny."

"I see," Dolores said, not having expected anything different.

"You should know the General intends to detain the father for questioning. I'm sure he'll tell you himself, when time presents itself."

"Ah," Dolores said, processing the words but not the meaning.

Looking out the window, Dolores absently watched a rocket being prepared on a distant launchpad. What could the child have told them if she were still alive? Danika was her name, she recalled. Did the child know what she played? If so, how? Did she know about the program, what it did? Those questions Dolores would never get to ask. But there was one thing she could do, and that was to run the alien program.

CHAPTER THIRTEEN

Large drops spotted the driveway, prompting me to look skyward. Gray clouds from an unseasonal storm had swallowed up the last patch of blue. A brisk wind kicked up to tousle my hair. The air smelled thick, as if it held its breath before a tempest. Gripping the umbrella, I began the eight-block walk to my office.

Like most people, I could feel when I was being watched. Usually this was nothing more than the visual cortex processing nerve impulses from the eyes, especially those received at the periphery. It was nothing more than a trait honed by evolution. But of late, for me, that sense was amplified a hundred-fold, even when the source of attention lay outside my visual field. A sixth sense, I supposed, a concept I had once scoffed at.

The first watcher sat behind darkened windows of a gray sedan parked at the corner of the cul-de-sac. There every morning, I considered him or her to be my gatekeeper to the outside world. After walking another few blocks the second watcher slipped in behind me, following on foot. When I crossed the intersection, I stole a glance behind me. With hands tucked inside of pockets and the lid of a cap lowered to hide his profile, the man, and I assumed it was a man due to his heavy build, paused and pretended to look in a store window. I kept walking.

Pedestrians streamed along both sides of the sidewalk as I approached the center of town. Some conversed with their companions, others talked on the phone, and more than a few were fully focused on an electronic screen. The ones paying attention dodged the others who weren't. An elderly woman in an alcove held out a cardboard sign, calling out to passersby. I tossed a bill into her cup. Then, as I did every weekday, I stopped at the French bakery across the street from my office.

One brave couple sat outside on the patio, rubbing their arms together while chatting amiably. Both sipped from mugs steaming in the frigid air. Blackbirds flocked around them, hoping for a stray crumb. A typical morning, only it felt like I was seeing it for the first time. All these people, accustomed to the same routine at the same time of day, assuming that what happened before would happen again. But as the foundations of my own life had turned to quicksand, I was proof the certainties of this world were an illusion. Stepping into the shop, I joined a queue of people waiting to order. Despite the crowd, my attention was drawn to a lone woman sitting at a table for two, picking at a bowl of fruit. She wasn't hard to single out, with the surreptitious glances directed my way. These agents might as well have had neon signs blinking over their heads. I wonder if they suspected I knew. Or cared if I did. Either way, I found her presence disturbing. Usually these agents kept their distance, but today they nipped at my heels.

They're on edge.

I didn't need the Stranger to tell me that.

You should be wary.

"I know," I said, trying to push the voice from my mind.

"Sir, the usual latte and bagel this morning?"

Surprised at finding myself at the head of the line, I could only stare at the puzzled expression on the barista's face. Then, to my horror, her pupils blossomed into a multitude of hues that circled like a vortex. I rubbed my own eyes to dismiss the hallucination. When I looked again, her eyes were as they should be. These hallucinations had been happening more frequently of late, especially when the Stranger came knocking.

"Sorry, I've got a migraine coming on," I said, covering my confusion. "I'll live dangerously this morning and go with a cappuccino. Actually, make that two." With an understanding smile, the barista went about preparing the drinks. Order in hand, I detoured toward the window and placed one of the cappuccinos on the agent's table.

"With my compliments," I said. Compressed lips and an impatient sigh were my thanks, which was satisfaction enough.

I exited the bakery and walked to the red-tiled medical building which housed my office. Once inside, I surveyed the mess. Papers lay strewn over the carpet, the file cabinets stood open and empty, and books were stacked into haphazard piles. The same hurricane which had ravaged my home had struck here as well. I just hadn't bothered to clean it up. Tossing what little mail I'd received onto my desk, I flopped into the chair and flipped on the computer. As far as Fran knew, I was preparing to reopen my practice. "Start small," she had suggested, "with one or two patients." Given the bills piling up, that was a reasonable request. But I hadn't done anything of the kind.

What I chose to do was learn more about Dolores McCann. So, I'd been digging through the internet, looking for any clue, any breadcrumb, that might supply an insight about her or the transmission. The amount of material I found was overwhelming: research papers, interviews, and presentations by the hundreds. Frustrated, I'd been tempted to contact my brother. Since he worked at Caltech, he might've known Dolores well. But ultimately, I chose to keep Eric at arm's length, as I didn't want him earning watchers of his own. Then, I came across an acronym, AMIGO.

Opening the internet browser, I searched *AMIGO gravitational observatory*. Already I had learned more than I ever wanted to know about this project, including that it had been abruptly cancelled. Skipping past pages of search results, I found the spot where I had left off yesterday, at an archive of presentations given at a conference sponsored by the European Space Agency. One of the presentations concerned AMIGO, authored by Dolores herself. While the archive remained, the link to the document no longer worked. I wasn't shocked, for this had happened before. Strange how sparse the information was for so large a project, or fiasco, depending on what one believed. Almost like somebody was trying to erase it from the world's memory. I paged through the search results, choosing to drill down on any links that caught my interest.

They're coming.

I clicked on a link, this one a press release concerning cancellation of the project. Scanning the article, I found it interesting that the supposed malfunction was described as an anomaly, the same term

Dolores had used when referring to the transmission.

They're coming. You need to move.

"What, who's coming?"

You know who.

I jumped to my feet. "How do you know?"

Touch the strands upon which you are entangled.

I felt it, an agitated strumming along imagined lines in my head. Two people approached from the front of the building and one from the back, like spiders advancing on their prey. Having rehearsed this moment in the fearful depths of night, I acted at once. Slipping out of the office I hustled along the hallway, pulling the fire alarm along the way. I flew down the stairwell leading to the subsurface garage. With my head bent, I climbed up the vehicle ramp and onto the sidewalk where I began walking in a direction opposite the strumming. Sensing another pair of eyes on the street, I ducked into the nearest alcove, where I came face to face with the elderly woman from before.

Wearing a baggy coat and knitted cap too large for her head, the lady broke into a gap-toothed smile. She held out a plastic cup. "Excuse me sir, I need five dollars for a bus ride home. Would you be so kind as to help out?"

My heart pounded in my throat. With nowhere to turn, I felt like a bug caught in the middle of a web. Eyeing the lady, a germ of an idea sprang from my desperation. Taking out my wallet, I pulled out all the bills and shoved them into her cup. "How about a trade, a hundred and twenty dollars for your coat and hat?" Spying a shopping cart, I added, "Along with your cart." With a suspicious glance, the lady leafed through the money. I took off my sports jacket and held it out. "You can have this too."

She took the coat and inspected it, critically. "Doesn't look nearly as warm as mine."

I shrugged, then moved my hand toward the cup.

The lady pulled the money out of the cup and stuffed it into her pocket. She then handed me her coat and tried on my jacket. "A little big, but I guess it'll do," she said. After giving me the knitted cap, she added, "I hope whoever's looking for you doesn't find you, mister."

"Thank you, ma'am." I pulled on her jacket and tugged down the cap, so it was just above my eyes. The smell was overpowering. To make the costume complete, I flipped off my dress shoes.

In the space of a minute I was pushing the cart along the broken sidewalk. It clattered along with the empty cans and bottles. Pedestrians parted to each side and a mother and child pointedly crossed the road before I came near. I scratched at my scalp, having felt something wiggle. After a block, I glanced behind me. Patients and staff loitered outside the office building with more trickling out of the doors. I heard the muffled bray of a fire alarm. Then I saw a sedan creeping slowly up the street in my direction. The windows were open.

Hidden deep within the folds of the parasitic cloak, I imagined myself as invisible. The vehicle passed within feet. A glance back confirmed it had government plates. Increasing my pace, I turned at the next corner, having no idea where to go or what to do.

What would Danika have wanted?

"For me not to have killed her."

The Stranger didn't answer but the question lingered in my mind. What would she have wanted? In vain my daughter had tried to get me to listen to her, but I would always cut her off, fearing her tales were symptoms of mental illness. Now I could only wonder at her purpose. One thing I knew for certain…Danika never meant her song to be a secret. But what could I do about it now? Even if I found somebody to listen, I was a nobody with a story not even my wife believed.

A helicopter whirred overhead and I spied a black and white police vehicle moving down the street. I stopped and rummaged through a trash receptacle, tossing bottles and cans into the shopping cart. The vehicle passed as the helicopter flew in a lazy circle.

Despite the risk, I wanted to see my brother. He would know what to do. But going home to get my car would be foolish, so I would have to travel by train. I was about to angle the shopping cart toward the train station when it occurred to me I had no means to purchase a ticket. I had given away my cash and using a credit card would surely strum an electronic cord within the watchers' web. That meant I would have to make a phone call. Reversing direction, I headed toward a boutique hotel a few blocks up the street.

I parked the shopping cart behind a bush. After shedding the coat and cap I ran my fingers through my hair and walked into the foyer. Pretending to be a guest, I asked the concierge at the front desk if I might make a call. With a puzzled look at my stockinged feet, which I explained away as, "Hey, I'm on vacation," the concierge handed me the phone.

I dialed the school where Fran worked. On the first ring the receptionist picked up. Keeping my voice level, I explained that there was an urgent matter requiring my wife's attention and asked if the receptionist would be so kind as to pull Fran from class and put her on. After a long pause, the receptionist—whom I knew would recognize my voice—asked who was calling. I hung up. I then called my brother's cell phone. Silence answered. Looking inward, I felt strumming along a distant thread and dropped the phone back into the cradle as if it were on fire. The spiders had caught up with my brother and wife. What would they do with them? The possibilities swelled my head with a helpless anger. With a "Thank you" to the concierge I exited the inn.

Once I had outfitted myself back into the old woman's clothes I continued walking up the street, intending to get as far away as possible from my pursuers. Under a darkened sky, drops pattered the concrete more forcefully. Pedestrians took cover under awnings or crouched beneath umbrellas. Vehicles swished over the asphalt. A block ahead and moving in my direction came two watchers, actively peering into every face and into every corner.

Resisting the impulse to bolt, I abandoned the cart on the sidewalk and sauntered across a grassy area toward the nearest refuge, the downtown library. I paused under the arched entryway of the building, feeling as if I were on the precipice of a cliff. My breath was short and the normal cautionary wiring inside my brain screamed for me to jump. As I entered the building the librarian scowled, no doubt due to the water dripping from me onto the wood floor. There was only one thing I could do. Studiously ignoring the angry stare from the librarian, I took a seat at a table set up with a line of computers.

I logged on using my library card. Using a public email service, I created a fictitious account. Then I collected email addresses from a number of major media organizations that I used to create a distribution list. Opening a new message, I crafted this note:

To whomever it may concern,

NASA's Jet Propulsion Laboratory is investigating an extraterrestrial signal emanating from the trinary star system, HR 7448. The message was detected by AMIGO, A Massive Interferometer Gravitational Observatory operated and funded by NASA. The government claims there was a malfunction and has taken AMIGO offline. But I assure you that is not true; it is only an attempt to impose secrecy on a transmission clearly meant for all. I need your help to make that happen.

Sincerely, Stephen J. Fisher

After pressing "Send" there was a satisfying *swoosh* as the message disappeared into the cybersphere. But I held no illusions. Assuming anybody read the note, I expected most people would dismiss my words as coming from somebody with an overactive imagination, if not the ravings of a lunatic. Even if someone chose to investigate, what could they do? Still, this was the only arrow I had in my quiver. As fast as I could type I repeated the same process until the message had been sent to a dozen media organizations. On the thirteenth, a spinning wheel replaced the cursor. A message appeared inside the browser – Page not found.

Groans erupted from the people sitting at the table. A man raised his hand in exasperation, the video he was watching frozen into place. I tapped furiously and futilely on the keyboard, picturing the blank face of a watcher staring back at me from the screen. It was over, and I didn't need the Stranger to tell me that they would be coming for me.

"It'll be back up in a minute, it happens all the time," said a young woman.

I turned toward the woman, and the moment I did, blue eyes captured my own. Fibers within each iris interwove and twisted around the black epicenter of each pupil. Colors of red, green and yellow coalesced amongst the strands, becoming currents that turned into whirlpools which enlarged and combined into a single vortex that filled her mind.

Don't' look away.

I didn't.

Take her hand.

I did. When she tried pulling away, I gripped her hand more fiercely. The vortex within the woman's mind rippled to viridescent. She was scared.

Ask for help.

"I need a favor," I said. The currents in her head smoothed to a glassy sheen, or so I imagined.

"What is it?" she asked, her voice a whisper.

Taking a pencil from the tray, I scribbled a message on a scrap of paper and wrote an address at the top. I placed it in front of the young woman. "If you'd be so kind, I'd appreciate if you'd place this in an envelope and send it in the mail."

"Why?"

"Because the people about to arrest me would rather the world not know what I know. Plus, I think it's what my daughter would have wanted me to do."

Without waiting for a reply, I rose from the chair and headed for the exit, shedding the coat and cap as I passed beneath the arch. Wind buffeted me, and the rain fell in sheets. I walked past an ornate fountain and down cement steps to come to a halt in the center of the lawn. Raising both hands over my head, I turned in a slow circle.

A sedan jumped the curb onto the sidewalk. Hudson popped out the passenger-side door, her hand gripping the butt of a sidearm. A man burst from the driver's side. Two dark suited figures approached from opposite ends of the building, one trotting, the other walking, both with weapons drawn. I heard the helicopter circling overhead.

"You've only made it worse for yourself, Fisher," Hudson said. A man, tall and unsmiling, forced me to the ground and pulled my arms behind my back. I felt the cold steel bite into my wrists. Hudson then rattled off what I'd only heard in the movies. "You have the right to remain silent..."

PART II – THE MACHINE

CHAPTER FOURTEEN

Soft blue light bathed Dolores as she hurried along the catwalk that overlooked rows of quiescent computer equipment stretching the length of the monstrous data center. The government's largest, it boasted computing power measured in thousands of petaflops, exabytes of memory, and zettabytes of storage. With the footprint of a large town and energy requirements of a small city, it was a monument to twenty-first century engineering.

Dolores had estimated, to the Vice President no less, that the effort required to turn the alien transmission into a low-level computing language would require hundreds of minds, years of effort, and machine intelligence bordering on cognition. To that end, this data center was placed at her disposal. She was also granted permission to bring in her own team, the first of which were due to arrive within the week.

Nodding to the Special Security Force agent guarding what was once the lunch room, now the newly christened center of operations, Dolores swiped her badge, heard the magnetic pop of the lock, and stepped through the door.

Michael was hunched over a keyboard with Tara at his shoulder, exactly where they'd been when Dolores left to get some shut-eye. Both were animatedly speaking while gesturing at the monitor. Squinting at the display, Dolores made out lines of machine code, the low-level instructions executed by the computer's processor. They had made progress, she noted. Slumped into a plastic chair with glassy eyes observing things he didn't understand was Connor, reminding her that the General was there in spirit if not in the flesh. Believing it best to be polite, Dolores lifted her hand, which he returned with a yawn. In the back, Megan plugged coins into a vending machine.

Two cans in hand, Megan crossed the floor and handed Dolores a Mr. Pibb, her very favorite. "Get any sleep?" Megan asked.

"If I did, I dreamed I was awake," Dolores answered. "You?"

"Like a baby. But these two"—she pointed at Tara and Michael—"have been here all night."

"Forty-eight hours straight," Dolores said, and raised her voice. "That's it, Tara, I order you to get back to the hotel and forbid you from returning here for at least twelve hours. I mean it this time. That goes for you too, Michael. I'm sure Obadiah would agree."

Tara turned, smiling with an enthusiasm at odds with the dark pouches under her eyes. "We came up with an algorithm to render output to the graphics driver."

"The program outputs imagery?" Dolores asked.

"We think so," Tara replied, "but it all depends on the input, which as far as we can tell is a random string of duodecimals."

Michael pushed the keyboard aside then made a nest with his arms and laid his head down. "It's done," he said.

Dolores sidled up to him. "What's done?"

Without looking up Michael tapped on the monitor. "I compiled the program."

Dolores bent at the waist to look where he pointed. It was an executable file, *Barbarella.exe*. "You did this overnight?"

Michael turned his head and gave her a tired smile. "Converting the operators into machine language was easy. The graphical output was the challenge."

"Really?" she asked, hardly believing it, especially since they had accomplished the feat using Tara's laptop, which she had brought along "to play games." If true, this feat was strangely disappointing in a way, but it reinforced that whoever sent the transmission valued one thing above anything else – simplicity.

"Really," Michael confirmed.

"Damn impressive," Megan said.

"Don't get too excited," Tara said. She tapped on Michael's shoulder and swapped places with him. "We haven't executed nor debugged it. The program almost certainly is going to crash. But for me to get any sleep I need to try running it at least once."

"Is the computer secure?" Connor asked, having grown alert.

"We pulled the wireless card and disconnected the ethernet cable. Any data exchange has to be done physically, using a thumb drive. There's no connectivity to the outside world, none at all."

"Go ahead, Tara. Let's see what you've got," Dolores said.

Tara's fingers moved over the keyboard. On the laptop monitor a number of charts appeared to replace the lines of machine code. "These gauge system performance," she explained, more for Connor's sake than anybody else's. "Processing power, memory, I/O, that type of thing." She then pointed at the large screen on the wall. "Output from the program has been redirected there." Crossing her fingers, she looked over her shoulder at Dolores. "I'm about to feed input from the transmission into the program."

"Do it," Dolores said.

Tara touched a key. The lines on every graph spiked but nothing showed up on the overhead screen.

"Something's wrong," Michael said, and laid his head back on the table.

Tara shrugged. "We'll take a look at it tomorrow," she said, then stretched her arms in such a way it seemed the adrenalin that fueled her these past days poured onto the floor.

Megan wandered around the table, then crouched down on her hands and knees. Fishing through cords snaking over the tiled floor, she held one up. "Might help if you plugged in the monitor."

Dolores sighed.

Megan plugged the cord into the wall. The monitor shook from side to side, acclimating to the power surge. An image slowly came into focus, roughly spherical in shape with waves of blue surging around a pinprick of light so bright that it hurt Dolores' eyes. A crest from one wave shone a paler hue as it rolled through the center and accelerated toward the edge where the surge dissipated into wisps of vapor that spiraled inward toward the center. Another passing wave consumed the remains then collided head-on with another pulse of energy, resulting in a flash.

Megan's mouth fell open. Tara's eyes radiated delight. Michael pumped his fist. Connor stepped up to the display.

"What is this?" Connor asked.

"It's beautiful, whatever it is," Megan said.

Dolores tried to make sense of the image. If millions of years were compressed into seconds, the waves might be interstellar gas, and the light a newly formed star. But the energies were unlike any astronomical phenomena she'd ever observed. "Could be an emission nebula," she guessed.

"Electromagnetic pattern doesn't seem right," Tara said. "Maybe it's the ejected shell of ionized gas caused by a nova, the remnants of a star."

"Or a message from a dead civilization," Megan said. "Destroyed by its own sun and having sent all it learned and loved to whoever might be listening."

Tara reached out a hand to seemingly caress the outer edges of the screen. "That's so sad."

Two buttons then appeared at the bottom of the display, one labeled True and the other False.

Tara snapped her hand away. Dolores' mouth fell open. Megan let fly an expletive. "They know our language," Connor said, stepping back a pace.

"No no no," Michael said, "the words are ours, translated from the Boolean operators decoded from the transmission. It's only the program asking for input."

Connor sniffed his discomfort, but otherwise remained silent.

Tara rose from the chair to stand beside Dolores. "Are they asking if we know what the image represents?"

"Maybe they're asking if we know *where* it is," Dolores speculated.

"Let's find out, shall we?" Before anybody could object, Megan took over the mouse and pressed True.

The image shrank and multiplied into three distinct clouds. Candy colored ribbons emerged and connected to one another, forming a triangle. The structure then began to swirl in an elaborate twisting motion that increased in velocity until the entire screen became a blur. Feeling a wave of vertigo, Dolores momentarily had to look away. When her eyes returned to the screen, she found the structure had manifested into a single opaque sphere glowing with an intense blue light. It seemed to churn with invisible forces from within. The same True/False choice appeared at the bottom of the screen.

"It's a star," Michael said softly.

"Could be a post-main sequence blue giant," Tara said.

"Or it's some sort of map," Dolores suggested. "Using astronomical phenomena as guideposts, like we do landmarks."

"Leading where?" Connor asked.

"Let's find out," Megan said. She positioned the cursor over True and pressed on the key.

The sphere shrank to the size of a dime. A magenta speck emerged at the margins and began spinning in a frantic orbit. True and False popped up below.

"I bet it's their world," Michael whispered.

"Their world is moving awfully fast around that star," Megan said.

"Time must be accelerated," Tara said.

"Could be a way to define a standard unit of time," Dolores said. "Makes sense that an orbit would serve that purpose, like we use a twenty-four-hour day."

Megan pressed again on the mouse. Three dime-sized spheres appeared in the center of the screen…making a total of four, two colored blue and the others orange. Each sphere paired off with its complement and circled one another, orange and blue, spinning in tandem. A second magenta speck emerged at the edge and began orbiting the four spheres in a wholly different trajectory from the first. The motion made Dolores' head spin. The True/False buttons materialized below.

"A quaternary star system with two satellites," Tara said, or rather, asked. "You'd think that would be unstable."

"Thought the transmission came from a trinary system," Megan said.

"We should take a closer look. Maybe it isn't."

"Keep going, Megan," Dolores said.

Megan obliged. And each time she pressed True additional spheres materialized in the increasingly crowded center screen, as did more satellites to circle them. Dolores wondered at the number of stars, the eccentric orbits of the planets, and the varying colors. Then a thought occurred to her, as disturbing as it was obvious. "This is a test."

"Yep," Megan said, as if she'd already figured that out.

"You can restart the program, right?" Dolores asked Tara.

DAVID HOFFER

"We wipe the drive and reload," Tara answered, and glanced at Michael, who nodded agreement.

"All right," Dolores said. "Megan, how about you choose False and we see what happens." Megan positioned the cursor and pressed False.

Materializing on the screen came the same waves of blue surging around a single pinprick of light, exactly like before. "Back to where we started," Dolores said.

"The alien equivalent of a failed grade," Megan said. "Not the most auspicious start to first contact."

"We'll figure it out. Keep pressing True, Megan, and let's see where they lead us."

As Megan paged through the screens, the images repeated themselves in the exact same order as before, with each new structure more complex than the one that preceded it. Dolores watched in fascination, her certainty fading that these images were astronomical in nature. Megan, however, nodded in rhythm to each of her keystrokes.

"You know what this is, don't you?" Dolores accused.

A mischievous smile formed on Megan's lips. "Come along Dolores, I bet you mastered this subject in elementary school."

Dolores looked again at the screen, puzzled over it for a moment, then realization dawned. She laughed. In response to a quizzical look from Tara, Dolores said, "Think small, Tara, *very* small." It took only a second before Tara slapped a hand to her forehead. She beamed at Dolores, who in turn beamed at Megan.

Connor looked to Michael, who only shrugged. "Ladies, I'd very much appreciate if you'd share your insights."

"We were looking at these pictures through the wrong lens," Dolores said. "Tell him what it is, Megan."

"They're walking us through the periodic table of elements. The first image—"

"What I thought was a nebula," Dolores interjected.

"Was actually a quark," Megan continued. "A building block of the building blocks that make up subatomic particles. It was those weird movements that threw me off the scent. The second image—"

"The star?" Michael asked.

"Right, but wrong," Megan replied. "It was a hydrogen ion. The

90

addition of the electron, what everybody thought was a planet, turned the element into helium. Then lithium, beryllium, and so on." Megan pointed at the current image displayed on the screen. "That's carbon."

"They're testing our knowledge," Connor said.

"Actually, this is the second test," Dolores said. "The first was to see if we could detect the signal. Until now, I've been wondering why they use gravitational waves to send the transmission. Believe me, there are far easier ways to send a message than warping space-time. But I think it was done purposefully, to determine if our technology was advanced enough to detect something so subtle. This latest test, I think, is for the very same purpose, to determine how far along we are technologically."

"And if we fail?" Connor asked.

"Then I expect we'll never know the purpose of the transmission."

"Enough talking," Megan said. "Let's advance to the last element, at least, the last as far as we know. Then we can see if anything other than ignorance is our reward." Connor nodded, as if he thought the decision to proceed were up to him. Dolores wondered if it really was.

"Go ahead, Megan," Dolores said.

And Megan did, barking out each element name as it appeared on the screen, "Carbon, nitrogen, oxygen, fluorine, neon, sodium…"

Dolores watched, listened, and marveled at the whirring specks and dancing spheres. Particle physicists would spend years making sense of these images, if they ever could. A wave of warmth rose within her. She had a front row seat to first contact, when humankind received a message from the stars. Children would learn about this moment, and hopefully, feel the same sense of the awe that she experienced as she watched the universe unfold before her eyes. They would also be told of the monitor they forgot to plug in, which made Dolores smile.

Megan advanced to oganesson, the last known element. There she stopped, placing the cursor on the False button. And with a solemnity befitting the occasion, Megan dramatically lifted her finger, and arched an eyebrow. "Say the word."

"Do it," Dolores said.

Megan depressed the key.

A simple element materialized on the display. But before Dolores could blink, it shrank in on itself, multiplied, and formed a three-dimensional lattice in the shape of a cube. A second element appeared, heavier than the first, which multiplied in number then all of them fit themselves snuggly within the lattice at equidistant intervals. The structure began to slowly rotate. True/False appeared at the bottom. Dolores heaved a breath, for it seemed they had passed one test only to take another.

"What do we have here?" Megan asked.

"An alloy," Tara answered. "Looks like copper and tin, the recipe for bronze."

"Metals," Connor said.

"Keep going, Megan," Dolores said, having an inkling where this test was going.

More structures arranged themselves on the screen. Tara named the metals as they appeared, only getting as far as steel before she shrugged. "We're going to need engineers to figure this out, chemical, electrical, metallurgical…"

Dolores nodded while admiring the images that continued to evolve into more complex structures. "Fail the test, Megan," she said.

Megan chose False and the screen went black, as if it died. But the charts measuring the computing resources were pegged at a hundred percent. Dolores experienced a rush of disappointment, fearing they had finally crashed the program. Minutes rolled by before Tara broke the silence. "I think the program is in an endless loop. Michael and I can take a look—"

Just then images spilled across the screen, so fast Dolores could hardly make out one from another. What she could discern looked lovely, like art, almost…like designs. "Is this being recorded?" Dolores breathed.

"Yes," Tara replied.

The images abruptly stopped. Two figures then materialized on the screen. Megan gasped. Tara placed a hand over her mouth. Connor clenched his jaw while Michael chewed on a cuticle. Dolores could only stare.

Sketched onto the black canvas of the screen were two ovals that were each trailed by three lines. Two of the lines were of the same length, roughly three-times the diameter of the oval. The third lay between the two and was longer by half. But what commanded

Dolores' attention were the multi-hued currents flowing within each oval. Silent seconds ticked past, each more pronounced than the last.

"Is it a spacecraft?" Tara ventured.

Dolores considered. The lines could represent propulsion and the ovals some sort of habitation module. But given the detail of the previous images, why show only the outlines?

"It almost looks like two people," Michael said. "Maybe they're explorers."

"Or colonists," Connor said, the edge to his voice betraying his true meaning – invaders.

Dolores shook her head, unsurprised at his interpretation. That was exactly what the General would think too. Trying to rid herself of predispositions, Dolores studied the screen anew. At first glance, the images did resemble a stick-figure depiction of two people, like a child would draw. She might even venture to say they were holding hands. But the heads were oddly shaped and the arms too long. Also, there was only one leg. Megan would accuse her of interpreting the images through an anthropomorphic lens. Speaking of which, she looked upon her friend, who had remained uncharacteristically silent.

"I think it's them," Megan said.

CHAPTER FIFTEEN

From his perch atop the raised bench the Honorable T. Rawlee Atkinson studied me from over the top of thin spectacles. "You have been charged by a grand jury with two felony counts, Mister Fisher." He lifted a document from the polished wood desk and used a finger to push his glasses higher up on his nose. "Count One: on October 13th, the defendant did knowingly and intentionally attempt unauthorized communication of national defense information as defined in 18 United States Code section 793(d). Count Two: on October 13th, the defendant willfully communicated classified communications intelligence information to an unauthorized person as defined in 18 USC 798(a)."

Returning the sheet to the counter the judge passed a quick glance over the prosecutor who stood before the bench, a pregnant woman who looked as if she'd been disturbed from a night's sleep. Hudson was at her side, her back held ramrod straight. Beside me a suited stranger faced the judge without expression.

"Do you understand the charges set forth in this indictment?"

I hurriedly looked at the paper handed to me by the bailiff, sending the chains binding my wrists and ankles rattling over the tile floor. Same words, same charges, same lies. About to object, I was stopped short by the spinning colors emanating from two almond-shaped holes in the judge's skull. There were also things moving under his skin. I rubbed my eyes with a thumb and forefinger.

A series of sharp raps sounded from the bench. "Mister Fisher, I would appreciate your attention."

Cautiously, I looked up to the bench and was relieved to find normal eyes and unremarkable flesh hanging from the judge's jowly cheeks. The prosecutor's gaze fell to the floor where I'd dropped a now crumpled sheet of paper. Hudson silently shook her head. "Sorry, what did you say?" I asked.

The lines on the judge's forehead turned to furrows. "I asked if you understood the charges."

"Perfectly," I said.

"Your Honor," the judge finished for me. "I hear you've chosen to represent yourself. Is that correct?"

"Hardly." Since my arrest I'd been denied access to the outside world. No visitors, no phone calls, not even a window in my cell.

"That's not quite true, is it?" the judge said. He nodded to the silent figure standing on my right. "A court appointed attorney has been made available at no cost to you. I suggest we take a recess so that you might consult with him."

There was no chance of that. This was a sham trial presided by a sham judge, the same judge who had signed the warrant authorizing the search of my home. I had no interest in dignifying these proceedings by working with a lackey who did the bidding for invisible others. "Pass," I said.

"Do you have any background in the law, Mister Fisher?"

"Only what I've learned from watching television."

"I see." The judge placed his glasses on the bench and regarded me in a way that might have passed for thoughtful. "Mister Fisher, each of these charges carries a maximum of ten years in prison. I'm told that further charges may be brought against you pending further investigation. Given the serious nature of your situation I urge you to reconsider."

"Considering and reconsidering the cause of my imprisonment is about all I've done," I said.

The judge forked his fingers through his copious white hair. "I've been in this business an awfully long time and have yet to encounter a defendant who has represented themself very well. I think it's foolish for you to do so."

I began to suspect this judge had no idea of the role he'd been recruited to play. "Your advice is appreciated, Your Honor."

The judge waited a beat, then sighed. "Very well, that is your right but know that I advised you otherwise. Consider the answer to my next question very carefully, Mister Fisher. As to the charges in the indictment, how do you wish to plead?"

What did it matter? I'd been presumed guilty since I was abducted from my home. "Your Honor, whatever you've been told concerning my revealing any supposed national defense information is a complete fabrication. I'm here because I stumbled across a big secret." With a clanking of chains, I pointed at Hudson. "This woman is part of a government conspiracy to bury news of an extraterrestrial transmission detected by a gravitational wave observatory operated by JPL. The project is, or was, called AMIGO—"

The judge's hand shot up. "I've not asked for a statement. The appropriate answer to my question is either guilty or not guilty"—he frowned— "Wait, what did you say?"

"Extraterrestrials, aliens. The government doesn't want the transmission made public. I'm curious what they're hiding. You should be too."

The judge reclined his generous frame, causing the chair to squeal in protest. With the peculiarity of expression reserved for those suspected to be out of their mind, he asked, "You think aliens are trying to contact us, Mister Fisher?"

"I know how it sounds."

"I'm not sure you do." The judge drummed his fingers on the desk. "Mister Fisher, I'm going to ignore your plea and deny the request to represent yourself. Though that is certainly your right, I'm not satisfied you are in the, um, proper state of mind to understand the consequences of your actions." Turning to the prosecuting attorney, he said, "I'm going to order a full psychiatric evaluation of Mister Fisher. I not only need to be convinced he can represent himself, I need to be convinced he is competent to stand trial."

The prosecutor concurred with a knowing nod. Hudson smiled.

CHAPTER SIXTEEN

An overhead lamp housed within a wire frame cast sharp shadows on the sickly yellow cinder block walls of the interrogation room. Dried stains bespattered the cement floor and the place smelled of ammonia and poor plumbing. On my left a one-way observation mirror stared back at me. The perfect setting to reinforce a prisoner's dependence and heighten their discomfort.

"I'm not here to talk about why you betrayed your country and what you hoped to achieve," Connor said. "That's your business."

"But you have a few questions," I said, my voice cracking. Since the arraignment I'd not spoken to another soul, other than thanking whoever pushed the feeding tray under the door of the eight by five-foot cell in which I was housed. A border-line psychotic might cross the threshold to a raging maniac if left inside too long. Something to look forward to.

"That's right."

I knew where he was going with this. After all, interrogation was the crudest form of psychiatry. "And if I cooperate you'll float the possibility of a reduced sentence. You might even consider dropping a charge or two."

"I'm empowered to do all those things," Connor said, and I think, tried to smile.

"I'll settle for a visit from my wife."

Connor raised a non-committal brow. "If you prove helpful."

Unlikely, given I couldn't help myself. Regardless, I hungered for answers. Did the same agents who arrested me question Fran? Was she told about the transmission? Did she, like me, wonder about the connection to our daughter? Or was Fran told nothing and left to guess what had happened to me when I didn't return home. I considered that likely. If true, I wondered if she tried to find me. Or did she assume I fled from my troubles as I had done before? That concerned me most of all.

"Won't that judge be expecting a psychiatric evaluation?" I asked.

"The assessment's complete," Connor said. "It concluded you're not competent to stand trial."

"Funny, I don't remember being evaluated. Did you decide to completely toss out legal due process? Thought your kind had a higher calling."

"Different rules for those considered a national security risk. That's what you are, you know. When we first met I warned you of the consequences if you chose to divulge classified information. I was quite clear about it. You even signed a piece of paper to that effect. But you just couldn't keep your mouth shut, could you?"

"I signed nothing."

"Rest assured, you did."

"I get it, you're trying to cover up the transmission detected by AMIGO. From what I've read, that must have come as a big surprise. Was it a message"—the vision of my daughter came to mind— "or something else?"

"I've not said anything of the kind."

"Yet you're upset that I tried telling others about it. What's got you so spooked?"

"You're the one who should be spooked, Mister Fisher." Connor considered me for a long moment. "Just curious, do you consider yourself mentally fit?"

"I'm undecided on that question."

Connor nodded. "I appreciate your candor, I really do, and you'll find I'm willing to reciprocate. But only if you answer my questions honestly."

"Pretty sure you're going to get an honest 'I have no idea' to most of your questions."

"That would be most unfortunate," Connor said, and lifted his hand. Through the door came Hudson carrying what looked to be medical instruments on a tray.

My pulse began to race. "I thought you'd be above torture, Connor.

Then again, maybe it fits."

"Calm yourself, it's only polygraph equipment. You know, to detect a lie."

"Those don't work."

"I disagree."

Hudson outfitted a blood pressure cuff on my upper arm then pulled apart my shirt and wrapped two breathing tubes around my chest. When I saw her reach for the metal plates on the tray I reared back.

"Stay still or I'll have you restrained," Hudson said, and attached the plates to the tips of two of my fingers. Once she was done Hudson retreated a step and crossed her arms.

Connor asked a series of what I suspected were control questions, rattling them off like a clerk reading a shipping manifest. I responded with nonsensical answers. He didn't seem to care. Connor then paused and straightened in the chair. His eyes bounced off the mirrored wall.

"I've been looking into your past, Fisher," Connor said. "I spoke to a woman who told me of an incident involving a young patient at a psychiatric hospital. Happened years ago. Tragic. There were two deaths during what should have been a routine treatment. The attending nurse, the woman I spoke with, suffered a stroke. Paralyzed half her body."

"That's a lie," I said.

"Surprised? So was I. I found it odd that no cause of death was ever determined. Stranger still was what this nurse said." Connor looked at Hudson. "Tell him."

Placing both hands over her knees Hudson pushed her face within inches of my own. "It was the child," she rasped.

I bowed my head. My father had never told me what happened inside that room. What few memories I possessed were scattered like tiles from a mosaic. I remembered a table, a silent scream, and my brother. Most of all I recalled the fire inside my head. Even now, the reminder sent my heart into spasms.

"Funny how people seem to get hurt when you're around," Connor continued. "Did you know the anesthesiologist had an infant son, the psychiatrist was a newlywed, and the nurse a mother of three?"

You were torn from where you belong, the Stranger said. *You were confused, scared, and didn't know what to do.*

Was it you? I asked. Did you hurt those people? The answer came in the form of terrible music, the soundtrack of madness.

"Stop it!" I said aloud.

There's nothing to stop, there is only you.

"Your hands are shaking," Connor said. "Is something wrong?"

A maelstrom formed inside Connor's skull, a kaleidoscope of currents that disgorged from a pinprick of darkness in the very center. It was as beautiful as it was terrifying.

"Nothing to say?" Connor continued, remorseless. "The body count stands at one injured and three dead. Make that four if I include your daughter. My job is to keep that from growing."

"I never meant to hurt anybody," I said, focusing on the floor.

"The transmission, how did you know where it came from?"

"You asked me that already. The answer hasn't changed."

"You told me a fairy tale about a little girl who couldn't possibly be involved. That's not an answer."

I shrugged. What more could I say?

"Did the people who sent the transmission contact you?"

"Are you seriously asking if I was contacted by little green men?"

"Were you?"

I raised my eyes. "Maybe."

Connor tightened his lips. "You've been charged with a serious crime, Mister Fisher. It's not wise to be a smart-ass. Tell me, how did your daughter know about the music? Did you teach her how to play it on a keyboard?"

"You found that on the phone Hudson confiscated. I call that illegal."

"I call it evidence that your ignorance is a lie. I ask you again, how did your daughter know?"

"I ask myself that question every minute of every day."

"Who sent it and why?" Connor persisted. "Don't lie, you're obviously involved."

"I've told you what I know."

"Your claim to ignorance isn't credible. You taught your daughter that music and directed her to take a picture. Then you convinced your brother to point a radio telescope at the coordinates. Any rational mind would find that suspicious. On top of that you ran off and tried telling the world about the transmission. Are you a foreign agent, Mister Fisher?"

"You're not that dumb."

"Then why do it?"

"It's not your secret to keep."

Connor raised his chin. "Nor yours to give away. You betrayed your country."

"Ever consider that's what you're doing now?"

"You're a traitor."

"You're worse."

Steadying his breath, Connor's gaze drifted to the mirror. It was then I saw the wire lodged in his ear. "Help yourself by helping me, Mister Fisher. I can reduce your sentence, even drop the charges. Don't feign ignorance. Tell me, what's the function of the alien machine?"

I blinked, and blinked again. Then I replayed the words in my head to make sure I had heard right. A machine, that's what he said. I recalled the disembodied form of my daughter inside a cavern filled with golden orbs – my vision. That was more than imagination. Of that I was sure.

"What does it look like?" I asked.

"I'm asking the questions here. You tell me. Better yet, what are the intentions of the ones who sent the transmission? Last chance, Fisher, I'm warning you."

"One for one," I suggested.

"What?"

"You answer a question of mine and I'll answer one of yours. But I get to go first."

Connor's eyes rolled to the side, I assumed listening to whatever the earpiece instructed. "Fine," he said.

"What about this machine, where did you find it? Is it related to the transmission? Did you find a map, a spaceship, what?"

"One question—" Connor began, then his eyes rolled toward the earpiece. He frowned. "The design of a machine was decrypted from the transmission. It's not yet built. Your turn, what does the machine do?"

"Who's talking to you through the earpiece?" I asked, stalling.

"You're breaking the rules to your own your game. Answer the question."

I had no answer. But to learn more about this blueprint I needed to tell Connor something. Out of options, I chose to address the Stranger. Do you know about this machine?

That answer was lost on a silver table, the Stranger said.

Does that mean you once knew about it?'

There is no me, there's only you.

Tell me.

All that's left of your memory is a hole where answers used to be.

"Hello?" prompted Connor. "What are you doing? Who are you talking to?"

"A voice," I admitted.

"A voice?"

"It comes from the disorder triggered by my childhood trauma you so helpfully reminded me of."

"All right then. What does this voice say about the machine?"

"It claims not to know anything about it." Or the Stranger refuses to say.

Connor's jaw clenched. "I knew it, you're screwing with me. Bad move, Fisher."

"I've told you the truth."

Connor's eyes narrowed to slits. "I don't think you appreciate the situation. If I can't get answers from you, where shall I turn, hmm, your wife?"

Blood rushed to my head. "What did you do to her?"

"Nothing, yet. She thinks you abandoned her, by the way. Which is what you did, wasn't it? You had to know the consequences of your actions, trying to divulge secrets that weren't yours to tell. Quite inexcusable if you ask me."

The accusation had barbs, and I shifted in the chair. Weeks spent in silence had me obsessing over the mistakes I'd made, one of which was not bringing Fran fully into my confidence. Despite her cynicism she would have at least listened. "She doesn't know anything about this."

"And your brother?"

"You going to interrogate him too?"

Connor took the wire from his ear and placed it in his shirt pocket. "Did you know that your wife contacted your brother when you didn't come home? She's at his place right now. He's consoling her in that special way only a man can console a woman."

I spat out two rude words.

Connor's voice took on a brittle edge. "You leave me no choice but to drag your wife and brother into custody. I'll ask them the same questions. And when they can't answer, which I fully expect, I'll send them into a cell smaller than yours. No telling what can happen to innocents inside a real prison, Fisher. And it'll be your fault."

"You wouldn't dare," I said, believing his every word.

"Your wife's pretty," Hudson said. "I expect she'll make quite the entrée for the prison gangs. Probably be passed around like a tasty treat." She smacked her lips.

Anger surged, my head pounded with it. Ripping the cuff from my arm I rose from the table. Hudson fumbled for her sidearm while Connor towered over me. With a meaty hand, he pushed me backward. But not before I gripped his wrist.

Don't do it!

Terrible white light burst from within me. Staggering backward Connor hit the far wall, cradled his head, then slid to the floor. Hudson stumbled back a pace while raising her weapon.

I turned and advanced to stand before the observation mirror. Three elliptical smears colored the opposite side. Placing a hand on the reflective surface I focused on one particular maelstrom that hid behind these cruel walls.

"You're going to find darkness inside that machine of yours, Dolores. There will be a spherical cavern filled with golden eyes focused as one toward the center. That's where you should take me because that's where I belong."

CHAPTER SEVENTEEN

Dolores pulled the casting mold from her oversized purse and handed it to the uniformed guard. With a puzzled frown he inspected the insides, blinked, pulled it closer, then rubbed his eyes. What he saw, or didn't see, was a darkness so complete it nearly emptied the mind. At least that was her experience. For some reason, the man sniffed it.

"Ma'am, I need you to explain what this is before I allow you to enter White House grounds."

Dolores hardly blamed him for being suspicious, given the wires and battery pack secured by duct tape on the side. And it was as dangerous as it looked, but for reasons these guards would never fathom.

The alien design included directions to create an unusual alloy. Forged with rare earths, heavy elements, and bathed in gamma rays, the instructions called for the resultant material to be subjected to a constant flow of current. Dolores had wondered why. So, she had the material moved to a desolate area, the power withdrawn, and measurements taken. After two hours the alloy had turned to slag and a quarter acre of the Nevada desert had become radioactive. Thus, the need for the battery case.

"Look," she said, "this material is highly classified. I was ordered to bring it along by General Beckman. You know him?"

"No, ma'am, I do not."

"Ah, well, anyway, I was told that the assistant deputy chief of staff,"—she reached into her purse and looked at her notes—"Samantha Peebles, was supposed to meet me here. Can you call her?"

"I did ma'am. She's not answering. And I do have your name on the list. But I can't let you in with this device."

"It's not a"—she used air quotes— "device," and glanced at her watch – ten minutes before the meeting. She took a second look at the note. "Is this the southeast gate?"

"Northwest, ma'am."

"Okay, fine," she sighed. "But you absolutely positively need to keep those wires attached to the container. Do you understand?"

"I do, ma'am, but I need to get clearance from the officer in charge." A second sentry moved close to Dolores while the other picked up the phone. Dolores impatiently tapped her foot.

Rushing across the lawn came the frazzled form of what had to be Samantha Peebles, flanked by a pair of what she presumed to be secret service agents. Emphatically waving a hand, Samantha asserted with labored breaths, "She's fine, she's fine, she's expected. Let her through..."

The guard pointed out the container. "Including this?"

"That in particular," Samantha said, barely giving it a glance. While the agents consulted with the guards Samantha introduced herself. "You're a little late, Doctor McCann, but it should be fine, just fine. Come along now, and don't forget the visual aid." Dolores plucked the container from the counter, stuffed it into her purse and hefted the bag over her shoulder.

Gripping Dolores' elbow, Samantha pulled her through the cast iron gate and whisked her over manicured grounds toward an awning leading to an entrance of the West Wing. Nodding to the sentry guarding the door, Samantha guided Dolores into the foyer, through the lobby, and along a corridor.

While trying to keep up, Dolores tried not to gape at the antique lamps, fine cabinets, and oil paintings hung on the walls, many of which she recognized. She also couldn't help but peek inside offices where people went about their day-to-day business. This was the fabled West Wing, and sorely did she wish to linger to take it all in. Pausing before yet another sentry, Samantha displayed her identification card and Dolores her green visitor badge, then both walked into a multi-level room blue lit by overhead displays where five serious minded individuals studied three times as many screens. They halted before a closed door.

"Here we are, the Situation Room," Samantha said.

"Why did you say I was late?" Dolores asked, the fact having just registered.

"Oh, don't worry about that. Better late than never." Samantha pushed opened the door and gestured for her to enter. "Nice meeting you, Doctor." With her heart pounding in her ears, Dolores thanked the woman and entered the room.

Stretching the length of the conference room were seated what looked to be the entirety of the President's administration, advisors included. Other attendees sat or stood beneath louvered windows and along the nearest wall. She hadn't expected the meeting to have started, nor the assemblage of VIPs. The Vice President yes, with a few others, but that was it. Had she missed a message, or phone call?

The General spoke animatedly just feet from where Dolores stood, his eyes fixed at the head of the table where President Kieran McAllister presided. Janise Martinez, the Vice President, was seated beside him, and both were engrossed with whatever the General was saying. The Cabinet, most of whom she'd never met, were clustered near the President: The Secretary of Defense, State, Homeland Security, directors of the CIA and National Intelligence. Others she recognized from the news and many she couldn't place at all. Victor, the Acting Administrator of NASA, sat at Beckman's side.

The General's eyes flickered to Dolores, but nobody else gave her a second glance. She picked out a friendly face in the crowd, Obadiah, who with a tilt of his head urged her to take a seat.

Face flushed, Dolores navigated toward the nearest vacant chair while murmuring apologies as she stepped over and around polished shoes and high heels. The green visitor badge dangling from her blouse felt like a lead weight. Nobody else wore one. With a final, "Excuse me," Dolores gratefully plopped into the relative anonymity of a seat.

Feeling completely out of place, she took a moment to compose herself. A quick scan confirmed these people had been here a while, as evidenced by the empty cups of coffee, water bottles at half mast, and open notebooks splayed on the table and over people's laps. A bone china cup sat untouched in front of the President. Rather than being late, maybe there was a designated time on the agenda for her to participate. That made sense. After assuring herself all was well,

Dolores turned her attention to where all others were focused.

To her surprise, on the overhead screen she saw the final schematic produced by the alien program, displayed as three nested spheres from which protruded a thin cylinder. What the schematic didn't communicate was the sheer scale, the kilometer-wide outer sphere and two-kilometer stem. The General had commented that it looked like a particle weapon. But for Dolores, if it resembled anything, it was a lollipop from which protruded an enormous uncircumcised penis.

She turned her attention to the monotonous drone emanating from the General. Not only did she recognize his words, she knew what came next. For he was presenting material she had prepared, and thought, would be presenting. With arms crossed over her chest, Dolores listened to the presentation she had agonized over.

"…twenty million square meter surface area of the two outer spheres is believed to concentrate as of yet unknown energy into the innermost structure which redirects said energy into a linear induction accelerator that utilizes ferrite-loaded non-resonant…" the General shook his head and dropped the sheet he held to the table – "Bottom line, Mister President, is I'm seeking your approval to move forward with planning and design for constructing the alien machine."

"You said the schematic was produced after some sort of test?" the President asked.

The crack between the General's lips formed into a smile. "Yes, Sir. My team deciphered the transmission using cryptographic techniques which produced a computer program that tested our knowledge of the periodical table."

Dolores suppressed a cringe, and couldn't help but glance at Obadiah, who sat stone-faced.

"We believe the objective of the test was to ascertain our level of technological sophistication so as to provide a workable design."

"Extraordinary, absolutely extraordinary," the President said. "Alex, you and your team are to be commended. But I don't quite understand what this thing does?"

The smile vanished. "For that analysis, I'd like to call on the head of the Council's science and engineering team, Doctor McCann, who's been grappling with that very question." With a curt nod directed at Dolores, the General picked up papers scattered on the table and promptly sank into his seat.

Having expected to give the presentation Beckman just finished, Dolores was surprised to be called upon. It felt like a torpedo had been launched her way. Was she there only to reinforce his credibility? Or was he ambushing her in an attempt to discredit her? Or both? For the most part they wanted the same thing, so why not just involve her in whatever game he was playing?

Fixing an upward curve to her lips she rose from her seat, large purse in hand. As she made her way to the head of the table she overheard the Vice President say to the President, "This is the one I told you about."

At the podium, finding herself scrutinized by every person in the room, she sank into a silence so deep that she felt she would drown. Raising his eyes, the President said, "Doctor," in a tone so devoid of emotion it seemed judgmental.

She got right to the point. "Mister President, the best minds in the country have studied the alien design. There are several hypotheses as to its function and about the only thing they agree on is that any explanation depends on this." With a low thud, she hefted her purse on the table. Pulling out the casting mold, she placed it before the Secretary of Homeland Security. "We call it draconium, after the constellation Draco, where the transmission originates. The engineers believe this could be a new element, though they've yet to work out exactly where it would fit in the"—she gave the General a sideways glance— "periodic table."

The Secretary leaned forward and gave the same puzzled stare Dolores had seen from every other team member who had studied the material.

"It absorbs electromagnetic radiation across the entire spectrum, including visible light. Your eyes can only perceive it as a hole in space," Dolores explained. "Touch it," she suggested.

He poked the surface with a finger. "It's cold," he observed, and lifted the mold, "and heavy." His neighbor nudged him until the Secretary turned over the container. Soon the metal had been passed around until it rested in front of the President, who picked it up and rotated it in his hands.

"What does this tell you"—he waved at the image on the screen—

"about that?"

"Given the structure's design, our engineering teams presume draconium to be a reflective material. We've yet to identify exactly what it reflects as nearly all the properties of this alloy are a puzzle. About all we know is that its thermal conductivity is off the chart, that it has a high melting point, and requires an electric current to remain stable."

The Secretary of Defense interjected, "JPL has done a superb job, Mister President, no doubt about it. The material alone will revolutionize stealth capabilities to potentially make our ships, planes, and even soldiers virtually invisible. The Department of Defense has the resources to exploit the technology now, as well as to answer those questions JPL can't. Sir, I recommend the science and technical aspects of this investigation be placed under the DoD umbrella."

"That makes a lot of sense," the President said. "What about it, Doctor McCann, shall I bring in another team?"

Ah, so this explained the General's behavior. The material's potential for warfare whetted their appetite for control. Same play, different quarter.

"Our physics can explain a tiny portion of the universe, Mister President," Dolores said, "and this alien device falls squarely into the other category. Stealth is a sideshow; the main act is the machine. And there's only one way to find out what it does."

"You want to build it," the President said.

"Yes, Sir, I do."

"And if it kills every man, woman, and child on the planet?"

Caught off guard, Dolores paused to collect her thoughts. "With all due respect, a similar argument was used to prevent constructing the first particle accelerator. But we overcame our fears and built it anyway. As a result, our understanding of the universe grew."

"Reckless to take even a small chance, don't you think?"

"I don't," she answered, wondering where this was going.

"Tell me, Doctor, what do you think this thing does?"

"I don't know, Sir."

"Best guess, I want to hear it."

"Communication, maybe," she hedged. This was also Tara's guess.

"And draconium, what does it reflect?"

She glanced at Obadiah, who cocked his head. He had posed the same question, had pressed her even, but Dolores refused to disclose a suspicion so preposterous she was embarrassed to give it voice. She shrugged.

"You want to stay on this project, Doctor, I need to know your mind," the President said.

"Gravitational waves," Dolores answered.

Voices bubbled around the table. Some of the people laughed, others shook their heads, and Victor whispered "impossible" to the General so loudly he might as well have shouted.

"What would it take?" the President asked.

"Sir?" Dolores said.

"What would it take to build it?"

General Beckman scrambled to his feet and waved her aside. "The alien designs were submitted to trusted partners in the private sector, Mister President. Engineering and system integration firms the Department of Defense has worked with for years. The engineering is straightforward, simple even, but it will take some time as construction requires utmost precision, and the scale is enormous."

"How long?" the President asked.

"The total estimated duration ranges from five to six years, depending on the assumptions regarding critical path. Some seem to think it would be the linear accelerator, others believe…"

Feeling increasingly awkward as the conversation progressed, Dolores returned to her seat. Though she had no part pulling together the estimates (and no idea it had been done), the duration sounded about right. Assuming draconium could be manufactured in mass, no small feat, constructing the accelerator would take time. There was no getting around that.

"Six years," the President said, and ran a hand through his hair. "I'm afraid we don't have the luxury of time, Alex." He turned to the Director of Central Intelligence. "Tell him why."

"Six hours ago, a fringe media celebrity posted an article claiming AMIGO had detected an extraterrestrial transmission. Further, he reported the decommissioning of the observatory was a cover-up and disclosed the coordinates of the star system where the transmission originates. He also dropped a name, Stephen Fisher, called him a whistle-blower."

Beckman slapped his hand on the table. "Discredit the source, pull down the website."

"Too late," the President said. "Apparently, this character has a following. Thirty-nine media organizations reposted the report. And this morning, one of the majors ran a story questioning the abrupt cancellation of the AMIGO project."

"A number of consortium partners have already contacted NASA," added Victor. To cover the smile creeping over her face, Dolores placed a hand over her mouth. For she'd advocated from the beginning that the transmission be made public.

"We need to shut down that leak," the General said, "before anything more is revealed." Dolores knew exactly what worried him…that the key needed to unlock the transmission would be exposed, the child's music.

"Yes, absolutely," the Defense Secretary agreed, and pointed at the casting mold. "That metal alone will upset the balance of power. Who knows what other secrets can be exploited. We need to build this machine before another nation beats us to it and uses it against us."

A woman two seats to the left chimed in, "Dispense with the usual protocols. Sole-source the contract, bill time and materials, and incentivize our suppliers…"

As if on cue, people began talking all at once, at each other and over each other. Many tried directing their words at the President, who listened without comment. One man, she had no idea who, pledged his agency's full cooperation. Another brought up funding, and more spat out suggestions where to find it. The Director of National Intelligence slapped his hand on the table to declare a need for absolute secrecy, which spawned exclamations of vociferous agreement. When the subject of congressional oversight was raised, the voices rose two octaves and a round of political handwringing began. After several minutes, the Secretary of State declared, "If we can put a man on the moon we can certainly do this," which quickly devolved into exhortations to "do whatever it takes" and "go the extra mile."

None of which would "move the ball an inch," Dolores knew. You couldn't just throw money at this problem. The General had done his homework. It would take six years, at best, to complete construction. And she would be seventy-eight years old by then, into the fourth quarter of her life. Already she felt the weight of her age and thought long and hard about what could happen in those intervening years.

"There may be a way to accelerate construction," Dolores said. But it seemed she spoke to herself as the agitated voices continued percolating throughout the room.

"What was that?" the Vice President asked. She touched the President's sleeve. The room instantly quieted.

Dolores took a steadying breath, for she knew the scientific community would disown her for what she was about to suggest. "We repurpose the Relativistic Heavy Ion Collider in New York. Take it offline, disassemble the components, transport them to an engineering facility where the components can be reconfigured and modified per the alien specs. Then we transport and reassemble at whatever location is ultimately chosen to build the device—"

"That won't help," Victor interrupted. "Even if you pulled that off, the critical path would only move to constructing the spheres." He looked to the President. "Heavy duty mechanisms are required to coordinate movement of the device…"

"Movement?" Dolores asked, interrupting. "The specification never called for that."

"It should have been presumed," Victor said. "The earth spins, Doctor, and the device needs to be directed at the origin of the transmission."

It took a moment to piece together not only his words, but what was implied. "You presume whoever sent the transmission made a colossal error of omission. I believe that to be extremely unwise, Acting Administrator." For her trouble, Dolores received a scowl.

"Why?" the President asked.

"Sir, whoever sent this signal is well beyond us technologically," Dolores answered. "Also, the design strongly suggests the energy being harnessed is little influenced by the angle of the reflectors. And it just so happens that's consistent with how gravitational waves operate."

The President fixed his eyes onto hers. "What's the alternative?"

Dolores didn't hesitate. "Dig a crater in the earth to provide support for the device. That eliminates the need to build a foundation. Then we construct the outermost sphere, which is by far the most difficult, by laying reflective panels onto bare ground, at least for the bottom half."

"Time-frame?"

Dolores paused, not caring to share what she'd only speculated in private. But what the hell, the President already implied she was reckless. "Twelve months, assuming you can move mountains, literally and figuratively."

"Didn't I tell you?" the Vice President said to him.

Unlocking his eyes from Dolores, the President swept his gaze around the room. "Thank you for your time," he said, the dismissal clear. Before she could rise to her feet, he added, "Not you, Doctor McCann."

The remaining assemblage, aside from the Vice President, filed outside, with many a curious glance directed at Dolores, some of them resentful. The Secretary of Defense and the General lingered near the exit, until told by the President he'd speak with them later.

Once the door was secured, the President swiveled his chair and tapped his fingers on the table. "Doctor McCann, I'd like you to take personal charge of building the alien machine."

Dolores heard the words, processed what was said, and could almost see the General's jaw drop in the other room, along with her own. She allowed herself a moment of exultation before it was rudely swept aside by the magnitude of the task before her. "It's going to cost a lot of money, Sir," she warned.

"Eight billion has been carved out of the national intelligence budget," he said. "If more is needed, you'll get it."

She considered the next obstacle. "We'll need lots of space, isolated and secure, near a large power source" – she did the figure in her head – "one point two one gigawatts."

"I can think of a couple places."

"And earth-moving equipment, construction crews, and somebody to direct them..."

"The Secretary of Defense doesn't know this yet, but the Army Corp of Engineers is about to be redeployed."

Her mind raced to the next problem, manufacturing the draconium. Smelting wouldn't be an issue but finding the materials could be problematic, especially the rhodium. Three tons would be required, and that mineral was beyond scarce.

"Doctor McCann?" the President said.

She looked up. "Mister President?"

"Is it safe to assume you accept the assignment?"

"Oh. Yes, Sir. Absolutely."

CHAPTER EIGHTEEN

The distant echo of footsteps pierced the lethargic wakefulness that now passed for sleep. With a squeal of metal on metal the security gate outside my cell opened. Then there was a rattle and ugly scraping of plastic over cement as a tray was pushed through the hinged slot at the bottom of the heavy door. It was feeding time.

I swung my legs over the bed anxious to be let out of my cage. Walking to the sink I splashed water over my face then looked at what was reflected from the stainless-steel mirror pasted onto the wall. Green eyes sunken inside the emaciated skull of a stranger stared back at me, a face I wouldn't have recognized when I'd been deposited into this place eight months, one week, and six days ago.

A malodorous smell led me to look upon the tray holding breakfast. Three strips of meat from a slaughtered swine bled fatty tissue onto a scrambled egg. At one time the meal would have tempted me, but now I found the thought of eating flesh repulsive. Far less revolting were the two pieces of toast and blueberry muffin that shared the plate. That should have appealed to the gnawing emptiness in my gut, but with the loss of freedom had come a loss of appetite.

I pocketed the toast and picked up the muffin. After forcing down a few bites I lifted the half-eaten pastry to a mechanical eye watching from the corner of the room. This was to assure whoever monitored my movement that I followed orders, the orders having come from a team of physicians who poked and prodded me each week. During their last visit they threatened to plug me into an IV if I didn't get calories into this body. And I hated needles, with a passion. More important was that my keepers wouldn't let me out of the cell until I ate something. After finishing off the muffin I stepped away from the door and placed both hands on the back of my head. This was routine.

The face of a guard looked through the acrylic square embedded into the upper half of the steel door. I wondered what he saw. Was it a thin bird of a man with eyes too big for his head? Or the Stranger I'd become? What I saw were translucent tendrils writhing through his flesh and a galaxy of color spinning through his mind, both of which were accompanied by the dull thrumming of music that echoed inside my head, like tinnitus. Hallucinations had grown powerful these past few months, so much so that it took a concentrated effort to focus on the shell of the man before me.

The electronic bolt securing the cell released with a startling bang. The door swung open to reveal a broad shouldered guard. He was one of three who escorted me out of the cell each morning for recreation. None of the guards offered their names, so I attached a number to each. This was number three, the only one who spoke to me. He was friendly enough, after a fashion. I never gave him a reason not to be. The others not only kept silent, they kept their distance.

"Fishing today, or shall we go for a hike?" I asked.

"Neither, I'm afraid," the burly guard answered. He then proceeded to hobble me with constraints while numbers one and two aimed tasers at my chest.

With the guards leading the way, I was shuffled along a windowless passage lined with empty and dilapidated cells. The scent of must and a deafening silence lent the already oppressive environment a desperate air, reinforcing that my family had no idea where I was being held. Having reached the end of the corridor a guard unlocked and pushed open an exterior door to reveal a blessedly open sky. I drank in the fresh air. I was then herded along a familiar dirt path leading to a half-acre of weeds and dirt, the closest thing to paradise that I had left to me. Number Three locked the gate behind me and retreated with his companions to station themselves at equidistant intervals around the perimeter, as if I might somehow sprout wings and fly away.

Walking to the far side of the enclosure I stared past the chain link fence to gaze upon the surrounding forest. Spindly trunks of pine glowing a warm ochre splintered into branches that vainly reached for the sky. While chirping praise for the morning sun, tiny streaks of luminescent shapes flitted within the leafy canopy. The multi-hued whorl of another creature scampered down a nearby tree to disappear into the tall grass. It wasn't only people I perceived differently; it was the entirety of the living world, and I reveled in the beauty of my psychosis.

Before I'd even taken the toast from my pocket a host of birds descended from the branches of the trees to surround me on all sides. Some chittered from atop razor wire, others from within links of the fence, while most hopped impatiently over the ground. Jays were the most vocal. The squirrel jumped through the fence and stood on its hind legs to beseech me with tiny hands. I acquiesced to the creature's demands by crushing the toast and scattering the crumbs over the dirt. Chaos broke out. Within seconds all the bread had been consumed. I lifted my hands to show the entourage there was no more food to be had. Taking the hint, the squirrel scampered out of the enclosure and back up the tree. But most of the birds remained, except for the jays who took off with offended jeers.

Clouds meandered through a sapphire sky and the rays of the sun warmed my skin. I lay myself prone on the ground and looked up into a realm where no fences surrounded me. Time released its grip as I embraced the illusion of freedom.

With a rush of wings, the birds darted away. Annoyed, I lifted my eyes to find guard number three looming over me. "Looks like you have visitors," he said.

Sighing, I clambered to my feet and dusted off my trousers. Visitors meant doctors. "Medical or psych?"

"They came by air," the guard said.

Turning my back on the forest I looked over the collection of ill-maintained buildings to see the slowly spinning rotors of a helicopter. For some reason, the medical doctors came by land and the head doctors by air. I was relieved, because every time a physician showed up some part of me went missing…a vial of blood or container of urine. One had dared asked me for a semen sample, which I refused. But I found the psychiatrists entertaining.

The last who had visited gave me a Rorschach test. The first inkblot had looked like a butterfly, the second had resembled two dancers wearing red stockings, the third a bat, and the fourth a tree. She then held up a stick-figure drawing that gave me pause. Clearly, it was meant to resemble the figure of some type of humanoid, which I found to be an obvious and clumsy attempt to get me talking about the transmission. But there was zero chance I was going to give her the satisfaction. So, I told her it looked like a spider. She asked what else I saw. Pretending to study it more carefully I said, "Maybe a flower." That psychiatrist left disappointed, as did every other so-called expert they sent to examine me. I wondered what was in store for today.

Through dank and dreary corridors, the guards escorted me to the room where I expected to speak to the psychiatrist. But instead, when I stepped through the door, I saw through the glass partition a man I never expected to meet again.

"F-f-f-fisher," Connor stuttered.

I could only stare. He stood well away from the partition, leaned heavily on a cane, and the left side of his face drooped. "Leave us," he ordered the guards, who nearly tripped over themselves in their haste to exit the room.

"Nothing to say, Fisher?"

I had convinced myself that what happened during the interrogation was just another delusion from a damaged mind. Schizophrenics often believe they have special powers, and in my case that included hurting Connor with a thought and a touch. Unable to stop myself, I asked him, "What happened?"

"The doctors say a stroke, but I know perfectly well what you did."

"I never meant—"

"I don't want to hear it. Denial seems to be a h-h"—he swallowed— "habit of yours. Has your stay here been pleasant? I hope not."

A whiff of the old anger reemerged, reminding me of past threats. "What did you do to my wife?"

"I'm not a monster, Fisher, despite what you think."

"Then why are you here?"

"To deliver a message. It's more a gesture, actually. In exchange Doctor McCann expects your full c-c"—he huffed— "cooperation."

Another memory from the interrogation popped into my head. "Dolores built the machine, didn't she?"

"I advised against what she intends," he said, ignoring the question. And I have a message of my own…step out of line and you won't see the light of day. Understand?"

A quiver passed through me, in equal parts anticipation and strangely, fear. "I want my brother with me."

"This isn't a n-negotiation," he spat, literally.

"He comes with me, or no deal."

"Enough," Connor snapped. The partition turned black.

"Wait," I pleaded, but to no response.

Uneven light flickered from the ancient fluorescent bulbs affixed to the ceiling. A minute passed, then another, yet the guards didn't come fetch me. Then from the other side of the darkened partition came a whirlpool of luminescence I knew as well as myself. My throat constricted and moisture welled from my eyes. The partition cleared.

Ignoring the tendrils writhing through flesh, I concentrated on the shell of the woman I loved. Slowly, a heart-shaped face framed by midnight hair came into focus. Red lips parted in shock and tender brown eyes widened with alarm. Fran placed an open palm onto the window and her chest heaved. "Oh, Stephen, what have they done to you?"

Whatever joy I felt was overcome by shame from the psychosis that I had fought all these years. I dropped my eyes and stammered two words weakened by repetition, "I'm sorry."

"No, Stephen, I'm the one who needs to apologize. She was as much my daughter as yours. I think it was, well, I just couldn't believe what you told me the day our home was searched. I should have believed you."

I shook my head, unable to speak. Believe? I didn't know what to believe anymore. What was it I once told my daughter, that the imaginary world wasn't the same as the real one? That was sound advice. "You can't trust what I say."

"I should have helped you," she insisted, sniffling loudly.

Horrified at the thought of my wife inside a cell, I raised my eyes and repeated what I'd been thinking every moment of my incarceration, "I should have gone quietly, told them whatever it was they wanted to hear."

Fran stared at me, then leaned within a hair's breadth of the pane. "Oh my god, you don't know."

I shrugged.

"You wrote a note, didn't you?"

"You read it?" I asked, recalling the young woman in the library.

"I did, Stephen, because it made the news a few weeks after you disappeared. The government tried dismissing it as a hoax, but I recognized your terrible handwriting. Your brother and I have been clamoring for your release ever since."

"Then you knew what happened to me."

"More than that, Stephen. Don't think these people are being kind by allowing me to see you today. It's only because your case is getting the attention it deserves." The line of Fran's jaw tightened. "Four weeks ago, the Chinese government announced to great fanfare that their new observatory had detected an extraterrestrial signal. It confirmed everything you said in the note. And I think you know what the transmission sounds like, because I certainly do."

"Our daughter's song."

"That's right," she said.

A surge of relief washed through me. What I had thought happened had actually happened. There really was a transmission. Not only that, my wife believed me. And all this time I had feared she was angry, had thought I was insane, or worse, had forgotten all about me. Did she, like me, dream of our daughter? Was the music also playing in her head? Before I could think to ask, Fran said, "I'm not sure how much time we have, and I've got something important to show you." She stood, cupping a hand under her protruding abdomen. "We're having a child, Stephen."

I placed my palm against the glass, watching the pale circle of amber flow counterclockwise within her womb. "She's beautiful."

◆ ◆ ◆

Without a word, guard number three tossed a pair of shoes and burlap-bound package onto the end of my cot. "Get dressed," he said.

After stripping the paper from the package, I found inside the outfit I had worn the day of my arrest. The clothes were neatly folded and smelled of bleach. I mechanically pulled on the shirt, drew on the slacks, and cinched the belt past the last notch. Once I slipped on the shoes, new shoes to replace the ones I had left with the homeless lady,

I dutifully held out my wrists. As the guard bound me with manacles he said under his breath, "I know who you are, you know."

That made one of us. "And?"

"You're Stephen Fisher."

I grunted, hoping he had a better answer. "Where are we going?"

"You'll find out soon enough," he said.

As if I walked within a dream, the guard escorted me along secure corridors and out the exit to where a helicopter awaited. Once airborne he released me from the manacles. I rubbed the soreness from my wrists. "You're taking me to the machine, aren't you?"

To my surprise, he answered. "I have no idea. What I do know are my orders."

I peered out the window. Unlike when I'd been brought to this place, in a windowless aircraft in the dark of night, I could now see where I had been incarcerated. Below us the ramshackle buildings of the compound gave way to rolling green hills. Up ahead a river snaked through densely vegetated landscape and soon we were flying over tidy geometric outlines of farmland. I guessed we were somewhere in the southeastern United States. Arkansas, maybe. But it didn't matter where I was, only that I was free. After an hour an airfield appeared on the horizon and grew large as we approached.

As soon as we landed the guard transferred me to a military cargo jet idling on the runway. We were the only passengers. Once the jet took off and reached altitude a steward emerged from the front cabin. To my utter astonishment he asked if I wanted anything to eat or drink.

My stomach rumbled. "Toast, if you have it." Toast was promptly delivered along with a smorgasbord of breads and fruits. The steward also brought a bottle of sparkling water, tangerine flavored. Like my friends in the forest, I consumed it all in a flash before asking for more.

"Is it true?" the guard asked.

"What's that?" I said, digging into the second helping.

"That you, well, you know…"

"Sorry, I have no idea what you're talking about."

"Never mind, then. For what it's worth, you've always seemed like a regular guy to me."

If only he knew. "Thanks, I guess." Feeling fatigued and more than a little sick I reclined into the seat and stared out the window, pondering what was to come.

I must have fallen asleep, because I was startled awake as the plane landed hard and bounced three times before steadying itself on the runway. With a muffled roar, the engines slowed the aircraft to a stop. Outside the window I saw a featureless desert. The steward then emerged from the cockpit, opened the hatch, and stood stiffly at attention.

I blinked bleary eyes at my guard. "What happens now?"

"No idea because you're no longer my problem," he said, and angled his head toward the exit. "Welcome to the town of Mercury, Mister Fisher. Good luck to you." He held out his hand.

I regarded the proffered appendage a long moment before deciding this guard was in no way responsible for my plight. In a strange way, he had made my imprisonment more bearable. I rose from the seat, shook his hand, then strode down the narrow aisle without a backward look. Nodding to the steward I passed through the hatchway.

Suffocating heat descended on me like a physical blow, taking my breath away. As I adjusted to the air I took in the surroundings. Sparse and desiccated brush stretched to distant foothills silhouetted against a setting sun. To the right were a cluster of white buildings surrounded by massive squares of equipment, supplies, and construction vehicles, all parked in symmetrical rows. My attention was then drawn to the living forms huddled near two vehicles parked astride the airfield. One belonged to the woman who had summoned me, Dolores. The others I didn't recognize. As I was about to descend the stairwell another presence raised the hairs on the back of my neck.

I turned.

In the failing light, miles distant, an enormous barrow of featureless black lorded over the desert floor. A moving band of black specks circled the edifice. I squinted, and the specks turned to pinpoints of color. They were birds, thousands upon thousands moving as if they were one. But what most captured my attention were the silver tinged diaphanous waves that entered the darkness that the birds circled. It was then that the faint thrumming inside of my head began to roar.

CHAPTER NINETEEN

Dolores watched as Stephen stared into the distance from atop the stairwell. What was he thinking, what did he know about the transmission? Despite Connor's crude interrogation methods, they had learned nothing about him or the alien device (other than that Stephen had a tentative hold on reality). In her judgement it was well past time to use the carrot rather than the stick.

Megan, standing beside her, observed, "He's awfully thin."

Indeed, he was, with the sunken cheeks and shirt hanging from his torso like a burlap sack three sizes too large. What were the guards thinking, treating him like this? Didn't they understand Stephen's value?

Dolores turned to face three agents of the General's Special Security Force lounging against a black sedan. Ostensibly assigned for her protection, she hadn't a doubt their true purpose was to assure that orders were followed. The General didn't approve of Stephen's visit. In fact, he tried to countermand it, forcing Dolores to spend what little political capital she possessed to convince the President otherwise. In exchange, she had promised to uncover the true purpose of the alien device, its raison d'etre, a reason other than the ability to burn through billions of dollars.

Dolores singled out the surliest looking agent. "Hudson, is it? Thought your people were feeding him."

Hudson pushed herself off the sedan. "He refuses to eat, ma'am."

"Maybe prison doesn't agree with him," Megan said.

"He gets better food than the security detail," Hudson said.

"Be that as it may," Dolores said, "I intend to raise the subject with the President."

"It's not my fault. We have physicians that check on him every—"

Dolores cut her off. "Agent Hudson, I would appreciate if you and your team remain here while I welcome our guest. It's important that Stephen be at ease."

Hudson tapped her watch. "I feel the need to remind you, Doctor, that you're permitted one hour before the inmate is returned to the incarceration facility…starting ten minutes ago."

Dolores stepped to within a hand's breadth of the woman. "Who is in command of this project, care to remind me?"

Into an unflinching gaze Hudson stared, giving rise to a silence so thick that it oozed. Passing seconds became an eternity. With a lick of her lips, Hudson blinked. "Those are my orders, ma'am. General Beckman made that especially clear, to the both of us."

"I give the orders here, Agent Hudson. If you have a problem with that you can take it up with the President of the United States." Not waiting for a reply, Dolores turned on her heel and began marching toward the aircraft.

Megan hurriedly caught up. Once out of earshot, she asked, "Is that true, what the angry lady said?"

"We have one chance at this," Dolores replied, more forcefully than she intended.

Megan tilted her head. "You know I'm with you, right?"

"I know that, Meg, and thank you. I'm just feeling a little…tense."

They came to a halt at the base of the stairwell. At the top, a steward tapped the distracted Stephen on the shoulder, signaling for him to move along.

"He looks worse the closer we get," Megan said.

"Hush now," Dolores said, and watched as Stephen stepped carefully down the ramp. It seemed odd that so innocuous a man had become such a political hot potato. She wondered if he had any idea how much trouble he had caused.

It started a few weeks after Stephen's arrest, when a little-known purveyor of conspiracy theories released a hand-written letter allegedly penned by Stephen that disclosed the detection of the transmission along with the cover-up. If that wasn't bad enough, it was made worse by accompanying footage of Stephen's home being searched by the SSF. Given the source wasn't reputable, NASA was able to easily dismiss the news as a hoax. Then came the leak of the transmission, reported through the same source. As Dolores knew well, the sound was compelling, otherworldly, and overnight the recording had turned into a sensation, becoming the most downloaded file on the Internet. As a result, the former purveyor of cockamamie theories became a celebrity. Victor felt compelled to repeat the lies concerning AMIGO's malfunction. Since anybody with a passing understanding of gravitational waves *knew* they couldn't be artificially generated, Victor was believed. Connor lost his mind. He began a witch hunt that continued to this day, questioning everybody and anybody who had real or theoretical access to confidential information.

Then four weeks ago all hell broke loose when the Chinese Space Agency held a press conference to announce that their gravitational observatory had detected an extraterrestrial signal. Cries were now being raised concerning Stephen's whereabouts, lack of due-process, and what role he played in detecting the transmission. The more responsible news organizations called him a whistle-blower while the fringier outlets were having a field day spouting all kinds of nonsense. She had even heard (through Obadiah) that the President himself was considering making a statement. All told, the committee's effort to keep the transmission secret had become a complete and total fiasco. And as far as she was concerned, it was totally deserved.

After climbing down the stairwell to the tarmac, Stephen stood at ease while solemnly regarding Dolores. She found his gaze utterly disturbing, as if she stood naked before him. Without thinking she placed both hands in front of her blouse. "Good to see you Stephen. You look…."

"Like hell?"

"Thin," she said. "This is Megan McCullough, a compatriot of mine."

Megan took Stephen's hand and shook it. "You poor man. I want you to know that Dolores and I had nothing to do with your arrest. In fact, we never wanted any of this business kept secret."

"Thank you, I appreciate that," Stephen said, and turned his disconcerting gaze back to Dolores. "You built it."

"We call it the Gravitational Wave Amplification Device," Dolores said. "G-WAD for short."

"You gave a presentation about gravitational waves. Didn't think it was possible to, what did you say, amplify them?"

"It wasn't," she said, surprised he knew anything about the subject. "Not until my team proved otherwise by passing a laser interferometer through the device. We detected huge wobbles in the fabric of space-time. That's not theoretically possible, but then again, neither is using gravitational waves to generate a transmission. Care to explain how that's done?"

"No idea," he said, and thinly smiled. "You're the one who wrote the paper."

"That's what I figured, but thought I'd ask. Look, Stephen, I'm not going to beat around the bush with you. I need help figuring out what the G-WAD does and how it works. In return there's a good chance I can convince the authorities to get you released." That wasn't exactly true, but Dolores did have the President's ear.

"I'll do what I can," Stephen said, "and make things up if I have to."

"That's the spirit," Megan said.

"Whatever you have to say we want to hear, made up or not," Dolores said. "First thing to do is take a little tour of the G-WAD, to see if that shakes loose an insight."

"Were you able to bring Eric?" Stephen asked.

"We'll meet up with him later."

"What?" Megan asked. "How did you get away with that?"

"I have my ways," Dolores said. Long ago she had learned that authority was taken, not given. As a result, she didn't bother asking permission to do what was right.

"Thank you," Stephen said.

"My pleasure." Taking his arm, Dolores escorted Stephen toward the waiting sport utility vehicle where she found, to her great annoyance, Hudson settled into the driver seat. Sidling around the hood she spoke through the open window. "I'll be doing the driving today, Agent Hudson."

"I'm here for your protection, ma'am," Hudson said. Meaning, General Beckman wanted an eye kept on her.

"I appreciate that but can assure you our guest won't cause any trouble. That right, Stephen?"

"No plans," Stephen said. Megan gently shoved him into the front passenger seat while she clambered into the back.

"See, told you," Dolores said. With a brittle smile she opened the driver-side door. "You're welcome to follow in your own vehicle, Agent Hudson."

After a moment's hesitation, Hudson slid from the seat. Stiffly marching back to the sedan, she immediately got onto the phone, no doubt to report Dolores' impertinence. Dolores hopped in, turned over the engine, and hit the accelerator. The SUV bounced off the curb onto the adjacent street.

"Good god, Dolores, this isn't a race," Megan said.

She eased up on the pedal. "Sorry." Passing the detritus of hurried construction – piles of rebar, concrete mixing plants, pyramids of aggregate, and fleets of construction vehicles – they sped toward the massive black hummock on the horizon. The sedan followed close behind. Soon, the high earthen walls protecting the G-WAD came into view, like the fortifications of a medieval town.

"What you see is the top third of the outer sphere," Dolores said. "The remainder rests inside a crater carved out of the earth."

"A hundred kiloton nuclear blast did most of the work in 1962," Megan added.

"A short cut," Dolores said. "Anyway, inside the outer construct are three smaller spheres, nested within one another like a wooden Russian doll. Based on the interferometer readings, we surmise their function is to trap and collect gravitational waves within the innermost sphere. Takes about two and a half days before the wobbles in space-time max out, like topping off a fuel tank. Again, this shouldn't be possible, but a property of a newly discovered material seems to reflect the gravitons. Finally, when the device is activated, all that accumulated energy is funneled into what we call the amplification tower. Think of the G-WAD as a giant lollipop, with the nested spheres on top and a stick at the bottom."

Dolores paused for a breath then focused her attention on Stephen, hoping for a thought, a reaction, anything. But his head was craned forward, looking into the sky. It was if he hadn't heard a word she had said. "Stephen?" she prompted.

"Sorry, what?'

Dolores sighed, as Stephen's purported ignorance was very convincing. Noting that she'd missed the turnoff for their tour, Dolores swerved the SUV off the asphalt road and onto the desert floor, prompting her passengers to grab the nearest handhold. She then proceeded to plow through sagebrush to reach the dirt track that snaked up the earthen mound. A glance in the rear-view mirror showed the black sedan following four car-lengths behind, a tumbleweed stuck to the grill.

"Maybe you should let me take the wheel," Megan said.

"Relax, I'm an excellent driver," Dolores said.

"Uh huh."

They crested the earthen mound and Dolores made a hard right onto the perimeter road that ran alongside a barbed wire fence. On their left rose a lattice of honeycombed steel struts holding together the great plates of draconium that sucked the life from the sun like a hole in the universe. Only an illusion, she knew, but it seemed miraculous, nonetheless. Stephen was still staring at the sky. "What is it you're looking at, Stephen?" she asked.

"They're beautiful, how they pulse and intermingle, almost like, well, like they're caressing one another."

She followed his gaze only to find the host of birds circling above, as they'd done since the G-WAD was constructed. It took a full maintenance crew just to clean up their mess. "Why are they attracted to this place?" she asked, having wondered that before.

"You can see them?" Stephen asked. "I never know sometimes."

"Well, of course—" she started, then reconsidered. "Wait, what is it you see?"

"Silver tendrils moving toward the machine, as if the darkness is sucking them in. I can hear them too, very faint, like somebody singing from behind a closed door. Can you hear them?"

Dolores' pulse quickened. Looking into the rear-view mirror she caught Megan's eye, who mouthed, "Oh my god."

"I can't hear or see them," Dolores said, "but I believe that you do." This wasn't the first time Stephen saw things he shouldn't. "Question, during your interrogation did you really know I was behind that observation window, or was it a guess?"

"I know when I'm being watched," he answered.

"You also mentioned a voice," she continued. "You weren't joking about that, were you?"

Stephen's eyes fell, and it took a moment for him to answer. "No, and I don't like talking about it because it only makes the voice louder."

"I see," she said, having no clue to what he referred, but unwilling to write it off as imagination. "Forgive my second question then. What does that voice of yours have to say about the G-WAD?"

Stephen drew in a deep breath and closed his eyes. "Nothing, but it only tells me what I already know, or in this case, what I don't know."

"I appreciate your honesty," she said, then broached the question for which she'd been waiting, "You said something to me during the interrogation—"

"I remember."

"You told me about—"

"A cavern, with golden eyes focused as one toward the center."

"That's right," she said. His description held an uncanny resemblance to the chamber located at the tail end of the lollipop stick, where energy from the amplification tower was poured. It was there that hundreds of sapphire lenses emitted a dull yellow sheen, like eyes from a horrifically large insect. "What do you think you're going to find there?" she asked.

Stephen didn't respond, at first, and just before she repeated the question he leaned over and whispered so silently that she barely heard. "Hope."

"Dolores!" Megan cried.

She yanked the wheel to get back onto the path, barely averting sending the SUV over the earthen embankment. "Sorry!"

"Feel free to drop me off anywhere," Megan said.

"Won't happen again," Dolores said, and drove on. Stephen silently stared into the black while Megan's eyes periodically darted into the mirror to catch Dolores's own, as if asking, "What now?" Exactly what she was thinking herself. Having completed a full circuit of the G-WAD, Dolores backtracked down the embankment. It was decision time.

The General had made it perfectly clear that under no circumstances should Stephen be allowed inside the perimeter of the G-WAD. The President agreed, both of them fearing what they didn't understand. But as expected, Dolores had learned nothing. The remaining choices were stark. Return to the airport and she may never understand the function of the device. Or turn toward the main gate and put everything she had worked for at risk. The choice was easy, and one she had prepared for well before Stephen's arrival. Looking at the side mirror she saw that Hudson's sedan had fallen behind. Arriving at the main road, Dolores turned sharply to the left.

"God bless America," Megan said, gripping the handle above the door.

"Sorry," Dolores said, and peeked behind her. Barely discernible within the cloud of dust kicked up by her abrupt turn was the shadowed outline of Hudson's sedan, only now slowing to a stop. She hit the accelerator. A quarter mile later Dolores brought the SUV to a halt at the main gate. She rolled down the window.

Buzz, part of the Federal Protective Service guarding the G-WAD, stepped outside the security booth. "Evening, Doctor McCann," he said. Placing a calloused hand on the door frame, he peered inside the SUV. His eyes flicked to Megan, who nodded a greeting, then swiveled to Stephen, where they widened.

"This is my guest, Buzz, the one I told you about. Tell the agents behind us that we'll be back shortly, within the hour. It's a clearance thing. Under no circumstances are they to be allowed inside. Understand?"

"Leave it to me, ma'am," Buzz said. The gate rumbled open. Dolores bounced the SUV over the metal track then looked over her shoulder. Buzz had stepped in front of the sedan prompting Hudson to poke her head out the window and angrily gesticulate at the closing gate. How long before her order to Buzz was countermanded…a day, an hour, ten minutes? Probably the time it took for Hudson to contact General Beckman, who would then have to escalate up one chain of command and down another. Regardless of the outcome, she didn't want company.

"Um, Dolores, are we not supposed to be here?" Megan asked.

"I'm exercising my prerogative."

Megan clucked her tongue, and Dolores could swear that Stephen smiled. Slowing the vehicle, they passed through a tunnel built through the earthen embankment and emerged into a wilderness of metal lattice struts. As always, she felt claustrophobic between the two walls. On one side was reinforced concrete and on the other were the panels of draconium that seemed to suck the sunlight from the darkening sky. She flipped on the headlights before descending the steep and curving path.

"Stephen, this part of the tour is where I show you our problem," Dolores said. "Your brother—"

"Is waiting below," Stephen interrupted.

"Yes, at the elevator with one of my colleagues. From there, we're going to descend toward that chamber of yours."

Stephen nodded.

The road widened and leveled off as they approached a square building illuminated by a single bulb affixed to a pole. A car was parked in front and Tara and Eric stood beside it. Before Dolores had even stopped the SUV, Eric was striding toward them. Stephen was out the door in an instant and both she and Megan watched the brothers embrace.

"You're running quite the risk bringing Stephen here," Megan said. "What is it you hope he's going to do?"

"Pull a rabbit out of his hat," Dolores said, not really joking.

"It's not like you to rely on magic. What's the real reason."

If Megan weren't her dearest friend, Dolores never would have admitted her true motive. She twisted in the seat to face Megan. "Remember what I told you Stephen said during the interrogation?"

"Sure, the golden eyes."

"After that."

"Something about that's where he belongs."

"What if he really does, Meg?"

"I'm not following."

"Remember the stick-figure images output by the alien program?"

"Hard to forget those."

Dolores hesitated, then gave voice to what she was reluctant to say aloud. "What if those images are part of the blueprint, an integral component needed for the device to function?"

Megan scoffed. "You think Stephen's a component?"

"More a catalyst than a component," Dolores answered.

There was an outlier of physicists who believed consciousness represented a fifth force of nature. While Dolores never accepted that premise, she did entertain the possibility that observation alone could precipitate a wave function collapse triggering quantum entanglement, a phenomenon allowing particles to interact instantaneously at a distance. Aside from scale, it wasn't fundamentally different from creating a wormhole in space, the perfect mechanism to enable interstellar superluminal communication, which Dolores believed had to be the true purpose of the device. And not just any consciousness would serve, but one inexplicably linked to the transmission. And maybe, just maybe, the brother was needed as well because there were two humanoid figures included in the blueprint. That was the real reason she brought Eric along. Her theory was far-fetched, even preposterous, but it wasn't any more unlikely than bending gravitational waves. In so many words, she explained this to Megan.

After a long pause, Megan said, "I think those images are a greeting card, Dolores, from our extraterrestrial friends."

"You're probably right," she said, and heaved a sigh.

"But what the hell. Let's give it a shot. I mean, what do we have to lose?"

Dolores' heart warmed. "Our jobs?"

An impatient tapping caused Dolores to look out the window. Tara, with cheeks flushed and frazzled hair sticking out like a broom, waved for them to join her. After slipping out of the SUV, Dolores ran her eyes up the outer sphere that loomed over them like a tribute to a pagan god. Though she'd been here many times she still felt insubstantial in its shadow. And despite being in the middle of a desert summer, goosebumps ran up her arms.

"Eric's upset," Tara said.

"He should be thankful," Dolores countered. When she first spoke to Eric about the possibility of this visit, she received only accusations in return: blaming her for Stephen's incarceration and betraying her professional integrity. It didn't help when she required Eric to sign a document to assure confidentiality.

Dolores walked toward the brothers, overhearing Eric saying something about a lawyer. Angry eyes pierced her as she approached.

"Don't you start up," she warned.

"You should speak out," Eric said.

"What makes you think I haven't?"

"The fact you're still part of that council."

Dolores wagged a finger in his face. "Don't you dare scold me, Eric Fisher. I'm your brother's only friend on that council, a council you're not supposed to know anything about, by the way." Tara joined them, standing especially close to Eric. Dolores shot her an accusing look, communicating with her gaze what she had already said to her face – *Yes, I know about you two, and don't think others won't take notice. Connor, for one. If he hasn't already, he soon will, then both of you will become the subject of unwanted attention.* Tara averted her eyes.

"Not too late to quit," Eric persisted.

"Give it a rest," Dolores said, and looked up the path fearing to see headlights barreling toward them. Nothing yet, but that wouldn't last. She took hold of Stephen's arm and half led and half dragged him to the entry of the building. Taking care to assure Stephen had a clear view of the access panel, Dolores tapped in her security code. "I use the same numbers for every one of these panels, otherwise I wouldn't remember any of them," she said. "An age thing, I suppose."

The elevator doors opened. Stephen said nothing.

"What do you intend on doing with my brother?" Eric asked, having followed close behind.

"Exactly what he asked me to do," Dolores said, not caring for Eric's tone. She entered the cabin and placed her hand over the rubber bumper, allowing Tara, Stephen, and Megan to step inside. "Come, go, it's all the same to me," she said, already wishing she hadn't brought Eric along. She stabbed at the down button while Stephen signaled that Eric should join them. As the doors began to close Eric hopped into the elevator. With an abrupt lurch, the car descended into the earth, making such a racket bumping and squealing down the shaft that it forbade further conversation. A blessing, as far as she was concerned. The moment they came to a stop Dolores stalked out of the cabin and began striding through the dimly lit corridor.

Having reached the reinforced steel barrier, Dolores again punched in her security code. With a metallic pop and slight groan, the door swung inward. She addressed Stephen, "This is system control, where my team operates the G-WAD."

Lights flickered to life revealing the low ceiling and half-moon shaped enclosure. Exposed wires hung from fixtures overhead and a toolbox lay open near the entrance. Plastic tables were crowded with computer equipment, monitors, and instrumentation, most of which hadn't been taken out of the original packaging. Against the wall were cages of laboratory animals, the unfortunate subjects of experiments meant to test the device. And in the middle of the far wall was a cylindrical glass lift. As they filed into the room, she focused on Stephen, whose eyes went to the lift before traveling to the ceiling.

"That's right, Stephen," Dolores said. "Above us is the chamber that we call the Injector. It's the beating heart of the G-WAD." She tilted her head toward the lift. "And that's the entrance."

Stephen pointed to the wire cages. "Odd place to keep your pets."

"They're tools, used to figure out the puzzle we're dealing with—"

Eric interrupted, firing off questions about the device, the design, what it would do, and what Stephen had to do with any of it. Basically, the same questions Dolores wondered about. Tara hushed him.

"You're here to keep your brother company, not to ask questions," Dolores said. "Tara, man your station. Stephen, beside me. Eric, you stay out of the way."

An overhead display lit up once Tara brought the computer equipment online. The middle screen showed a dimly lit circular platform that seemed to hover within empty space. "This is a live stream from within the chamber," Tara explained. "That platform lies in the very center and fifty meters above it is a dome."

"Megan, if you don't mind," Dolores said.

Walking with heavy steps Megan approached a cage and pulled out a gray rabbit. While gently stroking its fur, she made her way inside the circular lift. With a pneumatic hiss the doors closed, and the lift rose through an aperture in the ceiling that opened and shut like a camera shutter. On the live stream they watched Megan ascend to the platform holding tightly onto the rabbit. She pushed the animal into a waiting cage. Within minutes she had returned to the control room. "The creature's bound to the altar," Megan said.

Dolores frowned, not appreciating the morbid humor. "All right then, same drill, like always."

"How many times have you done this?" Eric asked.

"Too many," Megan replied.

Tara prepared the sensory equipment while Dolores took position at the adjoining table. Neither needed to speak, as the procedure had become routine. "The power is steady," Tara said. "Multispectral sensors are online. Readings are nominal. We're at the ready."

"Stand by," Dolores said. Reaching for the keypad above the main console she tapped in the security code then tapped on the control. "Stephen, when I activate the device you're going to hear a countdown. Once that expires a gigawatt of power will be pumped into the amplification tower. Then a shield, the only moving part in the device, will open, allowing gravitons to flow inside the chamber. You have only one job, and that's to keep your eyes glued to the display. Do you understand?"

"Got it," Stephen said, and fixed his eyes on the gray rabbit cowering in the cage.

"How about me, what can I do?" Eric asked.

"Wish us luck," Dolores said. Praying Stephen's presence would change the outcome, Dolores pulled the lever. Blue lights flashed, and a computer generated voice intoned, "Sixty seconds, fifty-nine, fifty-eight…"

When the countdown hit zero, there was a buzz of power that raised the hairs on her arms. The walls vibrated as gears ground to part the shield. Dolores held her breath, keeping her eyes pinned to the screen. A golden glow filled the inside of the chamber. The rabbit leapt into the air, slamming against the wire mesh. It frantically pawed at the cage, jumping as if stung. After excruciating seconds of this, the creature finally slumped to the floor, kicking twice before becoming still.

"Shit," Megan said.

Tara scanned the sensors. "No change."

Like an overinflated balloon, the air drained from Dolores' lungs. Truly she expected the result to be different. Instead, her theory was exposed for what it always was…a dumb idea based on desperate hope. Now her foolishness would be wielded by the General to rid himself of Dolores, clearing the path for him to leverage the technology for an unspeakable purpose. The General had observed these tests for himself, and she was sure, had noted the potential.

"It's dead," Stephen said.

"Now you understand the problem," Dolores said.

"Physically there's nothing wrong with the animal," Megan said. "It should be alive."

"What was supposed to happen?" Eric asked.

"Not that," Dolores snapped, and flipped up the lever. The buzz of power ceased, and the room again vibrated as the shield closed. With a sigh, Megan returned to the lift to collect the body. Stephen folded his arms and stared at the screen. Eric joined him, urgently whispering questions in his ear.

Tara tapped Dolores on the shoulder, then pointed at the security monitor. "What are they doing here?" A glance at the display confirmed Dolores' fear. Hudson was waving at the security camera while jabbing a finger at the elevator entrance. Two other agents waited behind. For the moment they were stuck outside, but Dolores knew that would change with a phone call.

"Tell me you had authorization to bring Stephen and Eric here," Tara said.

"It'll be fine," Dolores said.

"You never bothered to ask, did you?"

"You know the answer I would've gotten."

Tara's brows knitted together. "Dolores, you know the General is looking for any excuse—"

"Excuse to do what?" Eric interrupted.

"Never you mind," Dolores said. "Tara, you and Eric head back to the surface. Stephen and I will follow once Megan disposes of the animal. Don't worry, I can handle this." Tara tightened her lips. "Go," Dolores urged. Reluctantly, Tara herded the objecting Eric out of the room and into the corridor.

Stephen sidled up to Dolores. "I know what I have to do," he said, his voice faint.

A flutter passed through Dolores' mid-section. She knew exactly what he was talking about, had thought about it herself. But to allow it would be unthinkable. "Why does it need to be you?" she asked him.

Stephen's eyes drifted to the ceiling, as if listening to that inner voice of his. "I belong here, Dolores. I knew it the moment I stepped off that plane."

"That's no answer."

"I don't have a better one."

"I can't let you inside the chamber," she said.

Stephen stepped forward, forcing her to stumble backward into the corridor. "You can. It's why you brought me here. It's why you showed me the security code."

Dolores placed her palm against the door. "You saw what happened to the rabbit."

"I'm no rabbit." In one motion Stephen batted her palm away and slammed the door shut with the other hand, leaving him inside the control room and her in the corridor staring open-mouthed at reinforced steel.

Should she force her way inside and demand Stephen leave? Then she would never know the truth, to be forever ignorant of what could possibly prove to be humanity's greatest gift, and her greatest triumph. There was a cry from behind and she heard quickening steps racing toward her. Reacting on impulse, Dolores tapped five random digits into the security keypad. Not once, but twice, then three times. The LED light above the panel turned red.

Eric shoved her aside and tried forcing the door. But it didn't budge. He slammed his body against the metal while yelling for his brother. Tara arrived and punched in the five-digit combination, only to hear a rude beep. She tried again and again to the same result. But it was too late, for the keypad had locked after the first three failed attempts.

Tara turned astonished eyes to Dolores. "What have you done?"

CHAPTER TWENTY

I leapt away as the door of the control room violently shuddered. On the opposite side there was a muffled cry and I perceived the anguished whorl of Eric's mind as he pleaded for me to come to my senses. But the door held, as Dolores had done what I expected…given me time. I fought the temptation to explain myself, to tell my brother of the vision, and my hope that it meant I could reunite with my daughter. But how to convince him of something I didn't understand myself? Placing a hand on the barrier, I silently thanked him, for his presence had given me the courage to do what I must.

She's waiting for you, the Stranger said.

I knew that. Somehow, in some way, I could sense Danika riding one of two interlacing chords that echoed inside my head. But within the second chord there was a separate and altogether disturbing presence, one that had raised the hairs on the back of my neck when I arrived.

Moving to the table I eyed the controls Dolores used to activate the machine. In the center of the console, amongst the buttons, lights, and single keypad, was a red lever. I tugged on it, but it wouldn't budge. I didn't expect that to be a problem because I had noted the code Dolores had used to unlock the elevator. She made sure I knew the security codes were the same and made it easy for me to remember by using my home address. But before I was able to type those numbers into the keypad, I heard a voice.

"What is it you think you're doing?"

Surprised, I turned around. Dolores' colleague stood before the lift, coddling the dead rabbit in her arms. I had forgotten all about her. "It's

Megan, isn't it?"

"Megan McCullough, and there's no way I'm letting you in there, Mister Fisher."

"What makes you think I'd consider that?" I asked, pondering this new obstacle. Sure, I might force my way past her, but then Megan would let the others inside…which meant she somehow needed to be immobilized. Scanning the enclosure, I noted bundles of cable and rolls of tape lying under the tables. Tools enough to secure a small human, I supposed. I sized up Megan, considering how difficult the task would prove.

"No chance, mister. Forget about it."

I had to agree. Although just short of five feet, the woman was stout and her composure grim. Plus, I was weak from inactivity and had no experience with this type of thing. There might be another way, but the mere thought filled me with a sense of foreboding, not for myself, but for her. "I don't want to hurt you," I said.

Megan snorted. "Dolores had a wild theory that your presence would change the outcome. But it didn't, the animal died, like they always do. Her experiment failed, Mister Fisher, and your committing suicide won't change that. Why be such a fool?"

"Maybe I know something you don't," I said, hoping that was true.

"Doubtful. What I know for sure is that you're confused."

"Point taken," I said. "But I still need to get into that chamber."

"What would your wife think about that? I hear she's pregnant. Congratulations. That means you not only kill yourself, you deny that child a father. A terrible fate, Mister Fisher, and one I don't think your wife would appreciate. Her name's Fran isn't it?"

Megan's words pierced me like a sword, because I knew them to be true. Fran would never understand my actions. Then again, she didn't know the reason. I clenched my hands into fists. "Step aside, Megan."

Megan's feet sank into the floor. "Really? So, you could execute a death wish? No sirree Bob, I won't let you do it." Not taking her eyes off me, she bent sideways and tenderly placed the dead rabbit on the floor. "Move away from that console, Mister Fisher."

I stared at Megan. She stared back.

You know what you need to do.

"I can't."

You have no choice.

"I don't know how."

"Are you listening to that voice in your head?" Megan asked. I didn't answer. "Ever consider that voice might be lying? Especially if what it's saying will get you killed."

Fill your mind with the music.

From months of practice in the confines of a solitary cell, I'd learned to somewhat control the sound throbbing in my head. Though I couldn't stop it playing I could alter the volume. This I did, ratcheting it up until a white haze glazed at the edges of my vision.

That's enough. Now touch her.

Stepping toward Megan, I extended a hand. In one smooth motion she twisted my wrist, the sharp pain sending me to my knees. "Don't test me, Mister Fisher."

Redirect the pain into her.

"What?"

Do it.

I concentrated, imagining a band of white light creeping through my arm into Megan. Then I saw it, as fingers that wound themselves around the violet gyre that flowed inside Megan's mind. Her eyes widened. Forcefully twisting my wrist, I heard rather than felt a snap, causing the light to burn phosphorescent. Megan's breath faltered, she staggered backward, then crumpled to the floor. I hurriedly placed two fingers over her carotid artery. There was a pulse, thank god.

"What did you do to her?"

You're out of time.

As if on cue, the pounding on the door resumed, or maybe it never stopped. Jumping to my feet, I strode to the console and tapped my address onto the keypad. An LED light above the panel turned green. I pulled the lever.

Blue lights flashed as the countdown began, "Sixty seconds, fifty-nine, fifty-eight…"

I stepped over Megan's body and entered the lift. There was a single button which I pressed. Obediently, the lift ascended through a dilated opening in the ceiling. And the moment it closed an all-consuming darkness enveloped me. The cabin slowed to a stop and dim lights blinked on to illuminate a circular platform that seemed to float within empty space. A pace away was the cage where Megan had placed the rabbit, the door still open. I exited the lift and walked to the center of the platform. The countdown continued, "Ten, nine, eight…"

This is where we belong.

Was it? Despite looking forward to this moment a sense of anxiety paralyzed me, as if I had swum too far from shore with fearful creatures lurking below. What was I thinking coming here? Why did I listen to the Stranger? Shattering the silence came the rumble of gears. I looked up. Fist-sized medallions embedded into the dome began to glow like golden eyes judging me from above. Did they see an animal to be sacrificed, or something else? At the very least, one way or another, I would be reunited with my daughter. I raised my hands over my head, resolved to welcome whatever came.

The gears ground to a halt.

Swirling wisps of silver poured from the interior of each eye. They moved slowly, lazily, and tangled amongst one another in a churning mass that grew to fill the topmost chamber. Did the rabbit see this? I certainly didn't from inside the control room. As the mass thickened I could only watch helplessly as the cloud of silver slowly grew to engulf me. The wisps stung as they attached themselves to my flesh, feeling like an assault from a school of jellyfish. I whipped my hands back and forth, trying to detach the threads which bit at my skin. But they stuck fast and twisted their way inside. Within moments I could no longer discern my body from the cloud. Then, from two points of darkness sprang two sets of spiraling arms. Morphing into streams of red, blue, and green, they spun in tandem before me. The smaller one bounced in place.

It's her.

My heart raced, and my body tingled, for this was the maelstrom of my vision. Falling to my knees, I searched for a way to express my regret for never having believed her, and for causing the accident which killed her. But I only came up with those two inadequate words that I'd used time and again… "I'm sorry."

She didn't answer, only swirled in an increasingly agitated manner. The second set of arms swelled to monstrous proportions. It then morphed into a ghostly and grotesque shape, with an elongated head, appendages too long for arms, and a thick torso ending in a whip-like tail.

I stepped backward, stumbling over the cage. "It's you."

There is no me, there is only you, the Stranger said.

"You caused me to lose control of the car, didn't you? You wanted my daughter dead, so you could take her."

That's not true.

"You planted the vision as bait to lure me into your lair. Having invaded my mind, you now want to claim my body."

You don't understand. Can't you see—

"You're a liar!"

With my back against the bar at the platform's edge, there was nowhere to run and nowhere to hide. But I had no intention of doing either. Intending to fight the Stranger with every fiber of my being, I plunged into the center of the ghostly shape.

CHAPTER TWENTY-ONE
A lifetime ago on a distant planet

The countdown ended, the shield parted, and the Beacon harmonized frequencies between two overlapping universes. The membrane of space-time peeled away, revealing the eighth dimension. Music, the soundtrack of the conscious realm roared inside my head. Looking up, I saw wisps gathering at the top of the inner chamber, signaling that a tunnel to another world was about to come into being.

My child glided to my side at the edge of the platform. With shell-shaped eyes they scanned the dome overhead. "What are those strings?" they asked, the colors along the bulbous stalks of their spine flashing anxiety.

"A manifestation of the conscious dimension spilling into ours," I answered, the hues along my own back flashing reassurance.

"How long will it be before our future-selves appear?"

"Patience," I flashed. "It takes a little time for the dimension to unfold. Bear in mind, our future-selves will materialize only if we build a Beacon on the new world. I don't want you to be disappointed if we choose not to build it."

"I think we will," they flashed. "But how can we be in two places at once?"

My child was nervous, asking questions for which they already knew the answer. Understandable, as they would be the youngest to ever bind worlds. I glanced up at the cloud churning above us, gauging the time it would take to descend. We had a few moments.

"Remember, there is no time or space within the conscious dimension, only cause and effect. You might think that one is dependent on the other, but that's not true. Time, as we know it, only exists in this dimension. But time in the conscious plane is an altogether different matter, measured solely through cause and effect. Think of it this way, all the decisions we make in this universe have already occurred inside the conscious plane. They will just unfold with no clock time between them. That means we could soon come face to face with ourselves. That's the function of the Beacon, to—"

"Combine the past, present, and future," they finished for me, reciting the lesson.

"That's right," I flashed, pleased. "In effect, the particles making up our physical forms will be split between two points in time. Our job is to pull them back together. With your strength and mine we can punch a tunnel into the conscious plane, creating a path between worlds."

"It's the only way to fly," they flashed.

"What?"

"They travel through the atmosphere."

"These beings have wings?"

"No, they walk on the surface with two limbs."

"Oh," I flashed, wondering what that would be like. "You're very special, you know, having found this place."

They enthusiastically swirled their isocercal, creating a surge that forced me to grip the edge of the platform. "That was easy."

"Only for you," I flashed. After a single lifetime, my child not only managed to navigate the conscious plane but had discovered sentience on the planet we now tried to bind. I'd encountered precious few beings with this gift, including my own mentor. Not all used that talent wisely and none were as young as my child, which fueled a secret hope they would be able to take on the burden I'd borne for uncounted lifetimes. A true scout, not only able to bind worlds, but to find them.

"I'm proud of you," I flashed.

Their bulbs burned brightly. "You're going to like it when we get there. Plants are different shapes and colors, there are lots of animals, and it's very bright. You have to be careful not to look at the star too long, because it will hurt your eyes. And there's water, everywhere. It even falls from the sky. There are some places that are dry and sandy. Those are boring. But almost every other place is green. I can't wait to show you."

"That sounds lovely. But you need to understand that binding a world is never a certainty. Our first priority is safety. Not only for us and those that follow, but to protect the inhabitants at the destination - what did you call it, Earth? From what you tell me they're newly emerged from the wild. That means it's possible, even likely, that I'll judge their civilization not ripe for binding. We don't want the denizens of this world using our technology for, well, other purposes. If that's the case our future-selves won't appear inside the Beacon."

"I think they're nice."

"We shall see," I flashed, and looked up. The eighth dimension had fully manifested. In moments we would be drawn into its embrace. Desiring to reinforce the most important lesson, I asked, "Child, what happens if our future-selves don't appear inside this chamber?"

"We shut down the Beacon, before we..." An orange glow rippled down their spine.

"Before we are pulled into the crack between universes and are forever lost," I flashed. "But don't worry, that won't happen. I just want you to be cognizant of the danger because there may come a time when you'll be the one who's doing the teaching."

"Not until I'm old, like you," they flashed, flicking their tail. My child looked up, noting that the conscious plane was nearly upon us. "Will it hurt? I don't want to get hurt."

"You'll only feel a little sting, like from a jellyfish. It's uncomfortable but won't hurt. That's the conscious dimension trying to pull us through the crack between two universes. Just do what I taught you and everything will be fine. Better than fine, because we may well save the inhabitants of this new world. All you need to do is be brave."

"I'm very brave," they flashed.

"I know you are." With a bite sharper than usual, strings attached themselves to my form. "It just started, can you feel it?"

They waved three sinuous fingers before their eyes. "Feels more like a buzzing than a sting. It doesn't hurt, at least not as much as I thought it would."

The strings burrowed their way inside my body, pulling me into the embrace of the conscious realm. Then, coalescing before us came the coil of a single mind – not the two I expected. Slowly, it took on the form of a physical being, a small bipedal creature with two upper and lower limbs.

"That's what they look like," they flashed. "A tiny predator species. But who and what is it?"

I moved toward the apparition, confused. Only myself and my child should have appeared. In all my experience, I'd never encountered a foreign being inside the Beacon. More unusual was how this mind moved, in two distinct patterns, one side flowing with a corrosive anger while the other flickered in and out of existence, as if it held a tenuous grip on the conscious dimension.

"I thought you said only our future-selves would appear," they flashed. "Is something wrong?"

Despite the risk of lingering longer than we should, I couldn't resist studying this being more closely. That's when I recognized it for what it was. "It's me, split into two."

"What? How is that possible? How did that happen?"

"A very good question."

Their mind flared. "The strings hurt, like they're stabbing me. I think we should leave."

I felt it as well, like daggers burning into my flesh. Our life force was being squeezed. "You're right," I flashed, but before I could signal for the Beacon to be shut down, the being's arms reached into me. Music turned discordant, becoming strung together noises clamoring inside my head.

You'll pay for what you've done, a voice said.

Though I knew the voice came from my future-self, I was certain it was dangerous. "Get out," I flashed to my child, using brilliant hues reserved for mortal danger.

There's no getting out, the voice said. *This is for the people you killed, the torture you inflicted, and most of all, this is for my daughter.*

"There is no me, there is no you, there is only us," I pleaded.

Tricks won't save you now.

Spasms wracked my physical form as the warped version of myself tore into me. But I couldn't fight back, as any hurt I inflicted would only rebound. The tendrils animating my flesh began to peel off, each a past life whose memories were lost forever. Pain became something worse as the wisps blackened and floated away. How many lives had I lived? I didn't know but I was about to find out. More lives turned to ash, their remains surrounding me like a malevolent cloud. I sagged to the floor of the chamber.

My child wrapped long arms and isocercal around my torso, trying to reinforce what was left of my dissipating strength. Fearing my child would be destroyed if she stayed, I tried throwing them off, but I hadn't the energy, which caused me more anguish than the burning sensation I felt throughout my body.

"You belong with me," my child flashed.

My future-self reeled back, its mind in disarray. And for the briefest instant, less time than it takes starlight to reflect off a mirror, we connected.

CHAPTER TWENTY-TWO
Present day, Earth

I grappled with the disembodied form of the Stranger. Lightning flashed, discordant music howled, and the world spun. "You'll pay for what you've done," I said.

Get out!

"There's no getting out, not for you."

The anguish of a lifetime I poured into the Stranger, discharging my hatred and vengeance directly into the ghostly image that surrounded me. "This is for the people you killed, the torture you inflicted, and most of all, this is for my daughter." With satisfaction I watched as the outlines of the thing began to disintegrate into a black cloud.

There is no me, there is no you, there is only us.

"Tricks won't save you now," I said. But with every blow I landed on the Stranger, it returned the blow with double the ferocity, draining my energy to nothing. I couldn't keep this up, and knew the time fast approached when I would at last be reunited with my daughter. If not in life, then in death.

With the thought of my child, Danika appeared fully formed in the upper left corner of my vision. Wearing a red flower dress, she stomped her foot and shook her head. At the same moment, the second maelstrom lingering beyond the platform approached and merged into the Stranger.

You belong with me.

That voice didn't originate from the Stranger, but from my child. Shocked at hearing the words of my vision, hatred and anger dried up. And my body, having been animated solely by adrenalin, sagged to the floor. In the resulting quietude, a silver curtain covered me like a shroud. In my mind's eye, the small hand of my daughter reached down and peeled the curtain aside.

An avalanche of images, cacophony of sound, and deluge of sensation flooded into me, all of which were blurry and incomprehensible. The sheer amount of input was so overwhelming that it hurt, like staring directly into the sun. To stop the assault, I curled into a ball and clamped shut my eyes, but it kept coming and coming until I lost track of where I was, what was happening, and most confusing, *when* this was happening. Still, the torrent of sensation poured into me like a pot boiling over. I felt helpless, lost, and it seemed a life-age passed before I felt myself being dragged over the floor like a rotting sack of meat.

An eyelid was forced open. Then the face of my brother entered the shrinking circle of my failing eyesight. Having retained some sense of direction, or more like a sense of the present, I locked onto his image as a drowning man would hold onto a life ring. Confused and overwhelmed, three things from the debris in my head crystallized to the forefront of my mind. One – the Stranger was me and always had been. I was a fool not to have realized it. Two – the vision of my daughter was no vision, but a memory. And three – I had cracked apart a door that only death should open.

My brother placed two fingers on my neck, searching for a pulse I suspect didn't exist. His mind swam viridescent with anxiety. Eric wanted to save me, as he did when he pulled me from the table as a child. At least this was the last time he would have to come to my rescue, which gave me some small amount of comfort.

This life had been troubled, and I had regrets, but I'd do it all over again given the chance. If only I had believed my child and confided in my wife, perhaps things would have been different. Certainly, they would have been less painful. But at least the compassionate eyes of my brother accompanied me as the lights dimmed, and I slipped from this world.

PART III - THE CHILD

CHAPTER TWENTY-THREE

Four years later

Dolores found it easier not to think of the pixelated yellow figures flowing across the screen as people, but as an evil force intent on launching an attack against innocents. For the most part, that belief was supported by facts.

The enemy nation had manifested its usual bombastic threats by mobilizing their army along their neighbor's border, then lobbing a hydrogen bomb into international waters as a warning for other countries to keep their distance. The Director of National Intelligence, Obadiah Wallner, projected a sixty percent chance they would invade and gave eight-to-one odds the hostile nation would strike U.S. territory if we got involved. The President decided to act. Not only was an ally threatened, but more crucially, the enemy possessed intercontinental missiles capable of hitting the U.S. mainland. A perfect chance to field test "The Weapon," General Beckman had advised the President. Dolores felt sick to her stomach, both then and now. Not because she feared the weapon wouldn't work, but because she knew it would. After all, she had designed it.

"Satellite confirmed operational. Ten seconds until the shield opens. Opening complete. Locking onto the first target…"

The voice was that of Admiral Robbins, Chief of Staff for the U.S. Space Force. Other than his words being piped through a secure channel, all was totally silent within the White House Situation Room. Janise Martinez, inaugurated as President three weeks ago, gazed at the screen with dagger-like intensity, her body hunkered into the plush leather chair. In contrast, General Beckman, now Secretary of Defense, was splayed over his seat and tapping his chin with a clenched fist. The chair of the Joint Chiefs and Secretary of State stood behind him, their eyes fixated on the display, as was the gaze of every other member of the National Security Council.

Dolores tried telling herself this action would save lives, as the President had claimed, but the thought provided no comfort.

Trying to detect any emotion coming from Obadiah's dark and ageless face, she stole a glance at the seat beside her. Nothing, though she suspected below his indifferent demeanor raged a mind which evaluated every detail.

"Target acquired," the Admiral said. "The sweep begins in three seconds, two, one. Injector firing. Time to completion, twenty-four seconds, twenty-three, twenty-two…"

Odd that the Admiral's voice never changed inflection, conveyed concern, excitement, or any other sense that something dramatic was happening. A true soldier, she supposed. Unlike herself, who cupped a hand over her mouth so as not to scream.

Figures jerked violently about the screen, then went still. The satellite's thermal imaging camera zoomed out to take in a wider view of the target area, appearing to Dolores like a still-life of yellow humanoid forms painted onto a dark blue canvas. If intelligence estimates were reliable, thirty thousand people now lay dead outside the enemy capital city. Soldiers, yes, but also innocents who'd made the mistake of living near the military headquarters of their "Most Beloved," the dictator of the enemy nation. The President nodded with what seemed relief, and Dolores noted with distaste that Beckman pumped his fist, as if a goal had been scored in some stupid sport.

"Sweep complete," the Admiral intoned. "Locking onto second target. Acquired. Beginning in three, two, one. Firing. Time to completion, eighty seconds, seventy-five, seventy-four…"

Dolores didn't dare look at the display, only stared at her Mr. Pibb soda, watching the condensation drip down the can onto the polished cherry wood table. Under her breath, she asked Obadiah, "How many?"

Obadiah replied mechanically, "One hundred and sixty-thousand."

Two thousand dead for every second of the countdown, she calculated. And that was only a demonstration of what would befall every enemy soldier if they didn't bend the knee…which didn't include the birds, insects, mammals, and reptiles caught up in the forty-kilometer sweep of the enemy front-line. The "Death Ray," as the General named his precious weapon, took out all sentient life, with no evidence of their demise. As the countdown continued, and bodies piled high in her imagination, the General's fevered breathing turned into a grotesque whistling from his nostrils.

"Sweep of the second target area complete," the Admiral said. "Injector deactivating. Initial battle assessments coming in. Hold on…" Seconds ticked off the clock as every person in the room held their breath. "No movement within target areas, no radio communication. Mission complete."

The General slapped the table. "Congratulations, Madame President. You cut the head off the snake."

Janise Martinez unwound herself from the chair and ran her fingers through her hair. "To you as well, General." She then swept her gaze over the assembled council. "Though I realize the tragic significance of this weapon, I'm confident we used it to stop a war before it got started. In the process we've saved millions of lives. You should all be proud of the work you've done here today."

Heads around the room nodded somberly, except for Dolores. Did the President wonder, as she did, if "Most Beloved" had only been testing the mettle of a new President? Whatever the answer, tens of thousands had just paid the price.

The President approached her. For the briefest moment, Dolores recognized a desperate loneliness reflected in that gaze, the same Dolores saw staring back at her from the mirror each morning. "The world has especially you to thank, Dolores. Your hard work made this possible, and I daresay, this new capability marks the beginning of the end for nuclear weaponry."

Dolores acknowledged the ghastly compliment with an empty nod, and not for the first time, questioned her decision leading to this moment.

◆◆◆

Four years ago, Dolores had in every practical sense killed Stephen Fisher. "Insubordinate" was how President McAllister had characterized her decision to let Stephen inside the G-WAD. Dolores dutifully handed over her resignation. But, McAllister surprised her by not accepting. Rather, he extended an offer. In exchange for being allowed to continue experimenting with the G-WAD, Dolores would lend her expertise to a new weapons program to be led by General Beckman. The General even encouraged Dolores to accept, remarking he could use a woman with *balls*.

What choice did she have? By refusing the President's offer, her career would be over. And that was all she had left. No longer did she have friends to fall back on, at least ones that mattered. After the incident with Stephen, Tara accused her of manslaughter and refused to speak with her again. Last Dolores heard, Tara had resigned from JPL, married, and moved out of town. Megan, after a two-week convalescence in the hospital, deigned to speak to Dolores only to ask why she had left her inside the control room with Stephen. Dolores had no answer to satisfy thirty years of friendship. In the end, Dolores accepted McAllister's proposal. Not only was she terrified of returning to an empty home and hollow life, failure had doubled her resolve to discern the true purpose of the alien device, which she had failed to do, unlike her success designing the perfect weapon.

The weapon was space-based, making it hard to destroy, and a hundred percent lethal. With a half-kilometer kill-zone that swept the earth's surface like an apocalyptic broom, the device could kill millions in a single sweep. Due to the draconium, which reflected nothing along the electromagnetic spectrum, it was near-invisible. Best of all, according to General Beckman, the "Death Ray" could strike anywhere at a moment's notice. Worse, Dolores had found to her horror and his delight that the weapon punched through the Earth's core to sterilize both sides of the planet.

◆ ◆ ◆

President Martinez replied to Dolores' empty nod by firmly grasping her hand, as if she knew her mind. Maybe she did. For if Dolores would be remembered as the creator of the most horrific weapon ever built, the President would go down in history as having used it as an executioner. Both their tombstones might as well read, "The ones who turned the gift of first contact into a butcher's tool." With a forlorn smile, the President released Dolores' hand and moved on to exchange words of appreciation to others inside the Situation Room.

Dolores slumped into the chair, a bleak sense of a wasted life nearly overwhelming her. The younger version of herself would have despised the choices she had made as much as she regretted making them. But it was far too late for her to change course; the corpses on the opposite side of the planet assured that. All she wanted to do now was return to her townhome and lie in a tub to wash away the guilt, blood, and responsibility for this day.

CHAPTER TWENTY-FOUR

Two suns beat upon my brow, one smoldered a dull red on the horizon while the other burned white and hot directly overhead. Peering over the edge of a sheer cliff, I watched white water violently churn amongst the jagged spires of rock while foam from the last assault retreated into a green sea that stretched to the horizon. An enormous swell rose from the depths, crested as it approached the shore, then exploded over the rocks shooting a frenzy of luminescent spray into the atmosphere.

Feeling the ground tremble, I tried stepping back from the ledge, but my body refused to cooperate. Looking down, I was shocked to find a coiled flagellum connected to a muscled torso that glistened in the reflected light of the suns. Raising one of two long limbs, I moved three supple fingers before my eyes. Who was I? What was I?

"Hi there!"

I followed the sound to rest my gaze on a small simian-like creature. It was a child, I somehow knew, and a female at that. She wore a red flowered dress and the hair on her head was tied back with a ribbon that fluttered in the breeze. She tiptoed to the precipice, cautiously looked over the edge, then tapped her fingers together. "That's a really far ways down."

I wanted to ask who she was, but no words came out, only a flashing that came from behind. When I looked over my shoulder, I beheld stalks ending in bulbous heads that ran down my spine. They began to glow an aquamarine luminescence, perfectly reflecting the confusion I felt.

"I bet that's going to hurt," the child said.

Hurt? I returned my attention to the child, who was now on her hands and knees peeking over the ledge. A hand slipped on the coarse surface, sending pebbles skittering over the side. Concerned for her safety, I tried scooping her up only to grasp an armful of air.

"You've been away for a long time," the voice said.

I whipped around. But rather than finding a small simian I found that the child had morphed into a smaller version of myself, complete with flagellum and muscled torso. She stared up at me with bright shell shaped eyes.

"Where are we?" I asked.

The bulbs along her spine flashed, "Inside your head. At first you were lost, but then I found you!"

"Oh? What happened to me?"

"You stayed in the Beacon too long and hurt yourself. I think that's because you were confused. You didn't know me, you didn't know you, you didn't even know where we came from. That hurt my feelings." She flicked her tail. "But now you're getting better. I can tell. How are you feeling?"

"Fine," I said, and noted that I said that aloud. Looking down I found I had grown two legs. Out of nowhere, the word "human" came to mind. And for whatever reason, I used a hand to cover up what I suspected were genitals.

"That's good!" she flashed, "Because it's time to go back."

I ran my eyes over the area. We were on a spit of land surrounded on all sides by a seemingly endless ocean. Around us were crystalline stalks that branched toward a burnt orange sky. Glass-like shards dangled from the boughs, refracting light that danced on the ground. "Maybe I like it here. It's quiet. I like quiet."

Absentmindedly, the child batted at a cluster of shards, sending them rattling. "I know you do, but that's because your brain is still scrambled."

I felt mildly insulted. But given I had no idea where I was, who I was, or what body I was wearing, I had to agree. "You could be right about that."

The tip of her flagellum twisted, then before my eyes she transformed into the child I had first met, but this time wearing a dress patterned with strawberries. "I don't think we can wait any longer. You need to come with me."

Her plea sounded so utterly forlorn I couldn't help but agree. "All right. But I'm not exactly sure how we can get out of here."

"I know a way," she said, her voice small.

"Good, tell me."

She kicked at the ground, sending a shower of small rocks over the edge of the cliff. "You're not going to like it."

"Let me be the judge of that."

"Well," she said, and shyly glanced up at me. "It's hard to explain. I have to show you."

"Fine, show me then."

She stepped toward me. "Are you sure?"

"I guess."

"Okay, but I want you to remember that I'm sorry."

"Sorry, for what?"

"For this," she said. And with a force all out of proportion to her size she shoved me over the cliff.

The child leaned over the edge and waved as my body spun head over heels toward rocks thrust up from the sea floor like black knives. Unable to watch, I closed whatever passed for my eyes.

CHAPTER TWENTY-FIVE

Samantha Peebles, the President's Chief of Staff, burst into the room, beelined toward the President and handed her a folded sheet of paper. The President unfolded the note, went still a moment, then showed it to Beckman, who frowned. The room went silent. Walking to Dolores' side, the President handed her the note.

Dolores took her glasses from an inside pocket and read the handwritten message.

> *NASA is reporting that AMIGO has reacquired the extraterrestrial signal. The Chinese Space Agency is expected to confirm within the hour.*

She read it again, and again, then handed the note back to the President. The transmission had fallen silent five years ago, shortly after Stephen Fisher was injured inside the G-WAD. Could its reemergence be due to the weapon? Impossible, as the signal originated from over a thousand light years away. A coincidence? It had to be. But then again, there were far too many coincidences involving the transmission. That's when it dawned on her what this could mean.

"Ma'am, I need to make a call. If you will excuse me."

"Yes, I expect you do," the President said. "Let me know what you find out."

After exiting the Situation Room, Dolores pulled her cell phone from the cubby and glanced at the screen. There were a dozen missed calls, all within the span of a few minutes. She opened the browser and with a tap of her finger confirmed that news of the transmission had already made the headlines. Another call came through which she ignored. Taking a breath, Dolores dialed a phone number that she'd been told by the family to never use again. On the fourth ring, somebody picked up.

"Hold please—"

"This is the National Science Adviser for the President of the United States. I want you to put me through to the on-duty nurse on the second floor. Yes, that floor. I know it's restricted. Put me through please."

There was a moment of silence, then another voice. "Hello."

Dolores' stomach tightened. She identified herself, then said, "I'd like you to check on the patient in room two-o-six and report back to me what you see."

"Ma'am, I'm sure there's no change—"

"Now, please," she demanded. What else did this nurse have to do? She had one patient to look after and an entire floor to herself. The nurse quickly agreed. Dolores paced the corridor, the phone held tightly to her ear. What she imagined shouldn't be possible. After the incident, the doctors had detected no cognitive function. And the last report on his health, which she scrupulously checked every week, stated he remained in a persistent vegetative state, the polite term for brain-dead.

A flustered voice rang in Dolores' ear, "Ma'am, he's awake. I've got to go!" The line went dead.

Placing a steadying hand on the wall, Dolores lowered herself into an empty chair. She rested her forehead against a palm and stared at the carpet, wondering at the meaning. Stephen Fisher had come back to life.

CHAPTER TWENTY-SIX

All was black. But unlike the night sky where the occasional star gave meaning to darkness, this was pure emptiness. Not the absence of light, but its direct opposite, the place where light found a home…like this throbbing pinprick of white that grew into a bright round pill.

It didn't shimmer and wasn't beautiful like sunlight seen through a crystal decanter. This light was harsh, and the brighter it became the more uncomfortable I felt. Not exactly pain, more the sick discomfort of a viral illness, a burning in the throat, nausea in the gut, and an aching throughout the body. As the glare increased so did the roaring in my head.

I opened my eyes.

Daggers of light pierced my skull sending me into a flurry of blinking. Or more like scraping, as eyelids passed over corneas like sandpaper over wood. I slammed my eyes shut, creating a colorful light show on the back of my lids. When the whites faded to blue and eventually settled to black I again cracked open my eyes, but only to let the world in through a slit. As my pupils adjusted to the brightness, I was able to focus on the source of illumination…a light fixture directly overhead.

I lay inside a room staring at the ceiling. Turning my head, I looked through a window that perfectly framed the canopy of a magnolia tree set against an azure blue sky. The leaves glistened, and white flowers shone from the rays of a lone star settling on the horizon. A breeze slipped in through a crack in the window bringing with it the fragrance of freshly mowed grass and citrus-like blooms. As I took in the scents the roar in my ears receded.

Cautiously, I pushed a hand against the surface on which I lay. It was soft, like a mattress. Flicking my eyes from the window I saw a metal rail running the length of the...bed. And my body was covered with a sheet. Was I in a hospital? Had I been hurt? What time was it?

Through the tumbled detritus of memory came a sensation of falling, then of rocks sharp as knives. My heart raced. I lifted an arm. The limb looked skeletal, and a white ribbon circled my wrist. I studied what was typed onto it, "Fisher, J. Stephen." The name was familiar. A tube ran from the brachial artery to an IV set beside the bed. A monitor displayed my blood pressure and a mechanical beep kept pace with the beating of my heart. It was true, I had been injured.

"Hi there!"

I followed the voice to rest my eyes on a child sitting in a wooden chair. Fair hair bound into a ponytail bounced up and down while oversized and very white tennis shoes swung back and forth to the beat of a cheerful tune. Smeared across the front of her pink blouse was a handprint the color of chocolate, and the blouse was patterned with strawberries.

"You," I tried to say, but what came out sounded like the bleating of a sheep.

She popped out of the chair, sending the computer tablet on her lap tumbling to the ground. "I told Mommy you'd wake up today. She didn't believe me, and said, 'Honey, you say that every day. Eat your breakfast.' But I knew you would because I decided to come and get you!"

I blinked.

"Aren't you glad?"

So, it was she, I knew it. When I tried asking why she pushed me off the cliff my throat tightened and turned into a spasm of coughing. After swallowing a few times, the fit passed, leaving me exhausted. I laid my head back, to try catching my breath.

The child's face appeared inches over my own. Translucent tendrils writhed beneath soft skin and waves of blue and gold spun behind two irises blazing with a green light. There were also freckles on her nose. She waved a plastic bottle over her head. "I bet you're thirsty. Are you thirsty?"

The sight of water filled me with an intense craving. I licked my lips and managed to nod.

Retreating a pace, the child crushed the bottle against her body and twisted the cap until her cheeks flushed red. Liquid exploded from the container, drenching the front of her blouse. After wiping her hands on the bed sheets, she lifted the bottle to my lips. A lonely few drops fell into my mouth. It was heaven. She vigorously shook the container then peered into the bottle. "It's empty. Would you like some more?"

I did, badly, and nodded.

"Be right back!"

She skipped across the room, clambered onto the seat, and began ransacking through the contents of a large purse set atop an adjacent dresser. On the wall was a picture of this same girl holding hands with a dark haired woman. I studied it.

"Found one," the girl declared, and held a container above her head. The other hand darted into the bag and reemerged with what looked to be a candy bar. She then sprang from the chair, landing nimbly on the floor. Behind her, as if in slow motion, the purse sagged and fell to its side, spilling a waterfall of objects large and small onto the floor. At the sound, the child turned and scrunched up her nose, watching the spectacle unfold. A rivulet the color of a robin's egg grew from a pinpoint in her mind and spun a couple times before disappearing. She gave a helpless shrug.

She walked toward me while wrestling open the container, spilling half the contents in the process. When she reached my side, she raised the bottle to my waiting lips. Water rushed into my mouth like rain on a parched desert. I gulped once, twice, then choked as liquid spilled over my face and overflowed into my nose.

She tossed aside the container. "Do you feel better?"

I did, very much so, and tried to thank her by throwing up a garbled consonant.

"Good." She placed a hand over my forehead. "Do you have a headache?"

A headache? Golden eyes leapt to mind then slipped away just as fast. I glanced at the ceiling. No eyes there. But there was also no headache. Cracking my lips into a pained smile, I shook my head.

"Whew." She broke off a piece of chocolate and touched it to my lips. Though famished, I'd had enough trouble with the drinking and thought it unwise to try eating. So I shook my head. With a shrug the piece disappeared into her mouth. "Mommy says I give her a headache sometimes."

I bet. Wetting my lips, I tried asking her name, but it took three tries, broken up by coughing and interrupted by swallowing. When the words finally came out they sounded incomprehensible to my ears.

"My name's Melody. Do you like it?"

"Pretty," I managed to croak, this time somewhat coherently.

She executed a quick pirouette. "It is, isn't it?" Twisting to face the door, Melody placed both hands over her mouth and said through splayed fingers, "Mommy's going to be so surprised!"

Struck by the familiarity of the gesture, a tide moved within me, and I beheld an ocean.

The flood gates opened. Into my mind poured a host of disjointed images, a cacophony of voices, exotic tastes, strange scents, and emotions of every hue. They rose over my head to engulf me in a chaos of sensation. I couldn't make sense of any of it, though I was certain I had lived through it all. That's when I understood. Bobbing under the surface tension of existence, as impermanent and chaotic as the currents which roiled beneath the waves, were the uncounted lives which formed my very existence. I was intimate with death in all its forms, the inevitable destiny which slumbered under the illusion of reality. I was overwhelmed in the memories, each a dead voice vying for attention. I gripped the sides of the bed as a drowning man would a life ring.

Melody leaned over me. "Focus on the past and work your way up," she said. "At least that's what I think you told me. Or maybe you said to focus on the present and work your way back. I'm not sure, something like that. Anyway, I think you should try it."

I chose to embrace the present, focusing on the here and now. Looking past the freckled face hovering over me, I studied the maelstrom that moved within Melody. Arms spiraled from a pinprick in the center and churned with an intricate mosaic of changing hues and textures. I had seen the turn of this mind before. Not just inside the rascal who tossed me off the cliff but curled within the womb of a woman I loved. This led me to study the picture above the dresser.

A memory clicked into place: the name of the dark-haired woman was Fran, my wife. Lifting my wrist, I again read the ID tag. That was my name. Another memory clicked into place: of the events that had happened inside the chamber. They had built a Beacon on this planet, I suddenly realized, but why that filled me with dread I left for another time, for I needed to concentrate on the narrow avenue of the present. There was prison, injustice, and a lady who was very smart. There was a short-statured woman whose mind I had violated, and the face of the man I called my brother. It was then I recalled the birthday party, a funeral, and the daughter I had thought was lost. My eyes welled with moisture and I raised them to look upon my child.

Melody placed her forehead against my own. "Welcome back, Daddy."

I touched my hand to her cheek. "Same to you."

She smiled.

The door opened, and my wife stepped into the room carrying a tray between her hands. Her eyes went to the contents of the purse strewn over the floor. Puffing out her cheeks, she let out a long suffering sigh. With a shake of her head, she turned her attention to Melody, who expelled a high pitched squeal and pointed at me.

Fran dropped the tray, launching food and drink into the air. An errant spatter landed on my lips. I passed my tongue over it…chocolate pudding.

"Hi Franny," I said.

CHAPTER TWENTY-SEVEN

A bright light shone in my cornea, moved in a circle, then from side to side. "Arousal scale is a five," said the voice of a man leaning over me. I was in bed, having just awoken. Last thing I recalled was fighting to remain awake while eating dinner.

"Sorry to wake you, Mister Fisher," the man said. "My name's Anthony Patton, a physician. Would you mind telling me your name?"

I cleared my throat. "Stephen," I said, and tried sitting up, only managing to collapse back on the mattress. Melody, who was lying next to me playing a computer game, absently patted the top of my head. She had been attached to me like a limpet, refusing her mother's coaxing to climb out of bed. Fran, watching television, passed me a bottle of water, which I drank greedily.

"Your full name?" the doctor asked.

"Stephen Fisher," I said, then added the place I was born, my birthday, our home address, and for good measure, told him my favorite color was blue.

"Remarkable, a five out of five on the verbal scale," he said, speaking into a recording device.

"What did you say was your specialty?

"I'm a neurologist, here to assess your cognitive functions." He stepped to the end of the bed, lifted the sheet, and squeezed my big toe. "Can you feel that?"

"The neural pathway is intact," I said, wanting to fast forward to the point of the exam. I'd had enough of various "ologists" poking, prodding and testing me. Besides, I had a suspicion that most came only to gawk, as if I were an animal in a zoo. It wasn't every day somebody woke from a multiyear coma. Fran had suggested it was better to have too many doctors rather than too few. I found that argument debatable.

"Oh, that's right, you have some training." He increased the pressure on my toe. "A psychiatrist, I hear, specializing in severe psychopathological disorders."

"Once upon a time," I said, "and that hurts."

The doctor released my digit and dropped the sheet. "Would you mind raising your right arm?" Taking my wrist, he asked that I move each finger as he touched them. I did so, no problem. He then asked for me to make a fist, which I did easily. "Astonishing. Seems the physical therapy is helping."

What I needed more was to rehabilitate my mind, for the scattered memories inside my head bounced around like balls in a pachinko machine, so much so that I struggled to remain grounded in the here and now. The spirits of my former lives cried out from a churning sea from which there was no rock to lift me above the chaos, leaving me no place to survey the turmoil. In every other life I had time in which to acclimate the past and present. But here I had lost track of who I was, spawning the myriad of dead voices to manifest as the Stranger. Despite that, or because of that, I very much remained Stephen Fisher.

"I'm quite the wonder," I said.

"Also, extremely fortunate. I've been told you recall nothing of events leading to the incident. Is that true?"

What incident was he speaking of? Did he know what had happened to me? "A complete blank."

Though Melody continued playing her game, her mind quickened, because she knew without having to be told that I lied. But until I understood what the council had done with the G-WAD, I thought it wise to claim ignorance.

Doctor Patton nodded. "What's your last memory, if I may ask?"

I gripped Fran's hand. "The grill of a truck in a car window," I said, and the sorrow wasn't feigned. Melody placed her own hand over ours.

"Nothing after that?" he persisted.

"Not a thing."

"Hmm. That's not unusual, but take heart, memories can return as you heal."

"Not always," I said, and that's when I noted the metallic yellow sheen twisting through his mind – deception. I became wary.

"Let's hope they will. If I might, I'd like to try an auditory prompt to see if that shakes something loose." Not waiting for a reply, he pulled a mobile device out of his pocket and tapped on a key. "Does this sound familiar?"

From the speaker flowed the soundtrack of the conscious plane, the music used in the transmission. The man watched me carefully, but he watched in vain. I had no intention of admitting I recognized it.

"Sorry, nothing." I caught Fran's eye and yawned.

Fran flipped off the television. "I'm sorry, Doctor, but Stephen tires easily. I'm sure you understand. Can we do this another time?"

"Yes, yes, of course, my apologies Mrs. Fisher."

"I'll escort you out," Fran said, then looked to Melody. "I'm going to get us some breakfast. Will you take care of Daddy while I'm gone?"

"Yes, Mommy," Melody replied, still focused on her tablet.

"Good girl."

"Keep up the physical therapy," Patton said. "I'll check in on you tomorrow. Take care."

I lifted my hand. Fran took the doctor by the elbow and firmly escorted him out of the room. Taking a long draught of water, I rested my head on the pillow. Though I had just woken, I already felt tired.

"You never told me why a Beacon's not safe," Melody said.

Surprised, it took a moment to collect the relevant memories and formulate an answer. "Think of the travelers who would come here. How do you think they'd be treated?

"Very well," Melody said.

"Hmph, you haven't met the people I have. Sure, some might welcome them, but others would most assuredly not. And we don't want travelers being treated as invaders. That's why we won't be activating the Beacon. Not for a while, at any rate. Give people a few hundred years to work off the xenophobia, then we can reconsider."

"That's not what I meant," Melody said. "Why not safe for people, like Mommy?"

"You know why, because it almost happened to us. The Beacon forces the universe to crack open. Unless we close that crack by activating the Beacon, somebody could slip through, then there is real death."

"What if they use it?" she asked.

I had a bad feeling as to what she implied by that question, and a worse feeling about the person I sensed fast approaching. Did the council corrupt the gift of the Beacon? That would be unthinkable. Then again, I knew their history. "Why do you ask?"

"Someone's coming," Melody said.

"I know. Best that you stay quiet and let me do the talking."

Melody put a hand over her mouth and pulled the sheet over her head.

Into the room sauntered Hudson, the short-cropped hair and severe lines of her face forcibly reminding me of past events. And what spun through her mind was as dark as the pantsuit she wore. She walked to the dresser and took the picture from the wall. "Isn't this precious. Such a beautiful family, they must make you very happy."

I said nothing.

Hudson studied me. "Are you pretending?"

"Who are you, exactly?" I said, playing the part of the amnesiac.

"That's good, Fisher, really good, I approve of the strategy." With picture in hand she walked to the side of the bed, a little too close for comfort. "But don't think you can fool me. Though the charges against you were dropped, they can be reinstated at a moment's notice."

"Should I know what you're talking about?"

Hudson leaned down to look me full in the face. Like a fish swimming upstream, I perceived the uncertainty flowing within her mind. Was I or wasn't I faking it, she wondered. I shuddered to think what would happen when she decided. With an index finger Hudson tapped twice on my forehead. "That's right, best not to remember anything. But if you do, know that I'm waiting for an excuse to put you back where you belong."

Melody peeked from behind the covers. "Go away!"

"Such a precocious child," Hudson said, and ham-handedly tousled Melody's hair. "You also have quite the mouth, like your father."

"I think you should leave," I said, and pushed the call button for assistance. Not because the nurse could help, but it seemed the expected thing to do.

Hudson's lips peeled back into anything but a smile. "Though you claim to forget, I assure you others have not. Consider my visit a courtesy, Mister Fisher, and a warning to keep your mouth shut. You might want to heed it, if not for yourself, then for your family." She tossed the picture onto my chest, then searched my face an uncomfortably long while. Finally, she said, "Good bye," and strode from the room.

"Who was that?" Melody asked.

"That, my dear, is a perfect example of why we shouldn't activate the Beacon."

Without a word, Melody pulled the tablet from under the covers and laid it over the picture on my chest. I looked at the screen. Instead of a computer game there was a browser displaying a headline from the news: U.S. Denies Involvement. Below was an image of people lying face down on a frozen plain. I played the embedded video. The camera zoomed out to show bodies stretching as far as the lens could focus. Machines of war dotted the plain. In hushed tones the reporter speculated as to the cause of death. I dropped the tablet and looked to Melody.

"That's why I came and got you," she said, her face a mirror of anguish.

CHAPTER TWENTY-EIGHT

As morning gave birth to sunrise a faint hint of light snuck between the window curtains to paint a sliver of white against the far wall. Breathing deeply, Melody lay face down on a cot. Saliva dribbled from the corner of her mouth forming a circular stain on the sheet. Fran huddled in an armchair next to my bed, a blanket pulled up to her chin. Stray strands of gray within dark unruly hair echoed the years I had lost. I wondered what sacrifices she had made during that time to keep a job, raise a child, and somehow deal with a comatose husband. It couldn't have been easy.

Fran's eyelids cracked open. Arching her spine, she ran a hand along the back of her neck before noticing I was awake. "Morning," she said, bleary eyed.

"I've been wondering, why did you decide to keep me around?"

"What do you mean?"

"The doctor told me I was unresponsive with no discernable cognitive function. Though he didn't say this, I'm sure he would have advised you to pull the plug. Not that I would have blamed you. Had I been there I would have recommended you do the same thing."

Fran pulled aside her hair. "You're not wrong."

"Then I owe you my thanks."

"To be honest, I'm not the one you should be thanking." She pointed at Melody.

"She's a good girl."

"And more active than a spinning top."

"I've noticed," I chuckled. Though her eyes remained closed, Melody's mind stirred at our words. Did Fran observe that our daughter's every gesture, mannerism, and even the inflection of her voice were identical to that of Danika? If so, I'd like to think that brought her comfort.

"She's also happy, healthy, and unbelievably smart," Fran continued. "In no time she taught herself how to read and mastered writing with little effort. Kindergarten is going to be wasted on her."

"Can't say I'm surprised," I said. Recalling learned skills from a previous existence was just one of the advantages of being Melody. "Now, don't get me wrong, I'm glad to be here but confess to being curious why you didn't follow sound advice."

Fran bit at her lip.

"It's okay, you can tell me. After all, I'm not in a position to complain."

Fran lifted herself from the chair and parted the curtain to look out the window. "Every doctor who treated you told me it was cruel to let you linger. Looking back, I think the only reason I refused was my anger at the people who hurt you. Keeping you alive was my way of getting back at them." Wetting her lips, she twisted her wedding ring. "But as months passed and you wasted away before my eyes my will began to waver. I grew to believe I was being cruel, even selfish, for keeping you around. I also thought it dishonest to give our daughter hope when there was none. Two years passed before I finally caved in to the doctors' will." Her eyes moistened and her mind contracted in a painful whorl. "I brought Melody here for what I thought would be a final visit. Though I never told her what I intended she became hysterical and started banging her head against the floor. She wouldn't stop, no matter what I did or said. She kept screaming you'd come back. Stephen, you don't have me to thank for saving you, it was your daughter. I couldn't pull the plug because of her."

"She's an insightful child."

Fran turned from the window and stepped to the side of the bed. "Forgive me."

I took her hand and touched it to my lips. "There's nothing to forgive." Fran smiled, and a comfortable silence lingered. My wife confessed to considering an action she thought was a mistake. Now it was my turn to confess, but the mistake I made was all too real. But here was not the place because others eavesdropped on our conversation. I could perceive them now, faces at the end of a wispy string craning forward to hear our every word. I had a question of my own for those who listened: why did you turn a gift into a weapon?

"I wouldn't mind going outside," I said. "I'm sick of this room."

"You and I both," Fran said. "We'll go when Melody wakes up."

"She's listening to us now," I said.

At that instant, Melody's eyes popped open. Then, as if she'd been waiting for this very moment, she sprang out of the cot, beelined to the closet, and began wrestling with the wheelchair stored inside. Fran helped her set it up. Once I was situated in the chair, Melody insisted on pushing me out the door. She headed for the elevator, aided by Fran who corrected course, so I didn't hit a wall, a piece of furniture, or a support pillar. Then, from the station in the center of the empty floor, the on-duty nurse hustled around the desk and positioned herself in front of us.

"Ma'am, the doctor hasn't authorized this. The patient is not supposed to leave the building."

"Since when do I need permission to take my husband anywhere?" Smoothly taking the wheelchair from Melody, Fran swerved around the woman and entered the elevator. As the cabin doors closed, I saw the nurse stride to the station and pick up the phone.

"I don't like that new one," Fran said, referring to the nurse. Melody echoed that assessment. "Stephen, I spoke with Eric and we think it's time to get you out of here. We can bring the therapists and doctors to us. What do you think?"

"The sooner the better," I agreed.

Fran rolled me out of the building into the private courtyard. After turning the chair so I'd be facing a fountain, she took a seat on the cement bench set under the magnolia tree. The sun was a whisper on the horizon and we had the place to ourselves. I drank in the fresh air and scent of the blooms. Melody wandered off to stomp through a flower garden lining the wall.

"There's something I've been meaning to tell you—" I began.

"You remember everything."

"You knew?"

"You're a terrible liar, Stephen. Besides, I'm perfectly aware that certain people are concerned about what you may know. I assume that's the reason you kept things to yourself?"

"Yes," I said, surprised at how transparent I'd been. I hoped others weren't as insightful as my wife.

"Remember, I was questioned just as you were. Difference is, they believed me. You, on the other hand, they took to some damn machine. Why did you get into it? What did you hope to accomplish?"

I couldn't help but look at Melody, now picking flowers from the garden. "That turned out to be a mistake."

Fran bowed her head. "Yeah, I think so, a pretty big one."

"Did Eric tell you about the machine?"

"He told me everything. We haven't discussed it in a while...too dangerous, he claimed."

"Probably true," I agreed. "That nurse you don't like is looking at us even now, from a balcony on the second floor."

Her eyes flickered to the balcony. "How did you know that?"

"The same way anybody knows when they're being watched. I've just learned to pay attention."

"Why is that council so concerned about you, Stephen? The transmission is old news, or it was, until it returned. Do they think you have answers to questions they can't figure out for themselves? I have to admit, I've wondered if you might."

"Um," I said, having no idea how to explain myself. Despite having imagined this conversation a hundred different times in a hundred different ways, I found myself tongue-tied.

"Come on, Stephen. Think about what's already happened. There's nothing you can say that will surprise me."

"Let's see how you feel about that afterward."

"You know something about the machine, is that it?"

"Everything there is to know."

"Really, how could you?"

"I want you to hear me out, no matter how strange what I'm about to say will sound. Can you do that?"

Fran's mouth formed a line. "Are you kidding me? If four years has taught me anything, it's patience. Yes, I can do that."

"Okay, well, to start with I come from the place where the transmission originates—"

"You what?"

"See, what'd I tell you?"

"Go on," Fran said.

Feeling it best to lay everything on the table, I set loose a flood of words, starting at the beginning, or at least the beginning of my time here. I shared with her the incident I suffered as a child, how I was split into two, and grew up believing I teetered on the edge of sanity. I told her about the Stranger, of my vision, and how I expected to find Danika inside the G-WAD. Fran shook her head at that. I told her what happened inside the chamber, that I fought with myself until I realized the Stranger was the voice of my past, from lives I had lived before. What I didn't share was that I had been partially right, that my child was in the chamber with me, but at another time and in another place. Now wasn't the time for that revelation. I then explained the purpose of the two Beacons, and how they allowed a being to travel between the stars while retaining continuity with the past. Catching my breath, I paused to see how my words landed.

Fran broke into a patient smile, the one reserved for times she thought I'd side-stepped reality. "You think you're an alien, is that what you're telling me?"

"I get it, you think I'm nuts. I did too, for a long while."

"It's okay, we'll get through this, just as we always have."

Words were an imperfect means to communicate what can only be felt. I stretched out my hand. "This might feel a little weird."

"What are you talking about?"

"I want you to see the world as I do. Take my hand."

Fran hesitated, then placed her palm over mine. Emerald eddies disrupted the currents of her mind as I penetrated deep into her innermost psyche. I felt her distress that I was losing my mind and dread for what that portended for our future. There was compassion for me and fear for our daughter, whose father had returned only to sink into insanity.

And below the surface of her awareness marched an army of past lives, forgotten experiences that revealed themselves only as predispositions. All this I felt and more, as the emotional being that lived inside of Fran I experienced for myself. But this connection worked both ways, and I could feel the fingers of Fran's mind wrap around my own.

Her mouth parted, and her cheeks went pale. Fran now

experienced the world as I did: seeing trees that glowed with life and past lives that moved as tendrils throughout my physical being. Most of all, she felt that my mind spun very differently from hers. Releasing my hand, Fran clumsily rose from the bench and backed away until she was up against the trunk of the tree. "How, how is this possible? Who are you?"

"I'm the same person as before, Franny, your husband and a father to our child. The only difference is that I've experienced life in a different form and in different environments, all of which I recall and none of which originated on this world. You're much the same, though you don't realize it. You've been here before, but only here, and with no recollection of the past."

Fran gaped, first at me then at the trees and plants that before had pulsed with life. She now perceived only their shells. "What was that? Where did it go?"

"With my help you were able to peek into the conscious plane, for which this universe clings like a membrane. Eventually, you too can learn how to do this, but only after the blinders are off."

"I don't understand."

"It's a lot to take in, I know," I said, but there was more to tell. "You asked why that council was so concerned about me. It started when they took a key that enabled them to build a Beacon. Had I known, I never would have allowed that to happen, especially because they did what I most feared - made a weapon from technology they didn't understand. The thing is more horrific than they know, as it does more than just kill, it destroys what animates life…the soul, as you might say. That weapon deals out a true death, and anybody touched by it will never again be reborn. That council is concerned because they're afraid I'll disclose the key, allowing other nations to make this weapon for themselves."

The forced serenity of Fran's features warred with the crystalline chaos that spun within her mind. With a calming breath, she returned to the bench, and sighed. "Okay, so, you're not from here. That explains a lot, actually."

"This is my home now," I said.

"What's this key you're talking about?"

"The song Danika played for us on the keyboard. I had it recorded on my mobile phone."

"For four years I've wondered how she knew about the music. Were you the one who taught her that?"

"I did."

"How did that council get ahold of the recording of Danika?"

"The same woman who accosted me yesterday took my phone when they were searching our house."

"Why didn't you tell me what was going on back then?"

"Because I didn't know," I explained, and it was my turn to take a steadying breath. "Fran, it was me who taught Danika that song, but her name wasn't Danika, and it was a lifetime ago at a place far from here."

Sounding at once overwhelmed and fatigued, Fran asked, "What are you saying?"

Melody, who had been hovering behind the trunk of the magnolia tree, approached and took a seat on the bench next to her mother. She laid an ill-gotten bouquet of ragged poppies onto Fran's lap.

"It takes two to bind worlds," Melody said. "So, I came with him. Good thing too, because I had to wake Daddy up so we can fix his mistake."

Fran gripped the cross hanging around her neck. "What is she talking about, Stephen?"

"Danika never left us, Fran. She's sitting next to you."

CHAPTER TWENTY-NINE

From the second story window inside the rehabilitation center I pulled aside the window curtains to behold swarms of people cavorting near the entrance. The crowd was five times larger than yesterday, which was itself three times larger than the day before and that was when the headline from a major news organization broke the news that I'd woken from the coma. Not that my condition was a secret, but Fran and I had hoped to keep it under wraps until I returned home. Attention had snowballed since that first report, with articles in the news media speculating how I might be connected to the transmission. A couple came close to the truth.

Melody squirmed onto my lap. "You're famous."

"Apparently so," I said.

Most of the people wandering the parking lot were in costume, dressed as superheroes, villains, movie characters, and alien types. Sidewalk entrepreneurs peddled snacks and a few hustled headbands with antennas and pointy ears. A half-dozen news vans were parked on the street. The atmosphere seemed carnival-like, as if this were some comic book convention, except for the humorless zealots in blue t-shirts upon which the front was emblazoned with the words "Sword of the Lord." They walked in a slow circle waving handmade signs proclaiming, "God Created Man In His Own Image," "Christ Resurrected Here," and "Judgement Day." I took special note of the unkempt man with a beard whose searching gaze wandered up the side of the building. His sign read, "Stephen Fisher, Antichrist."

"Does this always happen?" Melody asked.

"Hardly," I said. Though I strove to be perceived as a messenger, civilizations on other isolated worlds insisted on treating me as something more, whether it were an envoy, or despite my strong objection and extreme discomfort, a figure of adoration. Regardless, all places celebrated their ascension. But my arrival here had spawned only confusion and fear. In part, that was due to my screw-up, but it was also a reflection of a still maturing civilization, the very reason a Beacon should not yet be built. In truth, I was as much a judge as messenger.

"What are you going to do?" she asked.

"The light of sentience often flickers," I replied. "This one may go out."

"But it's not their fault. You have to fix the mistake. It's why I went and got you."

"Better stand back, honey. I'd prefer that nobody see you."

Melody slipped from my lap just as Fran joined me at the window. She placed a hand on my shoulder. "People gathered here once before right after you were injured. Looking for who knows what, a miracle, maybe? Though, it was nothing approaching the size of this crowd."

"I don't like it," Melody said.

"Don't you worry about a thing," Fran said. "We'll slip quietly out the back, just like we planned."

I pointed to a figure getting out of a car that had pulled into the parking lot. "There's Eric now."

With his head down and using a suitcase as a shield, my brother snaked through the knot of people. His new wife (at least new to me, they'd been married two years) kept pace behind him. A scantily clad woman wearing a leopard-skin bikini with antenna on her head threw a cloud of confetti over Eric. If I weren't so concerned for his safety, I would have laughed. They disappeared under the awning at the front of the building.

Fran knelt beside Melody, now sitting on the worn rug arranging plastic animals inside a toy barn. "Uncle Eric and Auntie Tara are going to be here in a moment. They're going to help us with the bags and take you to the car. Daddy and I will meet up with you in the back. No fussing, understand?"

"There's somebody mean outside," Melody said.

"That's why Eric and Tara are here, to make sure we stay safe."

"Smart," she said, placing a chicken and a cow in the loft of the

181

barn.

With a broken smile Fran tousled Melody's hair, then bounced her eyes off of me. After our talk in the courtyard I'd been unsure how Fran would react to what I had revealed about our daughter. But my concern proved unfounded. Other than the occasional quizzical glance, especially when she said things beyond her years, Fran treated Melody the same as always.

Eric barged through the door, dropping the suitcase to the floor. With a string of invective, he shook the confetti from his hair. Melody's eyes sparkled at the forbidden words. Fran shook her head. Tara, having entered right behind, snapped, "Eric!" and angled her head at Melody. Melody sprang to her feet and ran to Tara, who picked her up and swung her around. Their easy familiarity reminded me of what I'd missed these past years.

"Ready to go home, pretty girl?" Tara asked.

Rather than answer, Melody grabbed Tara's hand and pulled her toward the toy barn where she proceeded to give her aunt a guided tour. She first identified the species of each plastic animal, provided highlights as to their behavior, then explained what name she had given each of the creatures and why.

After greeting Fran, Eric walked across the room and stood before me with his hands on his hips. "I think you should consider staying a little longer, at least until the chaos dies down. And maybe after you've gained twenty pounds."

"Nice to see you too," I said. Eric had visited before, and always took the role of nursemaid. "But I'm sick of this place, and besides, I'm stronger than I look."

"Mm-hmm," he muttered, which was the same response he'd given when I'd claimed ignorance of what happened inside the G-WAD. Tara, as had become her habit, slyly studied me out of the corner of her eye while Melody educated her on the finer points of animal husbandry.

Blowing a stray strand of hair out of her eyes, Fran declared, "We're leaving," the tightness in her voice betraying the tension that moved like rust-stained rivulets through her head. She tossed my personal effects into the suitcase and after stifling Melody's objections, swept in the barn and plastic animals as well.

Eric peered through the curtains with a frown. "If you insist. Nobody was at the loading dock when we arrived, so we should be okay." Taking the suitcase Fran had packed under one arm, he lifted the remaining bag with the other. Tara picked Melody from the floor. "You're coming with me, little one." While clinging to Tara's neck, Melody waved goodbye as the three left the room.

Rolling the wheelchair to the window I waited for them to exit the building. When they appeared from under the awning, the crowd parted and seemed to pay them no mind as they made their way across the lot. It was only after I saw Melody safely strapped into the booster seat and the car was underway that I expelled a breath.

"Are you ready?" Fran asked.

I looked around the room, imagining Fran grading papers and Melody playing with her toys. For years they had done that, with only my unconscious body keeping them company. Love for them both swelled within me. "Let's get out of here."

Fran kissed my cheek. Then, like another bag needing to be carried to the car, she rolled the wheelchair toward the elevator. I noted that the nurse wasn't at her station. The moment the cabin doors closed Fran pushed the button for an emergency stop. "What mistake was Melody talking about?"

"That I gave away the key to unlock instructions that the council used to build a Beacon. It operates by ripping open the fabric of space-time, which provides the killing power to that monstrosity of a weapon."

"How can we stop it"

"Fran, you need to understand I never would have allowed a Beacon to be built here. You know what the council has done, and you know what my father did to me. The same might happen to others who come here."

"Your father made a mistake, Stephen. He didn't understand you. And not everybody is like the people on that council. You know that. What I want to know is whether you can stop the killing."

I was of two minds about the solution and knew she wouldn't like the answer. "The rip can be closed, permanently, no matter how many of the weapons are built. But to do that I have to activate the Beacon."

"Fine, how do you do that?"

183

I sighed. "Melody and I have to enter the Beacon together."

"Wait, what? Melody. Why?"

"It takes the strength of two beings to bind worlds, Fran. But it doesn't matter because it's not going to happen. There's no chance what's left of that council will ever let me near the G-WAD."

The alarm on the elevator sounded, prompting Fran to release the stop. We began to descend. "You have to tell people who you are and why you're here."

"For what purpose?"

"To change minds on that council, or maybe, get somebody else to build one of those Beacons."

"You saw what happened before, when I tried telling people about the transmission. The minute I open my mouth you and Melody are going to be in danger, as will my brother and his wife. Whatever hope you had for a normal life will end."

"You told me what that thing does," Fran said. "We need to stop it."

"Nobody will believe me."

"You think too little of us. Tell people the truth, give us a chance." The elevator lurched to a stop and the doors opened. Fran placed a hand over the bumper then poked her head out to look up and down the hall. "Greg has an acquaintance, somebody we fed information to in hopes of getting you released from prison."

"Greg? Seriously? Who's he talking to?"

"A guy named Max, some two-bit hustler of conspiracy theories, the type of thing Greg loves. I don't like the guy, but he might prove useful in that he can give you an audience. And Max owes us because the information we gave him made him rich."

Fran pushed me into the lobby and turned right. We headed toward a door labeled "Employees Only." Few people were about, mostly staff, and those were gathered around the television watching live footage of the circus out front. The profile of the man I once resembled was pinned to a corner of the screen.

"I don't know, Fran. But if I do choose to talk, you and Melody need to be far—"

"We stay together," she said, cutting me off. "We're just going to have to rely on that sixth sense of yours to keep us out of trouble."

"Then be prepared," I said, feeling a growing disquiet.

"Is there a problem? What should I do?"

"Hurry."

Fran sped up and pushed through the employee-only door into a kitchen. The three workers inside barely spared us a glance, perhaps believing Fran was a nurse. Certainly, nobody recognized me, as should be expected given I was sixty pounds lighter than before. "Pull your feet up," Fran said. Using the wheelchair as a ram Fran burst through heavy-set double-doors to emerge onto the loading dock. Bright sunlight stung my eyes. I shaded them with a hand.

At the end of a ramp running alongside the building Eric waited. Upon seeing us he gestured toward the open rear seat of the car with an urgency that matched my alarm. Tara sat up front while Melody waved at us from the booster seat in back. Fran rolled the wheelchair down the ramp just as Melody's hand stilled.

A man turned the corner with a video camera slung over his shoulder. Beside him walked a well-dressed woman. The moment she laid eyes upon me, the woman pushed past Eric and ran up the ramp with a microphone outstretched. "Sir, sir, might I have a word?" Fran would have run her down had the woman not flattened herself against the wall. But it was too late, for the source of my anxiety had already rounded the corner.

It was the bearded stranger wearing the "Sword of the Lord" t-shirt. Within a mass of stringy blonde hair, two orbs focused on me like a laser. The purple stain seeping through his mind screamed malice. He jogged toward us. I pointed and yelled, "Eric!"

Eric instantly stepped into the man's path. Without slowing down Fran spilled me through the open car door into the back seat. Tara grasped my wrist and pulled while Fran pushed from behind. Melody took a handful of hair and ripped it toward her. Despite the help, I managed to push myself into a sitting position. Fran jumped inside beside me. Tara screamed. I looked out the window.

Eric was grappling with the bearded man only a few feet from the car. There was a flash of metal in the man's hand and a blow that made Eric wince. Out of nowhere a video camera smashed into the tangled mass of hair, sending the stranger to the ground. Quick as a rabbit, Tara assisted Eric into the front passenger seat then slid to the driver side and fumbled with the starter.

The newswoman yelled through the closed window, "Are you Stephen Fisher?"

"Go, go, go," Fran yelled.

With a squeal of tires Tara flew from the loading dock and bounced onto the street. A horn blasted as a truck swerved around us. The last thing I saw was the wheelchair on its side, the cameraman lying face down on the cement, and the newswoman kneeling beside him. The "Sword of the Lord" had regained his feet, a blind hatred coursing through his mind.

Tara sped through a traffic light and turned onto the main thoroughfare, her knuckles white from gripping the steering wheel. Fran breathed heavily while frantically looking over her shoulder. Eric leaned to the side with a hand over his ribs. Melody jammed two fingers into her mouth and sucked on them forcefully.

"Where should we go?" Tara asked.

"The police," Eric said at once.

"No," Fran and I chorused.

"Pull over and find someplace quiet," I suggested.

At the next block Tara pulled into a parking garage and found a vacant space. Peeling Eric's hand from his side, she examined the wound. Though Eric assured her he was fine, I discerned painful whorls of green and blue that suggested otherwise. Tara grabbed a first aid kit from the glove box and tended him. Fran surprised me by dabbing a napkin on my forehead which turned crimson due to a ragged cut that I'd somehow acquired. I asked Melody if she were okay. Melody nodded, never taking her fingers from her mouth.

Eric turned his head toward the back. "That nut job needs to be put away. Why are we discussing this?"

"Because he may not be working alone," Fran replied, echoing my thoughts.

"Even more reason to go to the police," Eric said, and winced as Tara pressed gauze onto his ribs.

"Not deep, but you'll need stitches," Tara said.

"Eric," I said, "an agent visited me the other day, checking up on what I remembered. Hudson was her name and I'm pretty sure she was sent by whatever remains of that council. They're afraid I'll talk."

I looked to Fran. "Which is exactly what I intend to do."

"Good," Fran nodded. "She threatened Stephen."

"Not a surprise," Tara said.

"Which is why we can't assume that guy acted alone," I said. "And Hudson didn't just threaten me, she threatened my family. You and Eric need to be cautious."

"Wait, wait," Eric said. "You remember what happened to you?"

"Everything and more."

He exchanged a quick glance with Tara. "We figured as much."

"Isn't Hudson the same agent who followed us to the G-WAD?" Tara asked.

"The same," I replied. "Have you heard anything about a weapon?"

"Only rumors," she replied. "Even though I quit the project I still keep in touch with a few friends back at JPL. Nothing is certain, but the silence from NASA is notable. How did you know about that?"

"They built it," I explained, "and it's far deadlier than anybody realizes."

"Deadly enough as it was," Tara said, and looked me in the eye. "When you entered the chamber, there was a surge of gravitational energy that went off the charts. Can you explain that?"

Fran interrupted. "Talk about that later. Eric needs medical attention and my family needs to find a safe place to spend the night. A motel, maybe up the coast..."

Tara chewed on her lip. "I know just where to go."

◆ ◆ ◆

Tara pulled into the driveway of a suburban home nestled against the foothills of the Santa Ynez mountains. Pink roses lined a picket fence bordering a meticulously maintained yard. Under a wide-brimmed straw hat a short-statured woman trimmed a branch. When she looked up her face bloomed into a smile and she waved the pruning shears at Tara.

"Give me a second," Tara said, and slipped out of the car. Eric followed. After embracing the woman, Tara pointed out the blood stain on Eric's shirt. With a shocked gasp, the woman immediately hustled them into the house.

"Is this a safe place?" Fran asked me.

I shut my eyes and quieted my mind. "Yes."

Within a couple minutes the lady marched out of the house and flung open the car door. Taking off her hat, she appraised my shrunken form. "Is that really you, Mister Fisher?"

"Megan McCullough," I said. "And call me Stephen. This is my wife, Fran." After Fran and Megan introduced themselves, Fran climbed out of the car and stepped aside.

"Well, I'll be damned," Megan said. "It's good to have you back. Thought it was bullshit when I heard news you were awake."

"I'm proof that it wasn't. I know it's a little late, but I'm truly sorry for what I did to you inside the control room. That was a mistake."

She wagged the pruning shears at me. "The idiots at the hospital said I had a seizure. But I knew better, I knew it was you. Had a terrible headache for two weeks, thank you very much."

"I'd imagine you would. Sorry, again."

"Apology accepted. Mind if I ask you a question, Stephen, something that's been gnawing at me for quite some time?"

"Feel free," I said.

"I often ponder what happened back then and come to the same conclusion every time, nothing else makes any sense. You don't need to tell me, but if you can, I'd appreciate it." She lifted her chin. "Are you some sort of, I don't know, emissary, from wherever the transmission comes from?"

Fran looked at me with a raised brow, as if asking - *What in the world are you going to say?* Melody slurped noisily on her fingers, her eyes darting between me and Megan. Birds chirped outside the car.

"Close enough," I said.

Megan scratched her nose with the shears. "Then I think we are the ones who owe you the apology, Mister Fisher."

"The unfortunate outcome of the most unlikely events imaginable."

"Even so." Megan moved to the side to get a better look at my daughter. "And who do we have here?"

Melody mumbled between two fingers, "My name's Melody."

"I've heard all about you, dear," Megan said, and waved the shears at the house. "You and your family are welcome to stay as long as you like. I have a little dog who'd love to meet you. Her name is Twinkles."

The depths of anxiety rippling through Melody's mind dissipated at those words, for which I was grateful. Melody took her fingers out of her mouth and smiled.

"Thank you," Fran said. "Three days, at the most, would be great."

"Three days, three weeks, three months, whatever you need," Megan said. "Tara told me she's going to help you and your family, and that promise goes for the both of us."

CHAPTER THIRTY

Dolores sat across the cluttered desk of the physician who would reveal her fate, a fate already hinted at by the MRI technician who had scanned her brain. The falsely casual way he suggested she bring along a family member for the appointment with the neurologist implied the news wouldn't be good. But Dolores came alone, as she had no family left.

The crop-haired blond neurologist, Doctor Browning, spoke to her in an all too professional manner, "Dolores, I'm afraid the breast cancer has—"

"Metastasized," Dolores said.

With a solemn nod, the doctor confirmed her worst fears. "I'm afraid so."

She dropped her eyes, ashamed to have the depths of her desperation revealed. No longer could she pretend the pain in her head was due to lack of sleep, not enough caffeine, or an allergic reaction to the pollen in the air. The cancerous lump in her breast had spread to her brain. Years of bathing in low-level radiation had finally caught up with her. Not to worry, she had once told others, the square kilometer of draconium produced far less radioactivity than a single dental x-ray. Problem was, by her count, she had been subjected to at least three thousand scans. Even if the exposure wasn't the direct cause, it surely would have amplified an already strong predisposition for the disease. Her aunt had died of ovarian cancer, her mother of breast cancer, and the disease had attacked her cousin's brain. All before they turned sixty. Dolores was seventy-six…past due.

"How bad?" she asked.

"The MRI showed two distinct metastatic tumors in the parietal lobe of your brain, twenty-three and forty-five millimeters in diameter." Doctor Browning touched her thumb and index finger together, making a circle the size of a ping-pong ball. "Probably the cause of your headaches. CT scans also suggest that the cancer has spread to your left lung and number four and five ribs, possibly the breastbone as well. We won't know for certain until a biopsy is performed. I suggest we schedule that as soon as possible…"

Dolores watched the doctor's mouth move, heard her words, but could no longer string them together to make sense of what she said. Death was supposed to happen to other people, not to her. Sure, she'd been to funerals, had mourned family and colleagues while giving comfort to the survivors. Even knowing her genetic history, never once had she given serious thought to the end. But it had happened anyway, which she found shocking despite the inevitability. Was that cowardice or courage, she wondered? Didn't matter. Like every other challenge she had ever faced, she would confront this one head-on.

"It's terminal, isn't it?"

With the practiced ease and distant manner of one who's had this conversation too often, Doctor Browning said, "Never give up hope. The options at this point rule out surgery, which leaves chemotherapy, and possibly hormone therapy depending on the receptivity of the cancer. We might consider targeted radiation in the lung and—"

"How long do I have?"

"Dolores, we can slow the cancer. But first we need to run some diagnostic tests—"

"I can take it, don't worry about that. How long?"

Doctor Browning heaved a sigh. "Hard to say. Much will depend on the treatment. I first need to see the results—"

"Give me a range, please."

Tapping a pen against the surface of the desk, the doctor gave her the benefit of an open and honest stare. "Two months, on the outside, given chemo is effective against the cancer. But patients often surprise the experts. Hope is your strongest defense against this disease."

Hope, hope for what? So she could sacrifice more livestock on the altar of the G-WAD, or further sharpen the blade of an already deadly weapon, or watch a sunset while wishing somebody was there to keep her company? No, hope had given up on her a long time ago.

"Thank you for being honest," she said.

"Do you have family or friends who might help out? Somebody who can aid with, uh, making you comfortable, and arranging your affairs?"

Dolores dropped her chin to her chest, frozen into place by an impotent desire to change the past. Most of her colleagues were either dead or retired. And the two people she considered family refused to speak with her. A day didn't pass that she didn't regret locking the control room door, leaving Stephen Fisher alone with her dearest friend. She longed to contact Megan and tell her she was about to die in the vain hope that she'd forgive her for what she'd done. But time for that was long gone and she wouldn't stoop to burdening her friend with such a desperate plea. "I can take care of myself," she said.

Doctor Browning shifted in her seat then checked her watch. "I see. Well, I've taken the liberty of arranging an appointment with the head of oncology. Scheduled it the first thing in the morning. I expect he'll come prepared with a treatment plan and will likely recommend it begin immediately. What I suggest is you take this evening to digest the news. We can meet back in my office to discuss next steps, say at eight a.m. tomorrow? How does that sound, Dolores?"

Dolores rose to her feet. Having watched her mother struggle with chemotherapy she had no intention of doing the same. Her only desire was to escape this office and find someplace dark to hide. "Thank you very much, Doctor Browning. I appreciate what you've done for me."

◆ ◆ ◆

The sound of a horn alerted Dolores that she had run a red light. Swerving to avoid a collision, her car bounded over the curb sending pedestrians leaping to the side. Wrenching the wheel to the left she heard the clank of the vehicle's frame hit cement before she regained the street. More horns sounded, and people yelled. One driver raised his middle finger. She raised a hand in apology. Would these people be less angry if they knew she was about to die? Probably not, for their only concern was that her erratic behavior had almost injured somebody. That mistake was an apt metaphor for what she had done with her life, except she had killed tens of thousands.

An image came to mind then, the same which haunted her dreams. From one of many satellite images collected after the attack was an overhead outline of four figures sprawled face down on a city street. Three were children outfitted in white and blue uniforms. One was an adult wearing a long dress. Given the time of day, she imagined this to be a mother escorting her family to school.

Collateral damage, Beckman had commented at the time. Then, having seen her reaction, he made a clumsy attempt to console her by claiming the body count would have been far higher had they wielded nuclear weaponry. Though she said nothing at the time, she didn't believe that for a second. Truth was that the attack never would have happened without her weapon. It made killing easy, too easy. And if history were any guide, other nations would inevitably learn the secret and wield it for themselves. Then how many more bodies would be lying face down on the street?

Her mobile phone rang, which she ignored, and a chime sounded, meaning whoever called had just left a message. She focused on the road. After a few moments there was a ding of a text. More out of habit than desire she instructed the message be played back. A silicon voice informed her she had missed a meeting concerning plans to construct a network of satellite weapons, like a string of venomous pearls that could strangle the earth. This was General Beckman's vision for the future, to defend this country with the threat of killing millions in seconds rather than minutes. Sadly, it wasn't a matter of whether it could be built but only how long it would take. What had she been thinking to have agreed to be a part of this?

She pulled into the narrow driveway of the elegant house with the brick façade that she never called home. Once in the garage she remained inside the vehicle, unwilling to leave. Seconds ticked off the clock and turned to a minute before the lights flickered off, leaving her in complete darkness. This morning, before she had left the house, the future still stretched before her as an unbroken promise. And the possibility of unraveling the mystery of the G-WAD still beckoned, which could salvage meaning from her life's work. She didn't yet know that this morning would mark the beginning of the end. But no more. Time was up. And the moment she left the car the countdown would begin.

What would other people do if they knew they had weeks to live? Spend time with family and friends? For her the thought was only a painful pang of regret. Travel the world? She'd had more than enough of foreign shores, foreign beds, and foreign food. It made her feel even more isolated than she already was. Take refuge in the church? She'd rarely been inside of one. It seemed disingenuous to start now. Keep working? The thought made her shudder. What she most wanted was to run from this hollow life as far as it was possible to run. At least death would accomplish that much.

There was another ring, another chime, and another ding from her phone. Without bothering to look she silenced the thing with a flick of her thumb. Taking leaden steps, she forced herself from the car and walked through the garage into the dining room. Unsure how to proceed, she stopped dead in her tracks. Usually she would have opened her laptop to continue the day's work. But not this day. She considered getting a snack from the refrigerator but wasn't hungry. Nor was she thirsty. Unsure of what to do she felt the grip of panic.

Striding to the closet, she pulled out the vacuum and turned on the power. The soothing sound of purpose filled the air as she moved the vacuum back and forth over the same piece of carpet, all the while fighting the desperation that threatened to overwhelm her. After some minutes, which might well have been hours, an insistent pounding snapped her out of her daze. It came from the front door. She had the vague sense it had been going on for some time. Usually she pretended not to be home, but today distraction would be a welcome gift. After quieting the vacuum, she stepped into the foyer and cracked open the door.

On the porch stood what had once been her closest friend, vigorously rubbing her arms to stave off the fall chill. Dolores caught her breath, not daring to utter a word for fear the apparition would disappear.

"It's been a while," Megan said. "Too long, I think." She craned her neck to look beyond the foyer. "Mind if I come inside? There're a few things we need to discuss. Plus, it's freezing out here."

Dolores threw open the door and managed to exclaim, "Megan," before her throat constricted. Unaccustomed moisture spilled onto her cheeks and her chest began to heave.

CHAPTER THIRTY-ONE

Megan reached for the crystal decanter and poured a generous amount of merlot into their respective glasses, taking particular care to fill Dolores' to the very brim. Raising her drink in a toast, she said, "Fuck cancer."

Dolores broke into a genuine smile and clinked her glass to Megan's. "Alcohol may be the best chemo," she said, and drained half the contents. Megan refilled her glass.

"Can't believe Stephen was right," Megan said. "There really is a weapon. That's terrifying."

"Afraid so," Dolores said. "And the General plans on building more. Did he learn about the weapon from Tara, or guess from the news reports?"

"Tara claims only to have heard rumors, so I don't think it came from her. As for the news, who knows what Stephen saw?" Megan lifted her shoulders in a non-committal shrug. "I can only presume he deduced there was a weapon based on what he knows of the G-WAD. Quite frankly, when I saw those dead bodies on the television, I had wondered about the possibility myself."

"Either way," Dolores said, "it's a comfort knowing that Stephen's memory is intact. I had heard differently. It's a miracle he's here at all, and for that, I'm thankful."

"He's fully intact as far as I can tell, and not at all pleased with what he discovered when he woke up. Had a lot to say about the council and what it did, which is the reason I'm here. Now, don't get me wrong, the moment I decided to visit was the moment I regretted not reaching out to you earlier."

"Doesn't matter why you came," Dolores said. "I'm just happy you did." She reclined in the chair and savored a mouthful of wine. Strangely, despite the cancer, she felt better at this moment than she had in an exceptionally long while. "What did Stephen have to say?"

Megan placed the glass on the table and folded her hands. "First off, he claims the weapon is far more destructive than you know—"

"The thing sterilizes every square meter of earth it touches, including microorganisms. It's hard to imagine worse than that."

"Holy crap! I didn't know that. Anyway, Stephen said it's imperative that another machine be built. He knows there's no chance he can get near the G-WAD and needs to find another."

"Why?"

"To disable that weapon of yours."

"Disable a satellite?" Dolores shook her head, unsurprised to hear something crazy coming out of Stephen. That seemed to be his modus operandi. "How in the world does he plan on doing that?"

"I don't know, he said something about the G-WAD ripping a hole in the universe. Only he can repair it, and to do that he needs to get inside the Injector – again."

"A rip in the universe, are you kidding me?"

"I'm not kidding at all. And you shouldn't be so dismissive. It's not like you know what the thing does."

The image of Fisher lying in a fetal position on the floor of the chamber leapt to Dolores' mind. "Any reason that his doing the exact same thing as before will result in a different outcome?"

"I hear what you're saying," Megan said, then sighed. "If it were you telling me this I'd think you were full of piffle."

"But you obviously don't, or you wouldn't be here."

"He's different this time around, Dolores. Physically fragile, for sure, you'd hardly recognize him. A breath of wind might knock him over. Then there are his eyes. When he looks at me it's—"

"Like he's looking through you," Dolores said, remembering.

"That's it, exactly. And unlike the bundle of insecurity from before, he's…I guess, more confident. Hard for me to put a finger on it. It's almost like the coma knocked some sense into him."

"Or out of him. He needs to drop this obsession with the G-WAD. If not for his own sake, then for the sake of his family."

Megan swirled the wine in her glass, intently watching the wave as it rose and fell. "He claims to be an emissary of the civilization that sent the transmission. Said it right in front of his wife. And she didn't blink an eye."

"He has a history of mental illness. Maybe it's contagious."

Megan raised her eyes. "And what if he's not crazy."

Dolores flapped a hand. "Oh, come on Megan."

"I know how you feel, but what if you're wrong? What if he is who he says he is?"

"What does Tara think?"

"Tara believes him, lock, stock and barrel," Megan said. "When I pressured her to tell me the reason, she told me I'd have to make up my own damn mind."

"The Tara I knew would demand facts, evidence, proof that what he says is real."

"She hasn't changed, Dolores. And I'm sure Tara knows more than she's telling. Same for the brother, for sure the wife. They clam up when I'm around, like a coven of witches."

"Fine. For the moment let's take Fisher at his word. Did you ask him what it does?"

"The G-WAD?"

Dolores nodded.

"He told me the device was meant for real-time communication," Megan said. "Just as we thought. But I can't shake the feeling that Stephen only told me what I expected to hear."

"Do you believe it, that he's some type of emissary?"

"What I believe is that Stephen told me these things in the hope I'd reach out to you. Which I did. Go figure."

"Admit it, you believe him."

"What if I do? It explains everything...his odd behavior, how he held the key to the transmission, and the things he knew. You physic-types have a rule for it, Occam's razor, that the simplest explanation is the likeliest."

"Convenient, that's what I call it," Dolores said.

"Yet you yourself thought Stephen was more than he appeared. A component, you called him, an integral part of the blueprint."

"And my mistake nearly killed him and devastated his family," she said, her good humor spilling from her like grains of sand from a broken hourglass. "Which is why I find it hard to believe Stephen Fisher is anything other than a man, however delusional."

"Don't be so hard on yourself," Megan said, patting her hand. "You may have let him into the machine, but he entered the chamber all on his own. Do I need to remind you that Stephen didn't die, like every other creature we sacrificed? And the gravitational energy spiked. Somebody I know might call that empirical evidence."

"Circumstantial, at best," Dolores said. "Sure, the energy increased, but the end-result remained the same…any animal we put in there died. What does it matter, anyway, especially now?"

Megan thoughtfully sipped at her wine. "Did you know they have a daughter?"

"Melody," Dolores said, choosing not to volunteer that she received regular reports on the family's welfare. From a sense of guilt, perhaps.

"The kid's cute, and very much like the father. She not only looks like him, she kind of acts like him too. Watches and listens to everything he or anybody else says or does. Seems to understand even more. My dog follows Melody around everywhere, even started sleeping with her in the guest room, the little traitor. Twinkles cried when they left."

"Left? They're not staying with you?"

"They left two days ago. Sadly, I don't expect to see them again. Probably for the best, as I fully expect Connor or one of his goons to show up at my door demanding answers to impertinent questions. Just so you know, I plan on lying."

A pang went through Dolores, not because what she said was likely, but because Megan would eventually return home. "What does the daughter have to do with anything?"

"It just so happens that I believe you were right about those figures on the blueprint being components of the design. But what if that second figure wasn't his brother, as you had speculated, but rather, his daughter?"

"That's a stretch," Dolores said. "I should know."

"Whether it is or isn't, I believe Stephen plans on bringing Melody with him into the Beacon – that's what he calls it – assuming he can find another machine."

Dolores was horrified. "No, he wouldn't do that, would he?"

"I confronted Stephen with that very question. Melody was right beside him at the time, staring up at me in that weird way the father does. All I got in return was a stony silence. The wife later told me their daughter was none of my business, leading me to believe she knows exactly what Stephen intends. And Fran, whom I've gotten to know somewhat, would never in a million years allow her child to be put at risk - never. Which to me is more convincing than any empirical evidence. I believe him, Dolores, I really do."

Dolores placed the wine glass on the table then tried massaging away the throbbing in her temple. In a convoluted way, what Megan said made sense. But what of it? With every minute the cancer spread further into her brain and body. She was out of time. "Why tell me this?"

"I thought you'd be interested," Megan said, refilling both their glasses. "Also, like I said, it was an excuse to come visit."

"It wasn't, perhaps, to give me a chance at redemption?"

Megan took a languorous sip of the wine. "That's entirely up to you, my dear."

"Way too late for that, I'm afraid," Dolores said.

Megan pulled a mobile phone from her pocket. Glancing at the screen she smiled widely. "You might want to take a look at the news, Dolores."

Dolores took the phone and read the headline. "Oh my god."

"Stephen has a unique gift for throwing excrement into a fan."

There was an insistent knock at the door. Dolores leaned to the side and peered through the window. She recognized the two secret service agents on her porch. "I'm being summoned," she said. "Will you stay, Megan, at least until I can return to say a proper goodbye?"

"I'll stay with you until the end," Megan said, then reached over to embrace her.

Dolores fell into Megan's arms, feeling an enormous weight fall from her shoulders. She wouldn't die alone, after all, which was the greatest gift any friend could provide. And though she would never earn absolution for her sins, she might at least aim in that general direction. Perhaps, by throwing a wrench into General Beckman's plans. Or even better, a grenade.

CHAPTER THIRTY-TWO

With a military bearing quite at odds with the usual short-shorts, flip-flops, and ratty t-shirt, Greg marched Fran and me along a meandering path within the five-star resort. Hidden amongst the dense tropical landscaping we came upon the entrance to a freestanding bungalow. This was where I would deliver my message. Scanning the sun dappled courtyard, complete with fountain, plunge pool, and outdoor fireplace, Greg clumsily patted me on the shoulder. "Give 'em hell, Stephen. You too, Franny."

"Do you trust this guy?" I asked.

Greg unconsciously puffed out his chest. "Max wouldn't dare jeopardize his best source. I'm the leak that can't be plugged."

Fran added, "Everything you or Eric told me I passed on to Greg."

"Which I relayed to Max," Greg said, "and it made him famous as a result. His show grew from a few thousand listeners to millions. You can't ask for a bigger spotlight than that."

I intertwined my fingers with Fran's. "There's no going back after this."

"I'll be fine," Fran said. "It's you I worry about."

Fran thought I wasn't ready. I could hardly blame her. In preparation for the meeting she had peppered me with every question imaginable. I replied with an edited-down version of the truth, only revealing what I wished to disclose. Achieving that balance proved tricky, and my uneasiness came to life in a flurry of ums, hmms, wells, and uhhs. You'd think I'd know how to deal with questions concerning myself and the Beacon. But knowledge of the past was useful only insofar as those experiences helped me navigate the future. And I found nothing about this situation familiar or predictable.

"I'll stick to the script," I said. "Easy."

Fran wrinkled her nose. "I suggest the less said the better." Pushing the wheelchair across the courtyard she stopped before a pair of French doors and rapped politely on the wooden frame. After tapping her foot a few seconds, she knocked again, and again, to no response. Worried lines creased her forehead, matching the whorl of anxiety racing through her mind. "Maybe his flight got delayed."

"I'll check with the front desk," Greg said.

"Hold on," I said, for I discerned the sluggish meander of a being within the confines of the structure. "He's sound asleep."

Fran pounded on the frame, prompting Greg to warn her that we shouldn't be drawing attention to ourselves. He needn't have worried, for the path was deserted and the nearest bungalow empty. But there was still no response. Hand poised over the door, Fran asked, "Shall I knock again?"

"No need," I said, for a flashing aura of white had emerged at the edges of the once meandering mind. "He's up, and not happy about it."

Two bleary eyes set atop two dark pouches peered between the window curtains. The polished head was offset by a jet-black goatee and a thin handlebar mustache protruding crookedly from his upper lip. If I added a mop of dark hair, subtracted a decade, and greatly reduced the flesh on his jowls, the man would vaguely resemble the image I'd seen posted on his website. After a moment of seeming confusion, he focused on Fran's face, then his eyes slid to her breasts, where they lingered. A semblance of life percolated within his pupils. Fran scowled. Then the man noticed me.

I raised a hand in greeting.

A veined nose pressed against the glass and he squinted, maybe trying to do the reverse of what I'd just done with him, adding years and reducing pounds to try matching the last picture he'd seen of me. Thick lips formed into a smile. Turning his hand into a pistol he pointed at me with his index finger then disappeared behind the curtains.

French doors swung inward to reveal a bare-chested man wearing boxer shorts that hung from his extended belly like a tent. With outstretched arms, he exclaimed, "Good god, I never thought I'd get to see this day, Stephen Fisher!"

I wiped the fleck of spittle from my cheek. "Yes, hello."

He admired me for a long moment before turning his attention to Fran. Grabbing her hand, he gave it a sloppy kiss. "And you, my dear lady, must be Francine."

Fran pulled her hand away and rubbed it on her jeans. "The name is Fran. Let me guess, you're Max Mystery."

With an elaborate swirl of his hand he proclaimed, "Maxwell Bartholomew Cooper, the one and only. My mother calls me Maxwell, my fans call me a mystery, and my ex-wives call me a bastard." He guffawed. "You, my dear lady, may call me Max, as do all my close friends." He bowed, and with a start, noticed his lack of apparel.

"This is supposed to be a secret meeting, people," Greg said. "It might be a good idea to get inside."

Max did the exact opposite, strode through the doorway and embraced Greg in a bear hug while rocking back and forth on his heels. "Greggy, you're my champion. I owe you one, buddy. Thank you, from the bottom of my heart."

Greg disentangled himself from Max's arms. "Take care of these two, like you promised, then we can call it even."

"Of course," Max bellowed, then turned his beaming visage onto Fran. "Come inside, Francine, and bring Stephen along with you." With a graceful twirl, Max waddled back into the palatial retreat.

Her lips sealed into a line, Fran gave Greg an appraising stare.

"It'll be fine," Greg said. "He's just excited, and I'm certain he'll do what I asked."

"Which was what, exactly?"

"To help you and your family any way he can." With a peck on Fran's cheek and a bump of my fist, Greg declared he would patrol the perimeter. After wishing us luck, he headed down the jungle path. Shaking her head, Fran pushed the wheelchair into the bungalow.

Adorned with elaborately woven curtains, fine furniture, and an antique rocking horse, the place looked more like a model home than a temporary shelter. Two lounge chairs and an upholstered sofa surrounded a polished oak table on which an empty bottle of gin lay on top of audio equipment. There was also a large cow bell. The sound of running water and a voice raised in discordant song flowed from beyond the bathroom door. Fran shifted uncomfortably on her feet. After some minutes, Max burst into the room, his generous frame now housed within a black silk caftan embroidered with golden dragons.

"I beg your pardon for my delay," Max said. "Though, to be fair, I'm fresh off the red-eye from Melbourne and haven't had time to recover from jet lag." He ambled toward a cocktail bar built into the wall and began preparing drinks. "When Greggy called, I thought he was pulling my leg. Practical joker, you know. But as he's my best source I decided to take a chance." Max spun in place with three glasses in hand. "And here you are!"

One drink he offered to Fran, who replied with a disgusted shake of her head. The other he handed to me, which I accepted. What the hell, might help me relax. Clinking my tumbler with his, Max roared, "Hair of the dog!" and downed half his drink in one swallow. I took an experimental sip: gin and tonic with a hint of lime. Nice.

Max gestured for Fran to take a seat and for me to approach the table. Instead, Fran perched herself on the edge of the sofa, as if preparing to bolt. Max collapsed into the lounge chair across from me. Taking hold of the second tumbler, the one originally intended for Fran, Max swirled it round and round with eyes that never left mine. "I've been talking about you for so long, I feel that I already know you. May I call you Stephen?"

"Please do," I said.

"Excellent. How 'bout we get some nibbles before we start? I admit to being a bit peckish and heard they have quite the spread here, especially the blue cheese quiche" —he smacked his lips— "which I'm dying to try."

"I'd rather we get started," Fran said, impatience adding emphasis to her words.

Max snapped his fingers. "Tell you what, we'll do both. Besides, a little food will help grease the rails of conversation." Picking up the house phone from the table, Max called room service and proceeded to order what sounded like most of the items from the menu. I had to admit, I grew hungry listening to him. Once finished, he placed both hands over the swell of his belly and beamed.

Fran subtly cleared her throat.

"Taking in the moment is all," Max said, and his grin widened. "I've

imagined this day for so long I can't believe it's finally happening."
Leaning forward, Max snapped a microphone to my lapel then tried
doing the same with Fran.

She reeled back. "Absolutely not!"

"Dear Lady, your story is as of much interest to my listeners as
Stephen's." Max lowered his voice. "Defying every obstacle, meet the
woman who stood behind her man, while death knocked at the door."
Fran informed him that she wouldn't submit to a single question,
prompting a lengthy appeal from Max.

"Perhaps," I interjected, "my wife would consider your proposal if
you prove true to your word."

Fran didn't hesitate. "That's right. First, do what you said, let my
husband say what he wants then you release the audio in seventy-two
hours. Maybe then I'll consider talking."

Max solemnly dipped his chin. "Very reasonable, very reasonable
indeed." He placed a hand over his heart. "Since I'm a man of my
word, I'll consider that a promise, from the both of you." He placed
the microphone at the edge of the table, nearest Fran. "But if you have
a mind, feel free to interject...."

"I won't," Fran said, and crossed her arms. "Let's get this over
with."

"Your wish is my command," Max said, then turned his attention
to me. "All right, Stephen, don't censure yourself. Think of this as a
chance to set loose those secrets others have imposed upon you. A
declaration of independence, of sorts."

"I only want to make a statement," I said.

"And that you will, no worries. Now, this show is usually broadcast
live, and I'd like my audience to not know the difference. So, I want
you to talk naturally, as you would when conversing with a good friend.
Because that's how I'd like you to think of me. Can you do that?"

"I suppose."

"Excellent!" Max swigged the remains of his drink and
straightened his spine. "Are you ready?"

I shrugged.

Max powered up the console and mouthed a countdown from five.
Then he began, "Greetings Mysteryites, we've got a special treat in
store for you today, an interview with a man we never thought to hear

from again. None other than…well, let us allow our guest to introduce himself." With an ingratiating smile, Max gestured for me to speak.

I cleared my throat, lowered my head to my lapel, and said too loudly, "Stephen Fisher."

Max rewarded me with an upraised thumb. "You heard that right, Mysteryites. Sitting right in front of me at this very moment is the man who alerted the world to the alien transmission. And he paid for that with his freedom. He's in a wheelchair, folks, with arms and legs as skinny as can be, come back to life so he can talk with us." Max inhaled a lungful of air, his complexion having transformed into a constellation of pink splotches. "I'll dig out the truth from behind the rumors, find the man behind the mask, and ask the questions for which you've been clamoring to know the answers. Today, we have an exclusive interview with none other than Stephen Fisher, the true man of mystery." He picked the cow bell off the table and clanged it overhead.

I cringed.

"It's an honor to have you as our guest, Stephen. Thank you for joining us. I have to say, I can't believe you're here. Let's start this right off, shall we? We were all very distraught when we heard you fell into the coma. How are you feeling today?"

"Thankful," I said, "and getting stronger every day."

"Strong enough to escape an assassination attempt, I hear. Do you feel that your life is still in danger?"

"A misguided soul," I said, "who needs to be brought to justice."

Solemnly, Max nodded. "Yet you chose not to go to the police. Why was that?"

"To be frank, I'm not sure whom to trust. As you know, there are people in powerful positions who fear what I'll say. I expect our little talk today isn't going to help matters."

"Let's hope it doesn't," Max said, beaming. "Okay, Stephen, let's get into it. My listeners and I know most of what happened before you fell into the coma: your house being searched, the council, the note revealing the existence of the transmission – you wrote that, yes?"

"I did."

"Then you were thrown into prison for trying to reveal what should have been disclosed to everybody, not just the powerful few. That about right?"

"I suspect I would have been detained regardless, but yes, your information is correct."

"My sources are the best," Max said, and winked at Fran, "though I don't know it all. Details are sketchy concerning how you were injured. The government claims you suffered a fall inside a prison yard. But I think that's bullshit. I've heard"— he jerked a thumb toward where Greg patrolled the perimeter — "that you were taken to some machine. Stephen, my listeners want to know what really happened that day. From leaks and photographs we know something unusual was built inside the Nevada National Security Site. Is that the machine you were taken to? Why were you taken there? Was that where you got hurt? Most of all, why does everything about this transmission seem to revolve around you?"

"That's a lot of questions."

"Start anywhere you like."

I looked to Fran, who nodded encouragement. Beginning with Connor showing up at the door, I talked Max through the chronology of events. I told him of the council, identified the locations where I was taken, named the people involved (though kept my family out of it), and told him of my trip to Nevada. Max nodded along, for I shared what he had already been told, though this time he was getting confirmation direct from the source, along with the credibility that came with it. When I described what Dolores called the G-WAD, Max interrupted.

"It's true then, they took you to some machine. Where did it come from, Stephen?"

"It's called a Beacon, built using instructions deciphered from the transmission."

Max leaned forward and rubbed his hands together. "So many questions. The most pressing first, what's your government afraid you're going to tell me?"

"I was getting to that," I said, and took a thumb drive from my pocket. "It's not so much what I can tell you, it's what I can play for you. This is the key, Max, and with it the secrets of the transmission can be unlocked. It's the real reason I was put in a cell, it's why my family is in danger, and it's why I wanted to talk with you today." I handed it over to Max.

Max fondled the drive between his fingers. "The key to building a Beacon, you say. How did you happen to come across this?"

I replied not to Max, but to his audience, in hopes that another nation would build a Beacon, one that Melody and I could activate. "I'm a messenger from the civilization that sent the transmission. I know that's hard to believe, but you don't have to take my word for it. Decipher the message for yourself, then decide. You'll find that I'm part of the blueprint, a required component needed to activate the Beacon. In the meantime, I ask that sanctuary be granted to myself and my family, from any nation willing to provide it."

I smiled at Fran, who nodded. That was it, that was all I had come to say.

"Wait, what, you're part of a blueprint? What does that mean?"

"There's an audio file on the drive," I said. I had recorded Melody singing over the soundtrack of the transmission just last night. She waited in the motel room even now, with Eric and Tara minding her. "That's the message I've come to deliver."

"Hold on, if you're truly a messenger, how did you get here? On a spaceship?"

I pointed at his hand. "Play the key, Max."

Max plugged the drive into a port on the console, found the file, and tapped it. A melancholy rhythm took over the room. Soothing as a lullaby, the pitch waxed and waned into solemnity like a tide advancing and retreating from a rocky shore. No longer did the music trigger me as it had done before. With the return of memory had come a cure for my trauma.

Max sank into his seat and his lips parted. Even Fran, who'd heard this before, listened with her head down and hands clasped. I casually sipped at the gin and tonic until the song ended.

Max rubbed his eyes then shook his head. "That was a kid, singing. Is this a joke?"

"Play that to your audience and you'll soon find out."

Smiling at me in that incredulous manner I'd become so familiar with in this life, Max said, "You claim to be an envoy—"

"A messenger."

"Then tell me how you got here. And what is it that machine does, anyway?"

There were two things I would not discuss. One was the purpose of the Beacon, for it would only inflame passions that were already high and had nearly gotten me killed. Second was any mention of the weapon, as I didn't want to encourage others to build one for themselves.

"Thank you for your time," I said, and unclipped the microphone from my lapel.

"Whoa, whoa, whoa, where're you going?" Max asked.

"The interview is over," Fran said.

Max's face underwent a series of contortions ending with his brows furrowed into a caterpillar-wide crescent. "Now, wait a minute. I won't be playing any of this, not until you first answer my questions."

Fran got to her feet. "Fine, we'll talk to one of your competitors. What's her name, Secret Sarah, or Suzie Secret?"

"That woman's a fraud, a fake, a copycat. Whose voice was on that recording? Was that your child? Does she have something to do with—"

Fran unplugged the power from the audio. "We're done here." Marching to the exit she flung open the doors.

Max hefted himself from the chair. "Understand, my audience expects me to be skeptical. That's my schtick, you know? No offense meant. I promise not to mention your daughter. Sure, I've got questions, but mum's the word. What do you say?"

Fran replied by grabbing the wheelchair and pushing me into the courtyard. Labored breathing caught up from behind us. Max then shoved his rotund form between us and the path. "Wait, stay, please. Say whatever you like. I'll play nice."

"You've done us a great service, Max," I said. "All we ask is that you play the interview. Be prepared, I expect you're going to get far more attention than you want."

Max's eyes shone. "I doubt that. It's legit, then, what you said, about the key, and your being some sort of messenger?"

"Truly."

Fran pushed the wheelchair, ramming my knees against Max's surprisingly firm belly. "Move aside," she said.

Max lifted his palms in submission. "Peace, beautiful lady, for I come bearing gifts." From within the folds of his caftan robe, Max pulled out a manila envelope. "Airline tickets and cash to deliver you and your family to one of a half-dozen cities. One set flies out of San Francisco and the other out of Los Angeles. And don't you worry, I'll play the interview." He extended the envelope to Fran, who regarded it as if it were a soiled towel.

"I'm no fool," Max continued. "Greg may have provided me information, but I can pretty well guess where it came from." He raised a hand to forestall what surely would be the denial forming on Fran's lips. "I don't need to know," he said, and dropped his gaze to my frail form. "I gotta say, other than looking like a guy who climbed out of a hospital bed, you look pretty normal to me."

"We have more in common than you think," I said.

"Then you're in more trouble than I thought," Max guffawed, the pink splotches decorating his cheeks turning red. He dropped the envelope into my lap. "You've been in the center of strange happenings, Stephen. I look forward to seeing where your journey ends." He stepped aside. "Goodbye to you both."

Not glancing back, Fran pushed my wheelchair along the pathway. "You did well, Stephen."

I reached behind me and squeezed her hand. "Practice makes perfect."

"Stay ahead of the bastards!" Max yelled at us from behind.

CHAPTER THIRTY-THREE

Dolores cracked open the door, desiring to slip unobtrusively into the Situation Room. She expected to find it packed with panicked cabinet members wringing their hands over repercussions from the interview. Instead, she found the solitary figure of Obadiah silently tapping away at a computer.

He raised his head. "Doctor McCann."

She stepped inside. "Where is everybody?"

"The President wants to talk with us before bringing in the full cabinet, the General included. I presume you heard?"

"Oh yes," she said. "Hard not to."

The interview with Stephen was the top story in the news. She had listened to it a full three times before being dropped at the White House gate. A quick perusal of the web found that most media outlets had dismissed Stephen's claims, calling him delusional while citing the injury to his head as the probable reason. Declaring himself as some sort of messenger only reinforced that impression. But if the right person chose to take Stephen seriously, the secret would be out. And that seemed a certainty, especially given that every major nation in the world had dedicated teams devoted to making sense of the transmission.

"When did the interview come out?" she asked.

"Zero eight hundred," Obadiah replied.

Eight in the morning, two and a half hours ago. That could be enough time for somebody sharp to have already figured out how to decipher the transmission. Even now, they could be scratching their heads over the meaning. "I think we have a problem," Dolores said, and eased into the nearest seat.

Obadiah grunted, his eyes falling back to the screen.

Beckman barged into the room, an ugly grimace disfiguring his face. Dismissing her with a glance, he placed both hands on the table and leaned toward Obadiah. "Goddamn it all to hell! How did your people lose him? He's a cripple, for god's sake. All you needed to do was put a bell around his neck!"

Not looking up, Obadiah said, "I find it curious he was able to slip through our net. Almost as if he knows when and where he's being surveilled."

"Curious? Are you kidding me? You're supposed to be the Director of National Intelligence, not the head of the Keystone Cops. Criminal incompetence, that's what I call it. Specifically, yours, made worse by the fact you should have had that man silenced a long time ago."

Obadiah raised his eyes, his motion languid, as if purposefully taunting the General. "I seem to recall that your Special Security Forces lost track of Mister Fisher inside a two-story office building."

Beckman stabbed a thick finger into Obadiah's face. "Don't give me that shit! That bastard gave away this nation's greatest secret, all because you couldn't make a hard decision. The minute he woke up you should have put a bullet in his head. I would have done that years ago, not only to him, but his wife as well…"

Dolores numbly watched him rant. As his head slowly lolled to the right she noted that an artery in his neck pulsed wildly, as if his heart were about to explode. Once, she would have been horrified by the General's temper tantrum, but now she felt detached, as if she watched through another's eyes. Through it all, Obadiah remained still and silent.

"…I hold you personally responsible for putting every man, woman, and child in this nation at risk. You're weak, Obadiah, unfit for duty. As far as I'm concerned you should be immediately removed from office—"

"That judgment's not yours to make, General," the President interrupted, having slipped quietly into the room. She closed the door then took her usual place at the head of the table where she looked Beckman in the eye. "Sit."

Beckman took a trembling breath. "Yes, Ma'am." With a glare directed at Obadiah, he dropped into a seat.

"I take full responsibility for what happened," the President said, then her eyes swept them all. "And now I'm making it your problem. What remains of our old council needs to untangle this mess. The secret's out, and to make matters worse, every unfriendly nation on the planet has offered sanctuary to Fisher. Not that they believe a word he said, more to rub our noses in it. Australia included, I might add." She focused on Dolores. "How long?"

"Sorry?"

"Before somebody deciphers the transmission."

Dolores glanced at her watch. "No later than say, two o'clock."

"Not funny," Beckman said.

"That was no joke. Remember, it took us only days, and that was with four people. There are now thousands studying the transmission: data scientists, cryptologists, engineers, mathematicians, you name it. And at least ten times that number of amateurs. Believe me, it'll happen fast if it hasn't happened already."

Obadiah shifted in his seat, his eyes on the screen. "I've just received a report that the Chinese Science Ministry cracked it. The intelligence source claims the team is now puzzling over exactly what it is they decrypted."

Beckman slapped an open palm on the table. "That's just great. And at this very moment Fisher might be informing the Chinese that what they have is a computer program. Then he'll describe exactly how it works and tell them which buttons to push."

Dolores was about to remark that Stephen didn't know it was a program, but the words caught in her throat. He might, for Tara was with him, and she knew everything. Megan as well. Given the chance, Dolores felt sure the General would kill the entire family along with both her friends. That brought to mind the assassination attempt. Did General Beckman arrange for that? The idea wasn't preposterous.

"That's not helping, General," the President said, slowly enunciating each word. "I summoned you for advice, not recrimination. Focus on the problem. How do we fix this?"

"For a start, we could claim the key as our own," Obadiah said. "Declare that we spent billions decoding the transmission and that Fisher stole it out from under us. In some respects, that's true. After all, we did build the G-WAD. Invent a motive by which he betrayed us, maybe evening the score for his incarceration. We reclaim the moral high ground."

"And put a bounty on his head," Beckman said.

"I don't care about Fisher," the President said. "By all means, go after him, hang him by his thumbs if you want. As for taking credit for the key, fine, do it. It won't hurt, but I fail to see how it helps. The cat's already out of the bag. I need real suggestions."

"Accelerate construction of the G-Net," Beckman said. "Ring the planet with enough satellites to cover every square inch of ground. Then we threaten any nation with destruction that tries to build a weapon for themselves."

"Or do the opposite," Obadiah said. "Come clean with what we've built and declare the weapon an existential threat. We then work with other nations to put an outright ban on the technology."

"Is it possible you're really that naïve?" Beckman said, contempt dripping from every word. "They'll do it anyway."

"I'm forced to agree," the President said.

"Sanctions, then," Obadiah suggested, undeterred.

"Maybe we do it all," the President said, "accelerate development of the G-Net while doing everything in our power to dissuade other nations from building one themselves."

"We'll need allies," Beckman said, warming to the subject. "Put them under the protection of the G-Net in exchange for support in punishing nations that don't comply." Surprisingly, Obadiah agreed, prompting the General to elaborate at length.

Dolores' mind wandered. This she wouldn't miss…the constant back and forth in the vain pursuit of imagined security, however temporary. Always the General shaped the discussion into the form of a hammer pounding a nail. At least he was transparent about it. As for the President, a practical woman, she was open-minded about any suggestion as long as it would "Keep America Safe," her administration's campaign slogan. Obadiah though was a puzzle. Sure, he cared about security, but Dolores had the impression that wasn't his passion, only his job. Did he care about rank? Obadiah was no better or worse than any other ladder climber. Money? Who knew? What then, love? As far as Dolores knew he had no significant other. Could be that Obadiah just didn't want to talk about it. Having

Beckman around certainly didn't help.

And what was it she wanted? To be happy, she supposed, like anybody. But misguided ambition had resulted in a life of loneliness and a legacy of death. Now, with ambition at an end, happiness might have a chance to take root. Maybe she should spend her last remaining days on the coast, curling her toes into warm sand while listening to waves whisper secrets of hidden currents flowing beneath an infinite sky. That sounded nice, but she knew that wasn't for her. It never had been. What she really wanted was to turn back the clock, having learned from her mistakes to do this life over again…which was to want the impossible.

"That may be the only tool we have," the President said, sitting back. "What do you think, Dolores?"

"Pardon?"

"I *said*, what about sanctions as a method to deter weapons development."

"Are we boring you, Dolores?" General Beckman asked.

It was then that a germ of an idea fell into the soil of her mind, so obvious that she blamed the ball of cancer growing in her head for not having thought of it before. Though she couldn't turn back the clock, she might at least delay the inevitable. And to do that, she needed a diversion.

"Better to focus on the iridium," Dolores said.

"The what?" the General asked.

"A key material for manufacturing the draconium," Obadiah answered.

"While all the metals may be critical," Dolores explained, "this one's particularly difficult to find."

Obadiah nodded. "We create a choke point. Stockpile the metal while cornering the market. Make it impossible for anybody to procure."

"Exactly," Dolores agreed.

"I like it," the President said.

Beckman suggested sabotaging foreign mining facilities, followed by the theft or destruction of stockpiled material that could fall into the hands of an enemy nation. Obadiah, after some frantic tapping on the keyboard, cautiously allowed the General's suggestion might be feasible. The discussion then turned back to constructing the G-Net, for which the General presented a surprisingly well-thought-out plan. Dolores waited for what she knew would inevitably come next.

"The problem," the General continued, "goes back to the draconium. We have the launch capacity, but the materials, as noted, can be exceedingly hard to come by. It'll take at least three years for full deployment. Unless…" In that condescending way of his, he angled his head toward her.

"I get it," Dolores said. "You want to salvage material from the G-WAD." For four long years the General had lobbied the President to repurpose the panels of draconium for his weapons program, calling the G-WAD a failed experiment. At Dolores' behest, the President always blocked him. But it now suited Dolores' purpose to give in. "You can have it."

Silence greeted her offer, not one of doubt, but of surprise. Beckman scratched his balding head. Dolores didn't dare look at Obadiah, for fear he would detect her duplicity. Janise pondered Dolores a long moment. "You sure about that? I can't promise we can build you another G-WAD, Dolores. That means never knowing what that thing is supposed to do."

"Desperate times," Dolores said, choosing not to elaborate. "In order to do what the General suggests, we'll need" — she lifted her eyes and pretended to do the math, then settled on a number which would work — "nine weapons strategically placed in geostationary orbit. That'll cover the land mass of unfriendly nations. One's already deployed, and another is nearing completion, which leaves seven to fill the gap. And it just so happens that there will be enough material once the G-WAD is scrapped. The General can have his G-Net up and running as quickly as he can assemble the weapons and launch them into orbit."

The President steepled her fingers and cocked her head. "Well, what do you think, General?"

"We should do it, absolutely," Beckman said, "starting yesterday."

The President's gaze went to Obadiah, who must have nodded, because she said, "Then we're agreed. How long will it take to disassemble the G-WAD?"

"Two months, Ma'am," Dolores replied, which was the same

amount of time the doctor had given her to live. "The electrical circuit needs to be sectionalized in order to safely dismantle, transport, and reassemble each grid. In our rush to build the thing, we never considered disassembly, which makes the task particularly tricky. Any mistake, any interruption in the power flow, and the draconium will turn to slag. With your permission, I'd like to personally supervise the salvage effort."

"Of course, it's your baby," the President agreed, smiling warmly across the table, showering Dolores with the approval she had once valued. But the President was in for a surprise, as were they all. Dolores had no intention of dismantling the G-WAD, but of destroying it.

It would be easy. One hole in the ceramic bushing atop a transformer in the electrical substation would interrupt power to the G-WAD. The little pistol she kept in a dresser drawer, her "peashooter," would do the job nicely. Batteries would then power up to serve the load for eight hours, more than enough time for a technician to install the spare transformer. But Dolores intended to put a hole in the spare as well. It would take at least a week for a replacement to be found, and by that time, the G-WAD would be a lake of radioactive sludge.

The plan was as simple as it was reckless. But certainty of death did wonders for anxiety.

CHAPTER THIRTY-FOUR

From atop the second floor balcony of the motel room we temporarily called home, I watched a gray silhouette materialize from within the retreating wall of fog. It slowly took on the shape of a great hummock of rock overlooking the glassy calm of the harbor. Sea lions barked morning greetings while gulls wheeled overhead crying their objections. Melody, nestled in my lap, pointed out a lone sea otter swimming between moored boats. Little arms pounded a mollusk on its chest sending a series of sharp cracks echoing throughout the bay. I inhaled deeply of the salt air, feeling an aching admiration for the beauty of this world...one I had put at risk.

"That bastard!"

I turned to look inside the room, where Fran sat at the edge of the bed staring open mouthed at the television. The beaming face of Max Mystery was splashed across the screen. Then I heard it, the audio of my interview. Max had broken his word, releasing the recording before the agreed upon time, which wouldn't have mattered so much except we were still in the country.

"I knew it," Fran said, with a rare obscenity exploding from her lips. "The moment I met him I knew we couldn't trust him."

"Then you saw something I didn't." Though I recognized his desire, I underestimated his impatience. "I should have anticipated this."

"This is nobody's fault but Max's. He betrayed us."

Footage appeared on the screen of Fran pushing my helpless form down the ramp of the rehabilitation center. The camera shook, crazily spun around, then fell to the ground, showing a sideways view of the reporter leaning over the cameraman.

Fran hurriedly silenced the television. Melody sucked on two fingers. Rising from the bed Fran took Melody into her arms and ran her fingers through her hair. "It's okay, it's okay," she said as Melody placed her head on Fran's shoulder. After a couple minutes pacing the room, Fran said in a falsely calm tone, "We can't chance going to the airport."

I nodded. It was all too easy to imagine dark suited agents waiting for us at the departure gate.

The original plan was for us to board a flight out of the Los Angeles International Airport late that afternoon, the destination being Melbourne, Australia. We chose the country mainly because they spoke English and it was across an ocean. Also, Melbourne was Max Mystery's home town. Ironically, I had hoped Max's celebrity might shield us from unwanted attention. Eric and Tara had arrived this morning, both of them having insisted they travel first to assure the path was clear. Our plan was now in tatters.

"Probably too risky for us to fly out of the United States," Fran said. "We might drive south to Mexico or even north to Canada, though that's quite a way. Does your sixth sense have a preference?"

My "sixth sense," as Fran called it, couldn't predict the future. What I felt was despair, being stuck inside such a frail vessel that it needed assistance to cross the street or go to the bathroom. About all I could do was to guess the obvious. "Once we don't show at the airport, they'll assume we'll head for the closest exit."

Fran nodded as she paced. "Canada it is, then. We fly out of Vancouver."

"Once we get there, we could just hunker down. Canada is a foreign country."

"Too close," Fran said. "Besides, I'd feel safer if we were with Tara and Eric."

"I would too, actually," I agreed.

"There's a business center downstairs. I'll go research the best route north and what to expect at the border. We'll figure out the flights later." She deposited Melody into my lap, saying, "It's going to be a pretty drive, honey. Lots of trees. I think you'll like it." While keeping her fingers in her mouth, Melody smiled.

Before Fran left the room, she and I exchanged a solemn glance. I felt sure we were thinking the same thing: if agents could watch one airport, why not another in Canada? For that matter, why not stop us at the border? Accompanied by a child and with my face broadcast on the news, we'd be hard to miss.

Early the next morning, before the sun broached the horizon, Melody was on the motel balcony squinting into the fog trying to spot an otter. Fran was trying to force the zipper closed on the last of our suitcases.

"We take the 101 to the 5," Fran said. "From there it's an eighteen-hour drive to the border, assuming there's no traffic. We don't stop for anything other than fuel and food. We pay cash for everything. I checked, we have enough. I'm thinking we cross into Canada at a place called Sumas, a little town to the east. Maybe they won't—"

"I think you should take Melody and go," I said.

"After what we've been through, absolutely not!"

About to argue the point, I perceived a complication climbing the stairs. "Hold on, we're about to have a visitor."

Fran froze in place. "They found us."

A machine gun rap sounded at the door. Springing to her feet, Fran's eyes darted to the left and right, as if expecting agents to burst through the walls. Before I could tell her it was a friend, Melody shrieked "Twinkles!" and bounded across the floor and threw open the door. A fluffy white cloud darted inside and began spinning in circles. Tumbling to the ground, Melody wrapped her arms around the dog and squealed with delight. Megan gingerly stepped over the pair and into the room.

Fran hustled around Megan and poked her head out the door. She looked up and down the hall before slamming the door shut and securing the lock. "You shouldn't be here, Megan."

"It's nice to see you too," Megan said.

"Somebody could've followed you," I said.

"I was careful," Megan said, and described how she took back roads and checked the rear-view mirror a lot. I didn't find that reassuring. Looking inward, I searched for unwanted attention. Nothing really, only a hazy thread leading from Megan to a distant someone, my brother, I presumed, who must have told her where we were staying.

"Eric shouldn't have told you where to find us."

"He didn't tell me a thing, Tara did. And if it makes you feel any better, she didn't want to. But I told her the choice was yours, not hers. Tara eventually agreed. After all, she's a sensible woman, which brings me to the reason I'm here."

Fran split apart the window curtains and peered down at the motel parking lot. "You've put my family in danger."

"I didn't mean to," Megan said, and surveyed the room. Her eyes landed on the packed bags sitting atop the dresser. "I actually expected you'd be long gone by now. That would have been smart, you know, to leave before the interview was played."

Fran dropped the curtain back into place. "You think we don't know that?"

"Don't get me wrong," Megan said. "I'm glad you decided to stay put. Where are you going, anyway?"

"None of your business," Fran said, her voice rising.

"What's this about a choice, Megan?" I asked.

"Well, you said you need to find another Beacon, so I took it upon myself to find you one."

"The G-WAD isn't an option," I told her, anticipating where she was going with this. "It's so out of reach it might as well be on the moon."

"That's what I thought too. But what if, and bear with me on this, what if there was a way to get at it?"

"Do I have to remind you that the people who built that damn machine are the ones we're trying to avoid?" Fran asked.

"I know, I know, but hear me out. I spoke with Dolores—"

"The woman who nearly killed my husband?"

Megan shifted on her feet. "She feels really bad about that."

"Does she now?" Fran asked, her voice dangerously calm.

"That's not totally fair, is it?" Megan asked, and bounced her eyes off me. "She allowed Stephen to do what he wanted. Remember, she locked me in there too. If I can forgive, then maybe—"

"I want nothing to do with that woman," Fran snapped. "Go back to your life, Megan. I appreciate what you've done for us, but you need to forget we were here."

"Only trying to help, like I promised," Megan said.

She pulled an envelope from a pocket and tossed it onto my lap. I unfolded the enclosed note. Inside was a phone number, a date and time, and the name of a city. The closing salutation read, "Forgive me, Dolores."

"Dolores intends to destroy the G-WAD," Megan said. "I have no idea how, but I guarantee she'll follow through."

I handed the note to Fran, who scoffed.

"She's dying," Megan said. "That's motivated her to focus on what's important. You were right about there being a weapon. Dolores designed it herself. Told me it was the biggest mistake she'd ever made. Now she wants to use what little time she has left to make amends. If you meant what you said about disabling the weapon, I urge you to meet her there."

Like Dolores, I was also intimate with regret. It was I who had allowed the Beacon to be constructed, resulting in tens of thousands of dead, their immortal beings shredded into nothingness. No word sufficed to describe the tragedy for which I was responsible, however accidental the cause and unintended the consequence. Worse, more were sure to follow. Did Dolores' gut wrench with that same pain?

Melody lifted Twinkles up by the forelegs and lurched across the room and dropped the dog into my lap. "You're a good doggy, aren't you," she said, gently running a hand over its head. With every stroke, ripples formed within the creature's mind, altering the texture to match that of my daughter's. Melody lifted her eyes to mine. "What if we get caught, or can't find another Beacon?"

That was the same question I asked myself. Even if we could leave the country there was so much more that could go wrong. This body I inhabited might not be strong enough to withstand the journey, the next assassin could succeed, or we could be extradited back to this country and into custody. Then there was the greater risk that whoever built the next Beacon might not let me near it. In order for Melody and me to disable their weapon, we needed to find a Beacon. And that required that everything go exactly right …which was worse than a long shot, because nothing ever goes exactly right, especially in this life.

I looked to Fran. "What do you think?"

"I think Dolores is the same as Max, she only cares about herself."

Fran was undoubtably correct. Every being ever born cared about themselves; that was natural, not selfish. The trick was understanding what one valued, which begged the question, what did Dolores want? Stripped of health and wracked with regret, I could take an educated guess – peace of mind. But I expect what she really wanted was something she thought to be impossible – to have a future.

CHAPTER THIRTY-FIVE

Dolores sipped at a mug of green tea inside her favorite café on the outskirts of Las Vegas. This was her usual stop before traveling to the proving grounds where she would continue banging her head against the enigma of the G-WAD. She had tried variations of the same experiment for years, killing hundreds of animals in the hopes of obtaining a different result. But nothing ever changed; death remained the inevitable outcome.

A family of four chatted amiably amongst themselves at one table, bleary-eyed tourists at another, and a young couple laughed nearby. Sitting at the counter were a smattering of locals engaged in their morning routines, whether it were reading, eating, or doing what she was doing…watching life pass by. Dolores drank it in, as she knew this would be her last visit.

"May I get you something else, ma'am?" the waiter asked.

"I'll take another Madeleine, Karl," she answered. And why not? No longer did she have to concern herself with calories. "Actually, make that two. And a refill of tea, if you don't mind."

"Celebrating something special today?" he asked, taking the mug.

"I suppose you might call it my retirement."

"Ah, then I have just the thing." Grinning affably, he flitted off to the counter and returned with a steaming mug of tea and assortment of pastries on a china plate, including a dozen of the shell shaped Madeleines. "My special gift, on the house."

"Why, thank you, Karl, that's very thoughtful."

With a wink and a smile, he hurried off to deal with a bleary-eyed tourist irately waving an empty coffee cup.

Dolores glanced at her watch. It was thirty minutes past the time

Stephen should have called. She felt a sting of disappointment, for she had hoped to hear from him, if only to gain closure by apologizing for the suffering she had caused him and his family. But it was probably for the best, because no matter how many times she turned it over in her mind the possibility Stephen could disable a satellite weapon seemed beyond remote. As for his claim to be a messenger for an alien civilization, well, that was nonsense.

Then how do you explain the music, the figures in the blueprint, and return of the transmission? her inner voice asked.

Familiar questions for which she would never know the answers. Though, she was sure of one thing: having rechecked the DNA results she had confirmed Stephen was as human as she, and just as flawed, a troubled man who had fooled himself and others into believing a fairy tale.

Tara and Megan aren't fools, insisted that same voice.

Maybe not, but Dolores had proved that she was. At one time she had believed Stephen was more than he seemed. Then she had made the mistake of allowing him to enter the G-WAD's injection chamber, not something she cared to repeat.

Dolores signed the check with an obscenely large tip. After scanning the room to assure nobody was watching, she peeked into her bag. At the bottom lay her little pistol, her peashooter. With the hot pink grip, it hardly looked dangerous. She disengaged the chamber and confirmed it was loaded with six rounds, more than enough to take out the two transformers at the substation.

She wrapped the remaining cookies into a napkin and had just placed them into her purse when a chime sounded from the phone. Her eyes went to the screen where she saw a local area code and unknown number. She fumbled for the device sending it bouncing across the floor. A young man sitting at the next table picked it up and held it out. With a quick thanks she snatched it from his hand.

"Hello, hello, are you still there?"

"Who is this?' a female voice asked.

"Dolores McCann. Whom am I speaking with?'

"Are you alone?"

"I came alone, if that's what you mean. I'm sitting inside a café."

"Do you intend on going through with this?"

"Before I answer, I'd like to know who you are," Dolores said.

"You know who this is," the voice replied, albeit irritably.

"All right, I wouldn't have answered the phone if I didn't intend on doing what I said. Where are you?"

The woman, whom Dolores presumed to be Stephen's wife, rattled off an address which she hurriedly scrawled on a napkin.

"Bring coffee and we wouldn't mind breakfast. Yogurt and fruit for a start." The line went dead.

Keeping the phone to her ear Dolores swept her gaze around the dining area. The patrons, intent on their drinks or their companions, heeded her not despite the pounding in her chest. She dropped the napkin into her purse. To relieve the first stabs of a headache, she fished out two capsules, one a steroid and the other a painkiller. With the last of the tea, she downed the pills and left the café.

◆◆◆

Dolores pulled under an archway that connected two wings of a decrepit two-story motel. She parked the rental car next to the kidney shaped pool. After exiting the vehicle, she looked around.

A neon sign advertised a vacancy while intermittently blinking the daily and hourly rates. Trash littered the grounds and the water inside the pool was an opaque green. A sign on the broken gate read, "No lifeguard on duty. Swim at your own risk." No kidding, she thought. Hot asphalt singed her nostrils and the roar of a passenger jet assaulted her ears. A man pushing a shopping cart briefly stopped to rummage through a trash can. Finding nothing, he moved on to the next building. No other life stirred within the courtyard, causing Dolores to wonder if she had the right address.

A door opened from a room on the ground floor farthest from the street and a woman stepped outside. She didn't beckon or smile, only looked at her with a disturbing directness. The face Dolores recognized from the dossier: Francine Fisher, wife of Stephen. With long-legged strides the woman crossed the parking lot, her eyes darting into every shadowed corner. She was right to be cautious, as General Beckman wanted her and her husband dead. Butterflies danced in Dolores' midsection. What had once been a hypothetical meeting discussed with Megan in the safety of her living room had become all too real.

Fran came to a halt five paces distant. Her hair was tied back into a scraggly bun and lines creased her forehead. A second jet roared overhead.

"Good morning, I'm Dolores McCann."

An unblinking stare was the reply.

Dolores swallowed, unsure what else to say. This woman's home had been invaded, her husband incarcerated, injured, and now she and her family were being hunted. "You have good reason not to trust me. For what it's worth, I'm sorry for what happened and ask your forgiveness for my part in it."

Fran's brows knitted together. "A little late for that, don't you think?"

"You're right, but I'm sorry nonetheless."

Fran paced around her, forcing Dolores to turn to keep eye contact. "Why did you bring us here?"

"I'd like to leave this world without taking others with me," Dolores answered.

"Seems like you've already failed at that," Fran said, an edge to her voice. Dolores said nothing because there was nothing to say. It was true. Fran peered into the back seat of the rental car.

"Can I ask you a question?"

As if she didn't hear, Fran opened the backseat and grabbed the bag of food and tray of drinks.

Dolores took that as permission. "Do you believe he's a messenger?"

With her hands full, Fran headed to the motel room. She said over her shoulder, "Decide for yourself."

Dolores watched Fran's back, feeling off-center and indecisive. Maybe she shouldn't have come, for all she was doing was chasing a dream in the vain hope Stephen might undo the harm caused by her actions. It wasn't fair to put that burden on him. It was selfish.

Movement within the motel room caught her attention. Beneath the window curtains were two round eyes that disappeared the instant she looked. Good lord, they had brought their child. A lump formed in her throat. It was Melody. Once only a name in a dossier, now a flesh and blood innocent dropped into a desperate situation. Shaking her head, Dolores dragged her feet across the parking lot. The moment she entered the motel room she froze in her tracks.

An impossibly thin man stared at Dolores from a wheelchair. His arms lay limp on the armrests and his feet were turned inward. A shock of dark hair fell to his shoulders and his chin was unshaven to the point of having the beginnings of a beard. But what held her in place were the unfocused green eyes that stripped her bare. She resisted the urge to raise a hand before her face, ashamed at what he might find.

"It's nice to see you, Dolores."

Dolores moistened her lips, gathering the will to speak. "Is that you, Stephen?"

"Don't worry, I feel better than I look."

Before she could deny that the very same question was on the tip of her tongue, the child's head peeked up from behind the wheelchair. Wide eyes captured her own. She felt naked under their scrutiny. Oh, my god, she thought, they're one and the same, father and daughter, just as Megan warned.

Cupping her hand around Stephen's ear, the child whispered distinct enough to be heard, "I think she's sick. Are you going to tell her?"

Stephen placed the back of his hand on the child's cheek. "She knows honey, she knows. Forgive my daughter, Dolores, she often says what pops into her head."

"Sorry," the child said.

"You're Melody, aren't you?" Dolores asked.

"And your name's Dolores."

"That's right. It's nice to meet you, Melody."

"My daddy told me about you."

"He did, did he? Well, I've come to see how I might help your dad."

"I don't think so," Melody said. "Pretty sure we're here to help *you*."

Fran handed Melody a bagel. She took a large bite, made a face, and spat it out. Cream cheese dribbled from her mouth and onto her chin. "Come over here," Fran said, and pointed to a table where she had laid out a meal. "Let's get some breakfast into you." After handing the bagel to Stephen, Melody clambered onto a chair. She picked out a large Danish which Fran plucked from her hand and replaced with a yogurt. While lazily spooning the food into her mouth, Melody kept her attention fixed on Dolores, blinking owlishly. Fran wiped her chin clean with a napkin.

Dolores forced her attention back to Stephen. "Is it true, that you want to get back inside the G-WAD?" His silent nod prompted an image to pass through her mind, of his limp body lying on the floor in the control room. "How can I be certain what happened last time won't happen again?"

"You can't, but I am," he replied, taking a bite from the bagel.

"That's not good enough, Stephen."

He gestured to an ancient armchair, colored a shade of orange with large rips in the upholstery. "Have a seat, Dolores. Relax." Fran handed him a coffee.

She did as he asked, sinking uncomfortably deep into the cushion of the sofa. "In good conscience I can't put you at risk without proof that what you say is true."

"Dolores," he said, patiently, "you, more than anybody, have seen that evidence firsthand."

"What I saw was Eric pulling your half dead body from the Injector."

"Where I learned the truth."

"You've changed, Stephen. I can see that for myself. What happened inside the chamber?"

With a drawn-out sip of coffee, he studied her with that disconcerting gaze of his. "A veil was pulled aside."

"And?"

"I learned who I was."

"Really, and who's that?"

"The same person you knew, but with memories of what came before. Like you, Dolores, I have been reborn into this world. Except I have come from the place where the transmission originates. I know you won't accept that. There's no empirical evidence, but it's true nonetheless."

Dolores didn't believe in rebirth any more than she did an everlasting soul. The illusion of consciousness was wholly due to a network of interacting neurons, nothing more. "You expect me to believe what you told Max Mystery?"

"I'm more than a messenger," Stephen said. Melody gurgled through a mouthful of food, "Me too," before Fran hushed her.

"What's the G-WAD for?" Dolores asked.

"Life is rare and the distance between worlds vast," Stephen replied. "Forget about starships and warp drives. The Beacon, what you call the G-WAD, harnesses what beings do naturally as a more efficient means of travel than anything that can be artificially created."

"Are you telling me that the purpose of the machine is tourism? Then what are you, a tour guide?"

Stephen chuckled, then coughed weakly, revealing his fragility. "Hardly, though, experiencing your world is…unique. I'll give you that."

"Then what's your purpose?"

"Sentient life sparks into being within isolated pockets throughout the universe, struggling to survive much like a flame flickers in the wind. My job is to find those pockets before they're snuffed out."

Dolores shook her head. "You think you're a savior?"

"No," he replied, his tone sharp. "You have to save yourselves. But it doesn't matter what I say because you've already decided what to do. All you need is an excuse to act on it."

"I see. So, you can read my mind now?"

Stephen shrugged then took another bite of the bagel. Chewing thoughtfully, he regarded her in that disturbing way of his.

"What excuse do you think I'm looking for?"

"You claim to be a scientist, but despite the evidence you can't overcome your preconceptions. The only person that can bridge that gap is you, not me."

Silence lingered, and in that space her confusion grew, as did her shame. Her ignorance of the G-WAD hadn't earned her the right to cast aspersions on Stephen's claims. She had to admit, the story made a strange kind of sense. And Stephen was unlike anybody she had ever met. That alone shouldn't move her, but it did. She couldn't deny it. Dolores looked at the child, now lazily chewing on the Danish. A chill ran through her body as she recalled Megan's warning…that Stephen intended to bring Melody inside the G-WAD.

"I need to hear from your wife that she approves of your doing this. Especially if you intend on bringing your daughter along."

A pained expression flashed over Fran's face, gone within a second. "I wouldn't be here if I didn't, now would I?"

Dolores nodded, her mind made up. She turned to Stephen. "Did Megan tell you what I intend to do?"

"Destroy the G-WAD," Stephen replied.

"You can't talk me out of it."

"I wouldn't think of it. In fact, I heartily approve. Your people aren't ready for a Beacon."

The comment took Dolores aback, until she reminded herself that she didn't believe his story. "I plan on taking out the power. After that, batteries will keep the G-WAD alive for eight hours. I presume that's enough time for you to do whatever it is you intend?"

"Once inside the G-WAD, we'll need only thirty-four seconds."

"No problem," Dolores said. "I want you to know that this could be a one-way trip. While I'm sure I can get us in, getting us out is another matter entirely. Traveling to the site won't be a problem; the pilot knows me and is accustomed to escorting guests, even those as infamous as you. But the sentry guarding the gate will be a challenge. That person is active military, which means there's a chance he or she will feel compelled to report your presence. If that happens, it will be prison for you, your wife, and foster care for your daughter. Don't expect sympathy for your condition because you won't get it. Still want to go?"

He thoughtfully sipped his coffee. "What would your answer be if you could undo your own mistakes?"

"I'd do it in a heartbeat."

"Then you know my answer. And you, Dolores, besides undoing the harm you caused, what more do you want out of this?

"That's not enough?"

"Think back to when we first met. What was it you wanted?"

Dolores reflected, thinking back to the time before despair, when hope of unlocking the mystery of the alien transmission outshone the compromises she had made along the way.

"To understand," she said.

CHAPTER THIRTY-SIX

The roar of the helicopter's rotors diminished to a moderate chuffing as the craft settled onto the helipad within the Nevada National Security Site. Out the window, scattered lights from the nearby town of Mercury defied a darkening evening. Beyond the town, kilometers distant, the dome of the G-WAD loomed over a desolate landscape.

Sitting with Dolores in the passenger cabin were Stephen and his family. Melody had her face pushed up against the glass, looking outside while trying to get her mother's attention by pulling at the hem of her blouse. But Fran stared straight ahead, absently twisting a strand of hair with a finger. Stephen's eyes were unfocused, as if lost in a meditative trance.

Through the headset the pilot said to Dolores, "Take care of yourself, ma'am."

A retired military pilot, Randy had not asked a single question when the passengers boarded the craft, had barely spared them a glance. For as long as Dolores had known him, his sole concern was collecting a paycheck to support his ailing wife. Never once did he concern himself with cargo.

"Let Kitty know I've been thinking about her," Dolores said.

"Thank you, ma'am, I will."

Melody ripped the headphones from her ears. "Are we there yet?"

"Almost, dear," Dolores said.

"Patience," Stephen said.

Slinging her purse over a shoulder Dolores slid open the cabin door. With Fran's assistance she helped Stephen down the steps and into the wheelchair. Melody hopped to the tarmac and her eyes wandered in the direction of the alien machine. Fran hustled her a safe distance away from the aircraft.

With a scream of engines and rush of air the helicopter lifted from the runway. As Dolores raised her hand in farewell, she felt a profound sense of inexplicable loss. While not exactly a friend, Randy had become a comfortable presence in her life. She would miss him.

"All right folks, follow me," Dolores said, and escorted the family toward the waiting sport utility vehicle, the same she had used when escorting Stephen to the G-WAD four years ago.

"First order of business is to drive to the substation where I'll knock out the main power. The batteries will keep the G-WAD alive for a few hours, then the draconium turns to slag." She looked to Stephen. "Plenty of time for you to do your thing."

"Better we go to the Beacon directly," Stephen said. "After that you can take out the power whenever you choose."

"We talked about this. That's not the plan."

"Plans change."

"Knocking out power will draw attention to us," Fran said.

"It's an unmanned substation far from town," Dolores said. "All I do is put a bullet in a couple transformers then we're off."

"Wait, you have a gun?"

Dolores fought a rising tide of impatience. "You and your family can stay in the car. I'll be in and out in less than five minutes. You'll be perfectly safe."

"That's not safe," Fran said, voice rising. "It's a gun!"

"Seems risky," Stephen said. "Unnecessarily so."

"Destroying those transformers is a sure thing, Stephen. Forgive my doubt, but as far as I'm concerned the chance you can disable the weapon is...how shall I put this, less than a hundred percent probability."

Stephen shook his head. Dolores helped Fran position him in the vehicle then stored the wheelchair in the back. Once everybody was situated, Dolores turned over the ignition and found the main road. So far, everything had gone as expected, the same routine as always. She had every intention of keeping it that way. They traveled in a tense silence. The child suckled her fingers while Stephen sat stone-faced. Fran anxiously watched the passing landscape.

A hundred meters off the thoroughfare Dolores spied the substation, glowing like an island in a gray sea. In the safety of her own home, her plan had seemed straightforward. But now that she was here, the reality felt far more complex. She hadn't fired a weapon in years, and the bushings on the main transformer were a smallish target. What if it took more than one shot to destroy it? With eight bullets in the chamber, she would need to be precise. Why in the world didn't she bring more? Also, a shot, even from a gun as small as hers, was going to reverberate through the still air. If anybody was near, they would certainly investigate.

"Thought you said the substation was unmanned," Stephen said.

"It is," she said, growing tired of the second guessing. She had enough doubts as it was.

"There are people inside the enclosure."

Dolores slowed as they approached the access road. "How do you know that?"

"The same way I knew you were present at my interrogation."

Melody leaned forward and extended her fingers. "There are five people in there...one, two, three, four, five. Can't you see them?"

Glancing in the rear-view mirror Dolores saw that Fran had grasped Melody's hand. So strange, this child, as was her mother's acceptance of that strangeness. Struck with indecision Dolores decided to keep the SUV on the main road. Behind them, the substation faded into the gloom, along with her plan.

"Stephen, how sure are you that there are people in that substation?"

"How shall I put this," he said drily, echoing the words she had spoken to him moments ago, "greater than a hundred percent probability."

Dolores considered. If there were a problem with the equipment, one or two of the maintenance crew would respond. But five? Only if something major needed repair. That was possible, but unlikely, especially at this hour. "If you're right, we should come back tomorrow."

"Too late for that; they know we're here," Stephen said. Fran put her face in her hands.

Dolores was about to ask how he knew that, but thought better of it. "Let's hope they don't or we're not going anywhere."

"Unless somebody is curious where we're going."

"Seems I have no choice but to do what you want, Stephen. You better be right about disabling that weapon."

"I am, but only if we're allowed inside the Beacon," Stephen said.

They drove on. Like a monument to an ancient god the outer sphere of the G-WAD grew to dominate the landscape. Though it had been years since the machine was constructed, it seemed terrible to Dolores, as if it purposefully mocked her ignorance.

"That's it, isn't it?" Fran said, her voice cold.

"The G-WAD," Dolores confirmed, and her eyes jumped to the rear-view mirror where she found Stephen's eyes staring back at her. Returning her attention to the road, she remained silent for some time, considering all she had been told, knew, or had guessed about Stephen. A rabbit dashed across the road, causing her to swerve into the other lane. "Assuming for the moment I choose to believe you, and I'm not saying I do, mind you—"

"Ask your question, Dolores," Stephen said.

"How does the G-WAD work?"

"That's not the right question."

"Humor me."

He didn't answer at first, and a glance in the mirror found him tapping his chin. "Think of the Beacon as an interdimensional gate, of sorts, that allows you to retain the thread of consciousness between one life and the next – a memory of what came before. Otherwise you're stuck in an endless loop, living, dying, and never knowing or learning from the past. You're stuck in that loop now, Dolores."

"A soul? Sorry, I don't buy it. Life is the inevitable output of a universe programmed by matter and energy. In other words, physics, a universal system based on rules and random constants. That's the truth of existence."

"Except I've been to a place not ruled by your physics, Dolores. You have as well, though you've yet to realize it."

"I see," she said, her standard answer when she didn't. The vehicle kicked into lower gear as they climbed the slope leading to the entrance of the G-WAD. "All right, you've got me curious. What's the right question?"

"To ask about the why, not the how. What's the true purpose of the Beacon, the reason the message was sent, not just to you, but to any sentient species capable of receiving it?"

"Okay, I'll bite. What's the answer?"

"Consider the long term, Dolores. Earth may be humanity's cradle, but it's also an island, which your people return to again and again, with no chance of escape. That's the physics of what you mock as a soul. There are precious few exceptions to that rule, beings not bound by the walls of space and time."

"Like you?"

Stephen dipped his head. "Think of the Beacon as an off-ramp to another world, Dolores, the only one your people have. Better yet, consider it a lifeboat. Because given time, life on this planet will be consumed, if not by your own hand, then by the dying breath of the sun."

"Did you tell Megan this?"

Stephen smiled. "She called it hogwash."

"That sounds about right."

"Shouldn't you be slowing down?" Fran asked.

Seeing that the main gate was upon them, Dolores depressed the brake. "Let me do the talking," adding a silent plea that Buzz was working this shift. If there was one guard she could talk her way past, Buzz was it. She brought the car to a halt and stepped outside. Nobody greeted her. Entering the shack, she found it empty. Maybe Buzz had been called to deal with some emergency at the power station. She wanted to believe that. After tapping in the security code, she watched the gate rattle open. Returning to the vehicle she drove through the entrance.

"That was too easy," Fran said.

Dolores didn't reply, just drove on.

Twilight darkened into shadow as they entered the tunnel bored through the earthen wall. They exited and turned onto a dirt road that wound its way down a steep incline. As they traveled beneath a forest of metal lattice struts supporting the massive panels of draconium, the air grew chill. The road soon leveled out and Dolores halted the vehicle next to the elevator shaft.

Dolores retrieved the wheelchair from the back of the vehicle and handed it off to Fran who helped Stephen out of the car and into the chair. Melody scrambled out of the SUV then stood stock-still as her eyes climbed the massive hummock of the outer sphere. Dolores followed her gaze to the flock of birds that endlessly circled the G-WAD. A slap of feces splattered the roof of the SUV. "What's with the birds, Stephen?"

"The Beacon thins the walls between two planes of existence, creating a focal point for which lesser creatures have an affinity. Birds especially, it seems."

"Hmm," she muttered, unsatisfied. Then again, what else did she expect?

Dolores herded Stephen and the family into the elevator. A few minutes later she was escorting them along the underground corridor. Fran asked no questions, kept her eyes forward, and seemed entirely uninterested in the whole operation, as if she resented everything about the place. Having arrived at the entrance to the control center, Dolores entered the security code. With a metallic clack, the door opened. Lights flickered to life. She stepped inside then ran her eyes around the room. The power still hummed, rabbits cowered in their cages, and a whiff of ammonia burned her nostrils. She let out a relieved breath. Inside her home away from home, all was as she had left it. "See, nothing to worry about. Come on in."

Melody pointed. "You have bunnies!"

"You can pet one if you like," Dolores said.

With the permission of her mother, Melody skipped to the nearest hutch and brushed her finger against one of the creatures. The rabbit closed its eyes and leaned into her. That was very unlike how they reacted to Dolores, jumping and clawing.

"What's the bunny's name?" Melody asked.

"Um, anything you like, my dear."

"Brownie," she said at once.

Dolores made a mental note that if they were able to get out of this place she would find Brownie a new home.

"Best that we hurry," Stephen said.

Dolores went to the console, manipulated the controls, then pulled down the lever controlling the shield. But the lights didn't flash nor did the speaker intone a countdown. Instead, a message appeared on the display – "locked."

"Damn it," she said.

"You've encountered a problem," Stephen said.

"Just the safety protocol," she said, and lifted the phone from the cradle. "I can release it with a call."

"Somebody's coming," Melody said.

Dolores looked to the closed-circuit television. And saw them, three suited figures entering the elevator from the surface.

"Get us out of here," Fran said.

Dolores felt as if she'd been punched in the gut. Not only had her plan failed, but her actions would cause this family more pain. "The only way out is the way we came in."

"Thirty-four seconds," Stephen reminded her.

"I'll talk to them," Dolores said.

"You better do more than that," Fran said, clutching at her daughter.

Dolores heard them before she saw them, a steady march of feet echoing from the corridor outside. The door flew open and three agents burst into the room. Dolores recognized one as Hudson, the agent who had dogged her steps when she first brought Stephen to this place

"Everybody stay where you are," Hudson commanded. The two other agents, one bald and the other huge, peeled off and wrenched Fran against the wall. She cried out as handcuffs were slapped onto her wrists. With a shriek Melody ran to her father. Hudson pointed at Stephen. "Watch him, but under no circumstances do you touch him."

For a crazy moment, Dolores considered grabbing the gun nestled inside her purse. Instead, she placed the phone back in the cradle and dropped her bag on the table. Hudson sauntered toward her, a hand casually placed over a sidearm. The agent with the shaved head, having finished with Fran, approached Dolores and patted her down. He found the bottle of painkillers in a pocket.

"Dolores McCann," Hudson said, "you're being arrested on suspicion of harboring a fugitive. You have the right to remain silent, speak to an attorney—"

"Consider the future of your career before you dare finish that sentence," Dolores said. "I'm here under orders of the President herself."

"Are you kidding?" Hudson looked at Stephen. "He's right there, the fugitive."

"The President authorized this visit," Dolores continued, unperturbed. That fugitive, as you say, turned himself in to me. You need to understand—"

"What I understand is how to follow orders. Step away from the console." The agent grabbed her arm and pulled her away from the controls.

Hudson picked up the phone. "We're secure here, sir. Yes, all of them, including the child. Thank you, sir." She hung up the phone then walked past Dolores to stand in the middle of the room before Stephen. "I figured you were faking the memory loss. Still, all you needed to do was keep your mouth shut. I told you that, but it seems you're immune to good advice."

Stephen calmly appraised her while Melody leaned against him. "Think about where you stand," Stephen said. "Ever consider this machine has a purpose other than killing people?"

"Is this the messenger speaking? Just so happens I have a message too…I think you're full of shit."

"Carefully consider the choices you make today, Hudson, because they'll follow you no matter where you go. Make the wrong choice and it will haunt you forever. Believe me, I know."

Hudson paused a beat before forcing a laugh. "You're good, Fisher. I can see how you fool people." Stepping back a pace her eyes flicked to the door. "Let's see if you can fool him."

General Beckman strode into the room. "Dolores, Dolores, what the hell were you thinking?" On his heels followed Obadiah, who spared her a glance before his gaze landed squarely on Stephen.

"We were wondering what you'd do," the General said, getting so close she could smell his acrid breath. "Obadiah thought you'd try to destroy the power station. But I knew better and had the shield locked prior to your arrival. You may not believe this, but I dearly hoped you wouldn't be so foolish as to come here. We had a partnership, you and I, a partnership that changed the world."

"Not for the better," Dolores said.

The agent handed over the pills he'd confiscated. The General read the label. "Opioids. Are you an addict, Dolores? That would explain your lack of judgment."

"As usual, you've reached the wrong conclusion based on incomplete information."

"Have I?" He jabbed a finger at Stephen. "Then explain that."

"Alex, you've seen what the weapon can do. And you know what an arms race would mean, for all of us. Stephen claims he can put the Genie back in the bottle."

"You're a fool, Dolores."

"For once, open that mind of yours and listen. What do you have to lose?" She nodded to Stephen. "Tell him."

In a resigned voice, Stephen said, "For every person that falls to your weapon so does the accumulated experience of a multitude of lives. A true death, never again to be reborn. Your language doesn't have a word for that crime."

The General arched an eyebrow. "Hear that, Dolores? He says *your* language. The man's a foreign agent, something I recognized a long time ago. Thought you were intelligent, but apparently book smarts don't translate into common sense."

"You'll learn the truth soon enough," Stephen said.

The General pointed at Hudson. "Aim your weapon at Fisher's head. If that bastard says a word you pull the trigger."

"Sir?"

"Did you have trouble understanding me, Agent Hudson? That was a direct order."

"Yes, sir, I mean, no, sir…sorry, sir." Hudson leveled the pistol at Stephen's head.

Melody's fists bunched into little balls of fury. "You're mean!"

The General dropped his gaze from Stephen to the child. A puzzled expression crept over his face. He blinked then shook his head. "And you're a creepy little shit."

"Tell Hudson to holster that weapon," Obadiah demanded.

"The man is dangerous, and his words are poison," Beckman said. "Can't you see that, Obadiah? But of course not. You're squeamish and weak, always will be. As a result, you can't make the tough calls. That's why I insisted on accompanying you today…to assure that no further mistakes are made."

"You're making one now," Dolores said.

"Oh, I think not, Dolores," the General said. "In fact, I think I have it all figured out. I found it odd that you agreed to salvage the G-WAD, especially to build a weapon you so clearly despise. So, I had my team check up on your math. Seventeen of the weapons are needed to cover hostile territory, a far larger number than you told the President. Since you don't make mistakes like that, I had to ask myself, why would she lie?" He looked at her inquiringly. "I had you watched, Dolores, and only let you enter the G-WAD so you could hang yourself. Not even our little lady President can explain away your actions. You'll get five years, at least, for aiding and abetting a known criminal."

"I'm not spending five years anywhere, General."

"I beg to differ, especially when I add treason to the charges. I'm curious, Dolores, what did Fisher say to convince you to betray your country?"

"You've seen what I've seen, Alex. He led us to the transmission, gave us the key, and has done things we can't explain." She looked at Stephen. "I believe him, I do. Let him enter the G-WAD. Let him undo what we've unleashed on this world."

The General's lips cracked into an unnerving smile. "You've always thought I was a fool, but you're the one who doesn't understand. Open your own mind, Dolores, and see what's right in front of you. We were sent instructions to build a weapon, the most powerful in existence. Think on that for a second, past whatever naïve preconceptions you cling to."

Dolores scoffed. "You're imagining an invasion, aren't you?"

"Why is that so hard to believe? The world's a dangerous place. Why would the universe be any different? We were meant to build the weapon in the hope we'd use it against ourselves. So, when the invaders arrive, they need only mop up what's left. Like smallpox did to the Indians. But despite his ill intentions, the technology fell into *our* hands, *safe* hands, *American* hands." Beckman extended an accusing finger at Stephen. "Then he told our secret to the world, increasing a thousand-fold the chance the weapon would be used. Not only against us, but against our allies, our friends."

"Be reasonable, Alex, that makes no sense."

"No, hmm, then why does he want to get back inside the machine? To signal an invasion, arm a bomb, something worse? Open your mind, Dolores. He's an agent of a foreign power whose actions betray the intentions of an enemy."

Beckman turned on Stephen, the artery in his neck pulsing.

Stephen kissed his daughter on the forehead. Then, with a force all out of proportion to his thin arms, he pushed her from his side. Melody flew backward, landing on her butt with a surprised yelp. Fran screamed. Stephen expelled a disconsolate sigh, so deep his body seemed to shrink by half. "The Beacon is a gift, not a tool of conquest."

Beckman's head snapped to Hudson. "Well?"

Hudson looked to Obadiah.

"Stand down," Obadiah ordered.

Hudson's arm trembled.

With a giant stride and in a single motion Beckman stripped the weapon from Hudson. "Grow some balls," he hissed.

"What is it you think you're doing, General?" Obadiah demanded.

Beckman pointed the gun at Stephen's chest. "What you won't."

To Dolores' horror, the muzzle flashed.

CHAPTER THIRTY-SEVEN

Sprawled on the ground with the fallen wheelchair at my side, I placed a hand over the numbness spreading across my chest. Lifting my hand, I saw my fingers dripping crimson. Then came the pain, like fire burning from the inside out. Voices rang out in consternation, sounding muffled to my ringing ears. I stretched my neck toward the most vocal of those cries, the one belonging to my wife. One arm was handcuffed to a table near the door and the other held over her mouth.

General Beckman stepped into my field of vision.

Death never came easy and it was no less so when I could see it coming. And I saw the end of this life approach in the form of a black worm that burrowed within the General's skull. He intended to finish me off.

"Let this be a lesson to you, Fisher, you and your kind aren't welcome here." Lifting the pistol, I saw rather than heard a burst come from the barrel. Pain exploded in my left shoulder.

Melody scrambled to my side and threw herself over my body. Despite the eddies disrupting her mind, she repressed a snuffle. "You can't die, not yet."

Oh yes, I could. But I could also cling to this life as if it were my last. Exiling pain to a distant corner of my mind I pressed on the hole in my chest trying to staunch the blood pulsing with every heartbeat.

Wielding a high gloss Oxford, the General swept Melody aside. I tried grappling with his shoe but only managed to get my fingers ground under his heel.

"Help me," I said to Melody, or thought I did, for I couldn't hear my own voice. The quickening of her mind told me she understood, and the widening of her eyes made it clear she was appalled, which caused me more anguish than the pain I repressed, for I was about to sacrifice my daughter's innocence.

Glaring at me from beneath hooded brows the General sighted the gun to my head. Quick as a viper Melody slipped a hand beneath the cuffs of his trousers and with the other gripped my arm.

Time slowed.

The General's weapon wasn't the only thing that caused true death. I was another. Using my daughter as a conduit, I coiled the fingers of my consciousness around the arrogance that called itself General Beckman. Fear disguised as anger coursed through his mind, a warped caring for those he imagined he protected. Who was that? Did he have children, grandchildren, or others he loved, and thought protected from the demon that came to this world? Or was it something else entirely, perhaps notions of loyalty he used to create a veneer of nobility to justify his monstrous actions? Whatever the reason, however noble the intent, I would impose my own justice.

Rising like bile from the corners of my mind I brought forth the destructive emotions I'd accumulated throughout this life: fear of losing my sanity, anguish at having lost a child, and anger at the injustice done to my family. I poured it all into this vessel of a man like molten lead into a paper cup.

The coils powering Beckman's consciousness quivered then disintegrated into a thousand shards of gray. At the same moment, the gun went off…once, twice, then clattered on the floor, as did the husk of a man.

Time regained its urgency.

Fran screamed. Frantic shadows painted the walls. Hudson fell to her knees and ripped open the General's jacket. She then began pushing on the sternum of what I knew to be a corpse. Melody whimpered, but other than reel from the horror at what I'd done she was otherwise unhurt. "We need to go," I said.

"Okay," she said, nodding. Her mind had regained its usual symmetry and her voice held that same firmness of intent as the child who had pushed me off the cliff. I was proud of her.

I examined the injury to my shoulder. Only a scratch, as they say, nothing compared to the wound in my chest. To lengthen what time remained to me, I slowed my breath and quieted my pulse. I had played God, acting as judge, jury, and executioner. However deserved the punishment may have been, it left a hole inside of me larger than the one pulsing in my chest. In order to fight Beckman, I had become him. But it wasn't the loss of his corrupted soul I rued, it was the ease in which I had done it….and would do so again.

Curt orders from Obadiah cut through the clamor. He instructed one of the agents to call an ambulance and the other to tend to his partner. Having grabbed a med-kit from the wall, Obadiah knelt at my side and held a mass of gauze on my wounds. He directed his chin toward the General's body. "You do that?"

"Had to," I coughed, tasting blood.

"You nearly died the last time you were here. Why come back?"

I shook my head, lacking the strength for what would be a long answer.

"To fix his mistake," Melody explained. Obadiah's eyes flicked to my daughter. "He didn't bring me. That was the mistake. It wasn't his fault, not really. He just forgot. And I wasn't here to remind him. Because I was dead." —her words gathered steam— "He didn't know I'd come back. I mean, how could he? He didn't know who he was. But he does now and won't make that mistake again because I won't let him." She squinted. "Unless my daddy dies then you're the one who made a mistake, the biggest ever."

Obadiah blinked.

Dolores stepped to my side and looked upon my broken form, clutching her purse to her breast like a shield. "The child's like the father."

Obadiah lifted the bloody gauze from my wound and replaced it with another from the med-kit. "What does that mean?"

"It means they come from where the transmission originates. I suggest you let Stephen finish what he came here to do – disable the weapon."

"And what else would happen, Dolores? However much you dislike him, the General had a point."

She glanced at Beckman's body. "No, he didn't. Paranoia warped his judgment and blinded him to what should have been obvious. Think about it, the beings who sent the transmission can manipulate gravitational waves. The power to accomplish that feat is... astounding. If they had a mind to, they could wipe us out in a millisecond."

"They'd have to get here first, and a thousand light years is a long way to travel. Could be the G-WAD offers a shortcut."

"Good lord, Obadiah, for what conceivable reason would they have to come here? To take our land, enslave our people, suck the oceans dry? Those are movie scripts, not sound thinking. Ours is one world in a galaxy filled with billions. The entire concept is nonsensical..."

As they spoke, I studied Obadiah. Despite Dolores' efforts to convince him of the obvious, the rivulets within his mind bespoke a will that wouldn't be overcome by mere words. And time was running out. Gathering my dissipating strength, I raised myself up on my elbows. Obadiah and Dolores fell silent.

"You have to show him," I said to Melody.

Melody opened her palm and raised it to Obadiah. Warily, he considered the hand poised before him.

"They've given us no reason to fear them," Dolores said.

"You saw what happened to the General," Obadiah said.

"She won't hurt you," Fran said, her voice cutting from behind. I craned around to look at my wife. Her calm tone was at odds with the flare of crimson that colored her mind. Steps away, one of the agents lay on the ground, his slacks bathed in blood, I presumed due to one of the stray bullets the General had fired. Tending to him was the agent who had searched Dolores.

"I won't, I promise," Melody said, radiating serenity. "Don't be afraid."

As if testing a burner on a hot stove, Obadiah cautiously placed two fingers on my daughter's palm. And with his touch the currents within Melody slowed, reversed course, then accelerated to match the velocity of the whorl turning within Obadiah. The texture of her mind changed to match his as well, like ice crystals flowing atop a fast-moving stream. He would now see Melody as I did, with tendrils animating her flesh and the golden glow of her mind reflecting her caring nature.

Obadiah whipped his hand back. "What are you?"

"I'm a girl!" she replied, offended.

He looked doubtful.

"Let me be with my husband," Fran said.

Obadiah rubbed his forehead. "Are you one of them?"

"I'm her mother, if that's what you mean."

"You better do something soon," Dolores urged, looking at the massive red stain soaking my shirt.

Obadiah looked me in the eye. "Is it true, can you disable the weapon?"

I replied with a weary nod.

Obadiah addressed the agent tending his compatriot. "Release his wife."

"But sir—" the agent started.

"And take your injured colleague to the surface and wait for the paramedics. Tell them about the General. No arguing. Do it now."

There was movement. In a flash, Fran appeared over me. Blanching, she knelt at my side and cradled my head in her hands. "Oh, Stephen, you can't go through with this. You need a doctor..."

"Once we're done," I said.

With a sigh that pierced my heart, Fran said, "Quickly, then." Hooking her arms under my shoulders she began dragging me toward the lift. Melody followed. Obadiah did nothing to stop us, only watched the bloody smear trailing behind me. Dolores crouched down to take over pressing on the gauze.

"You better be right about this," Obadiah cautioned.

"I haven't been right about a lot of things," Dolores said, "but this isn't one of them. Why don't you do something useful and go unlock that shield?"

Sweeping the pistol from the floor Obadiah rose to his feet. Hudson bolted upright and placed herself between him and the console. "We're supposed to take these people into custody, Director. We need to do our jobs."

"Shooting an unarmed suspect in the chest doesn't qualify as taking somebody into custody, Agent Hudson," Obadiah said. "Thought you would've learned that at the academy." He waved the pistol in her face. "Along with not losing control of your weapon. But rest assured, you can place them under arrest once their chore is complete. For now, tend to your General."

"He's dead. You saw who did it."

"What I saw was attempted murder. It was wise not to make yourself an accomplice, otherwise you'd be in handcuffs right now. Step aside, Hudson, and the quicker you do it the greater chance you'll earn back this firearm." With a clenched jaw Hudson did exactly that, scowling at me the entire time.

While keeping a wary eye on Hudson, Obadiah strode to the console. Lifting the handset, he told whoever was on the line to release the shield. Then he pulled the lever. Red lights flashed, and the countdown began.

Dolores tapped on the security panel and the elevator door opened. Fran pulled me inside the cabin with Melody close behind.

"Come with us," I said to Dolores.

Dolores paused, on the threshold of uncertainty. I expect she was thinking of the rabbits she had sacrificed inside her G-WAD. As the cabin door began to close Dolores placed a hand over the bumper.

"Make up your mind," Fran snapped.

"Embrace your future," I added.

The countdown hit zero and the rumble of ill-mannered gears vibrated along the walls. Without comment, Dolores squeezed into the cabin. Leaning my head on my wife, we began to ascend through a dilated opening.

I gripped Fran's hand. "I love you."

"Save that for later," she said, not unkindly. "After this we'll get you to the hospital. Right?"

"Right," I lied, for I felt the chill of death swirl around me.

The lift came to a stop once it reached the platform set in the middle of the chamber floor. Fran pulled me from the cabin while her eyes tried to pierce what to her would seem to be a blanket of impenetrable darkness. The gears of the shield ground to a halt.

Melody and I lifted our eyes. Silver wisps spilled from gold medallions embedded in the dome high above as the eighth dimension began to manifest itself. Music, ever present, rose to a crescendo.

"I can hear it," Fran said.

"It's the music which animates us all."

Fran cringed, gripping the rail at the platform's edge. "What's happening, Stephen? It hurts."

"Whatever you intend you better do it fast," Dolores said, placing the butt of her palm against her forehead.

What they felt, what I felt, was the inexorable pull from a crack in the conscious plane. Like forcing an apple through a pinhole, we would soon be pulp, our remnants flushed into the crevice between two universes.

"This is what we've come to fix," I said.

"One to find and two to bind," Melody said, repeating the lesson.

"You're very special," I told her.

Pride shone in Melody's mind and she gave my hand a fearful squeeze.

Two clouds of silvery wisps coalesced before us. Slowly, they took on the forms Melody and I inhabited when we floated within the Beacon on our faraway home. Fran fearfully leaned away while Dolores did the opposite, moving closer and waving a hand through the tendrils that acted as brushstrokes to the ghostly paintings. This was the conscious plane made visible.

"What are they?" Dolores asked.

"That's us," Melody piped, "from a long time ago."

Disembodied arms extended from each maelstrom and reached out to the platform. Dolores quickly backed away. Melody grasped both my hands as the arms took us within their gentle embrace. A buzzing sensation traveled from my head to my toes. Then with a shimmer, the images faded away into nothingness.

Using physics as a language, Dolores surely would have had a complicated explanation for what just occurred. But for me it was simple: we had bent the universe in upon itself. The path was now clear, their weapon defanged, and beings could travel through the conscious plane while retaining a memory of what came before.

Melody jumped in place and clapped. I sagged to the floor, my energy spent.

◆ ◆ ◆

"What happened?" Dolores asked. "Where did those…things go?"

Stephen didn't answer, or couldn't answer, for he collapsed into a thickening pool of blood, more blood than Dolores imagined a body could hold. It was a testament to his will. Fran huddled over him. Melody however, stood up and leaned over the railing. Odd the child seemed so sanguine with her father dying at her feet. Must be the shock.

As if on cue, a blue luminescence materialized over the chamber floor and rose to the level of the platform on which they stood. Dolores stiffened. Shuffling to the edge of the platform she knelt down and passed her hands through the haze. She felt nothing, though the movement created little ripples which darkened into shades of violet as they passed through the sea of blue. An illusion? She bent closer and saw or imagined infinitesimally small threads writhing through the air. She also heard, or thought she heard, music. Very faint, like a gentle breeze rustling through the leaves of a tree.

"Look up," Stephen croaked.

Raising her eyes Dolores found the same bluish haze as on the floor. Medallions lining the dome glowed gold and heavy drops of opaque material gathered within, like tears about to drop. One stretched toward the floor, broke free, took the shape of a sphere, and gently spiraled downward until an abrupt upwelling from the haze swallowed it with a subdued flash of light. More drops parted from the medallions. Rising to her feet Dolores studied one that drifted nearby. Multi-hued arms spiraled from within, and the more she stared, the more intricate the patterns became, the more fluid the movements, the more varied the hues. As if… "They're alive, aren't they?"

"Yes," Stephen breathed.

"What are they?"

Stephen swallowed, shook his head, then looked to Melody.

"People-types," Melody said, "from where we come from."

"Coming here, inside these drops?"

"That's right."

"But…how, how do they get here?"

"We explained that. They use the Beacon on the other side."

Dolores felt her grip on reality slip. "I know, but, I mean, how?"

"Oh, you mean *how* do we get here." Melody rocked on the balls of her feet. "The same way I did. Actually, I don't remember coming out of my mommy because my brain was small. But it had to happen. We

249

have no choice. That's how it works."

Dolores stared, then looked to Stephen, who she could swear was trying to repress a smile. Then it hit her…Melody as much as told her. "Babies, you came here as a baby."

"I'm not a baby!"

"No, no, of course not, dear. You are very grown-up."

"We need to get to a doctor," Fran interrupted, though the hopelessness in her plea matched the reality of Stephen's condition.

"Too late for that," Stephen said, while caressing Fran's cheek. With a tired nod, he added so softly as to be barely discernable, "You can go, Dolores, if you like…"

Her heart skipped a beat. "Wait, what did you say?"

Stephen's eyes closed, prompting a heart-felt sob from his wife.

Melody tugged on Dolores' blouse. "My daddy meant you can go to where our home used to be."

Dolores knelt to be eye-level with the child. Blue mist washed around them. "Melody, dear, are you telling me I can travel to your world?"

"If you want."

"How exactly would I do that, that is, if I wanted?"

Melody clasped her hands together and looked to the side. "Well…you've done it before, lots of times."

A shiver traveled up Dolores' spine. "I have to die. Is that what you're telling me?"

Melody shrugged, not with uncertainty but embarrassment.

She took Melody's small hand into her own. "Just to be clear, dear, you're saying I need to die, right here, right now, inside this very chamber. Then somehow, I will be transported to what used to be your home. Do I understand that correctly?"

Melody nodded. "You become a drop on the other side."

It sounded crazy. But despite that, or because of that, Dolores let go of what wasn't supposed to be real. "I see," she said, and meant it this time. "I'm sorry about your dad. He's a good man."

"I don't like it when he dies," Melody said, turning to look at him. "Excuse me, I have to go say goodbye now."

"Of course. Thank you, Melody, thank you very much."

"You're welcome."

Melody returned to her mother who wrapped an arm around her. Placing a hand over Stephens forehead Fran began a whispered recitation. Dolores averted her gaze, ashamed at having subjected this family to more misfortune…yet more anguish added to her terrible legacy.

Hiking the strap of her purse over a shoulder, Dolores ducked under the rail of the platform and trod onto the panels of draconium. She waded through blue haze across the chamber floor until silence reigned so completely that all she could hear was faint music. Whether it was coming from inside or outside of her head she couldn't tell. Spheres dropped like rain into the surreal sea where waves plucked them out of the air with flashes of green, pink, and violet. It was as mesmerizing as it was beautiful.

Taking the peashooter from her purse, Dolores held it to her temple.

◆ ◆ ◆

A great fatigue washed over me, forcing my eyes to close. Fran kissed my cheek. "Rest easy, Stephen. Melody and I will find our way, don't you worry. I love you and will forever."

Melody approached her mother, then both gently placed their hands on my cheeks. I took comfort from their warmth, and for the first time in a long while, experienced a sense of peace. Very dimly, as if Fran spoke from miles away, I heard her recite a prayer.

Taking refuge in a tear upwelling from the floor of the Beacon I watched my wife mourn over what had been my body. Melody sat in her lap, offering silent solace to her mother and my departed being. I called out to her.

Melody tapped Fran's shoulder and pointed to the essence of my being that hung between this world and the next. Leaving my body further and further behind, I peered beyond this world into destinations unlimited and mysteries unknown, forever tempting me to leap into the beyond. I took one last glance at this life, then turned to the future.

EPILOGUE

Years later

Melody lifted the computer tablet over her head. She snapped a picture of the night sky and showed it to me. It was a boring picture of stars.

"So?" I asked.

"That's where we come from," she said. "Our home."

No, it wasn't. Our home was where I stood, in the backyard of my house. "I don't think so."

"Maybe you're right," Melody sighed. "But you're also kind of wrong. How do you feel when you look—" she pointed up— "well, you know where?"

I didn't need to follow her finger to know where it was that she pointed. It was a place that tugged at me, as did an avalanche of images, voices, textures, and smells. There was pain, and a dream of dying inside a scary place. It didn't make sense to me.

"I don't know," I said, not wanting to talk about it.

"You don't want to discuss it because you don't understand. That's because you're small."

"I am not."

"You won't stay small for long," Melody said. "That's for sure. Memories are going to come fast as your brain ripens. That happened to me and it will happen to you. When the memories do come, don't be scared. What you remember is real and what you will experience is natural. You once told me that."

I watched the myriad colored whirlpool spin faster inside my cousin's head. "I'm not afraid, but you are."

"I'm very afraid," Melody admitted. My heart beat faster, not understanding why she felt that way. She erased the image from the screen and handed the tablet to me. "When you start to remember I think it's best that you not tell my Aunt Tara. At least, not yet. Maybe not for a long while. That goes for Uncle Eric too."

"I know," I said, and somehow, I did. Turning around, I looked at my mom and dad, sitting at the patio table with Aunt Franny. My mom waved at me. I waved back, feeling my love for her.

"You especially can't tell *my* mom," Melody whispered. "When the time comes, it has to be me who tells her what happened. That's important. Agreed?"

I didn't quite understand why I couldn't talk to Aunt Franny, but I felt that was the right thing to do. "Okay," I said.

"I'm glad you came back," Melody said, and grabbed my hand. "Now I understand why you didn't want to activate the Beacon."

"What's a Beacon?" I asked.

"You'll remember soon enough," Melody replied, and released my hand. She wrapped her arms around herself.

"What are you afraid of?" I asked.

"They're coming, Stephen," Melody said, "I don't know what's going to happen…to them, or to the people who are already here."

I peered up at the sky, to the place of my dreams. Usually I found comfort there but today the sight filled me with unease.

"I don't either," I said.

AUTHOR'S NOTE

Starting a book is easy, but finishing it is an altogether different matter. The support of my family and friends is what got me to the finish line.

To my lovely and long-suffering wife, thank you for buttressing my confidence with encouraging words and insights that made the story better than it otherwise would have been. I appreciate your patience while I labored over the intricacies of the plot. I thank my daughter, Emily, who lent me her skills as developmental editor, beta reader, and artist. I thank my dad for copy editing and proofreading the book (and apologize for asking him to do the same for my first novel - now trunked). Also, I have to acknowledge Princess Freckles, our dog, who gifted me with hours of loyal companionship while becoming a literal writer's block as she demanded attention by lying across the computer keyboard.

Then there's my writing group, the Inkwells. Thank you, Sarah Beauchemin, Michelle Fogle, Dani Heinemeyer, Ramona Josephs-Horton, Steve Nickell, Carol Pope, Valerie Power, and Ruth Roberts. I appreciate the energy you poured into the story, the discussions we had around Ruth's patio table, and collective guidance that helped level-up my writing and shape Stephen's journey from human to alien. Thanks also to Tammy Greenwood, who made me a better writer, and the San Diego Writers, Ink, a community from which I met so many wonderful people. Other people who lent their insight include Helga, Lana, Maureen, and Will.

A couple of notes the reader may find of interest. AMIGO is based on a real project called the Laser Interferometer Space Antenna (LISA). The project is led by the European Space Agency and scheduled to be launched in 2034. I hope LISA detects something as unusual as did the fictional AMIGO. The U.S. Space Force was formed after I finished this book and it was only good luck that Space Operations Command is based at Vandenberg AFB.

Lastly, a word about the mode of interstellar travel used by the aliens. The 14th Dalai Lama claimed that if rebirth were true for one person then it has to be true for all. After hearing this, I recall thinking, "Well, if that's the case then it can't be limited to Earth but has to occur throughout the universe." Shortly afterward, I began writing a tale about a little girl taking a picture with her father.

Thank you again to those who made this novel a joy to write. Hopefully, you the reader, found this story worthy of your time and attention. If you enjoyed the book, I invite you to leave a review then visit david-hoffer.com to join my mailing list.

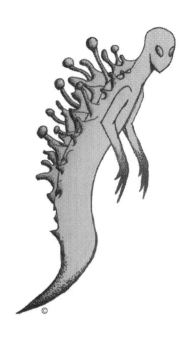

Printed in Great Britain
by Amazon